Love Hops

Christine Layne

Edited by NICE GIRL NAUGHTY EDITS
Edited by D.P. Lehan
Cover Designer COFFIN PRINT
Formatting Christine Layne

Love Hops

Copyright © 2023 Christine Layne

*This book is dedicated
to those who
need a change.*

Chapter 1

*H*appy *birthday to me*, Lena wistfully thought as she watched the ribbon-like clouds move slowly across the blue sky.

Lying on her back in a canoe with a bright orange life vest strapped to her chest while she nursed a cheap bottle of Pinot Noir was not how she pictured her 40th birthday. She was supposed to be on a luxury cruise, sailing the Caribbean with a fruity mixed drink in her hand, not drifting across a man-made reservoir in Aurora, Colorado. Alone.

At least it's fairly quiet.

Other than children's laughter from the swim beach behind her, all Lena could hear was the hum of jet ski engines in the distance. She propped up against the canoe's back and flung a leg over the side. Her toes dipped into the cool water. Watching a group of men jet skiing out in the middle of the reservoir, Lena's adrenaline pumped as they sped across the water's surface, making sharp turns and narrowly missing each other.

You'd never catch me on one of those dangerous things. She took another swig of her wine, leaned her head back and closed her eyes. With a deep breath, she flooded her lungs with earthy lake-scented air.

She grimaced and took another drink. This may not have been her first choice of birthday celebrations; hell, it wasn't even her fiftieth choice, but it was what she had.

A cloud passed over the sun, giving her a quick reprieve from the heat. Lena's memory served her well as she remembered mid-May in Colorado being plenty warm, but this seemed worse than twenty years ago when she'd moved away. Maybe because of global warming? Whatever the reason, the sun was doing a good job of baking her olive skin. She would tan nicely. With another swig of the wine, she swished it around in her mouth before swallowing.

This is a rocking party.

A truer statement had never existed.

As soon as she thought it, the hum of the jet skis became a roar. The water slapped the canoe's side, rocking it back and forth as someone yelled, "Watch out!" The next thing Lena knew, she was under water.

She kicked her legs furiously, flailing her arms around until her head popped above the surface. Lena sucked in a breath, coughing and spitting lake water from her throat. With her eyes shut tight, her hands searched for the canoe. They came up empty.

Lena's heart pounded in her chest. She employed what little swimming knowledge she had to tread water. The life vest was doing its job, but whenever Lena stopped kicking, it rose up, smooshing her face so her cheeks puffed up like a chipmunk. It was terribly uncomfortable.

Right as Lena felt the panicked urge to scream, the canoe bumped her hand, and she gripped it tighter than she'd ever gripped anything. Now stable, Lena rubbed her eyes, thanking herself for skipping the makeup today as she blinked them open.

"That was a mighty spill you took," a man's deep voice said. "You okay?"

Lena whipped her head up, her long black hair flipping into her face. A man, a few years her senior, leaned from his jet ski to hold on to the other side of the canoe. His bright blue eyes stayed trained on hers, and Lena's breath caught in her throat.

From the lake water, I'm sure. "Uh, I'm okay. Thanks."

"Good to hear." The man's mouth twitched behind his dark beard peppered with graying hairs. "Sorry about my son. Apparently, he needs more lessons."

"No, I'd say he handled the jet ski fine," Lena said, peeling her wet hair from her face. "He didn't crash into me." She grasped the canoe, throwing her leg over the side, but the already bulky life vest was now wet, and heavy. When her struggle to get into the canoe ended, she was out of breath.

The man shook his head. "I meant lessons about watching where he's going so he doesn't endanger the lives of pretty ladies such as yourself, miss...?"

Lena's cheeks flushed slightly as she fought a flattered smile. "Lena. Lena Bouras."

"Nice to meet you, Lena. I'm Del Stratton." They stared at each other for a moment until Del cleared his throat, letting go of the canoe and straightening up on his jet ski. "What were you doing floating aimlessly around in a canoe?"

Lena licked her lips before pulling her bottom one between her teeth. She turned away from Del. "Celebrating my birthday."

She heard Del chuckle. "Well, happy birthday, though you have interesting ideas on celebrations."

Tucking her knees to her chest, her toes curled in on themselves as she lifted her gaze to his once more. The warm smile on his face made her stomach flip, but she chalked it up to her adrenaline settling. Del wasn't Lena's type.

Handsome in his own right, Del was certainly what one would call a silver fox. Mid-to-late forties, with rippling shoulder and bicep muscles and a full head of salt-and-pepper hair matching his thick beard. Even if he wore his hair in a man-bun, he was nothing to laugh at. He just wasn't who Lena usually went for.

"Would you like a tow?" he asked. "Or are you planning on drifting along some more?"

Lena chewed on her lip, and checked the sun. With it getting lower, and her being dripping wet, she'd be cold when sunset came. Plus, her wine was almost gone.

Oh no! Her eyes darted around the canoe. She reached under her seat and blew out a breath as she felt the bottle on her fingertips, but her cheerful face dropped when she pulled the bottle out. It was empty. Lena hung her head and said, "A tow would be great, thanks."

Del hummed a laugh through his closed lips, shaking his head as he took hold of the rope tied to the end of the canoe and drug it across the reservoir to the dock. He tied it to the pier before beaching his jet ski. Lena watched him dismount, her eyes trailing up his tattooed calf to his swim trunks straining dangerously tight across his ass, and her heart rate quickened. When he took off his life vest, Lena snapped her gaping mouth shut. The man was cut, and that was being conservative.

She averted her eyes to keep from gawking at his sculpted torso adorned with more tattoos as he walked down the dock to extend a hand to her. Lena swallowed roughly and stood, but the rocking canoe proved to be a worthy adversary. She nearly tumbled back into the lake, and she would have, had it not been for Del's strong hand wrapping around her wrist.

"Whoa, careful." The rumble of his deep voice made her throat run dry. He helped her onto the dock, where the world spun, and she tripped on a splintered plank. Del caught her again, but not before she crashed into his firm chest, the top of her head brushing his bearded chin. He cocked an eyebrow. "How much wine did the lake get?"

Lena pushed away from him, straightening her posture before she shrugged. "Only like a quarter of the bottle."

"You know, if a ranger would've caught you, you'd have gotten a hefty fine."

"Honestly, it was the least of my concerns." She ran her hands up her arms, shivering from the breeze blowing across her damp skin. "Thank you for the tow."

Lena took another wobbly step, but Del leaned into her space, stopping her in her tracks. "Did you eat before you went out on the lake?"

"I had an early lunch, but I haven't eaten since."

Del pursed his lips and eyed her from head to toe.

Not wanting to squirm under his intense gaze, Lena busied herself with removing her life vest. As she fought her swaying, she noticed Del staring. She worried he was judging her for being intoxicated, but when she finally looked into his eyes, she saw something warmer than judgment.

A soft understanding lingered there, and he turned to look at the parking lot where several food trucks sat parked. "How about you eat something before you try to drive home?"

Lena thought for a moment. She wasn't in the best shape to drive, and satiating her grumbling stomach would delay having to go home to her empty house. With a nod, she followed Del to the reservoir parking lot.

"What do you like?" he asked.

Lena eyed the Mexican food truck, her mouth watering. "Tacos."

"Perfect." Del strode to the truck, taking his wallet from a zippered pocket in his swim trunks.

Lena skipped to catch up and put her hand on his forearm, the touch of his warm skin burning her fingertips. She shook it off. "I can get my own."

"Call it a birthday present." He winked and Lena turned her face away to hide her pink cheeks, but a quick gust of the breeze chilled the air, making her shiver. "Do you have extra clothes with you?"

She nodded. "In my car."

"Why don't you go change clothes while I get the food? Otherwise, you'll be freezing your butt off out here. Just tell me what you want."

"Okay, thank you. Um, may I have two veggie tacos, please?"

"Sure thing."

Lena hurried to her car, scanning her surroundings. There wasn't another car anywhere near her, so she crawled into the trunk of her Honda CR-V and changed. Stripping off the wet tank top proved arduous inside the cramped space. It was form-fitting already, but sopping wet, it stuck to her like glue.

Too bad there wasn't a wet t-shirt contest.

Lena smacked her forehead. Del hadn't been staring at her because he was judging, he stared because of the wet shirt. Her chest had probably been staring at him first. Embarrassment flooded Lena for not realizing what was going on, but it turned into flattery the more she thought about it.

I may be forty, but I've still got it. Even without makeup.

"Makeup!" Panic took up residence in her chest once more. She climbed into the driver's seat and quickly pulled out her emergency mascara and lip gloss from the glove compartment. Usually, she'd have her whole face done, but even Lena knew it would be moot at the lake. A little something never hurt, though.

After checking herself in the mirror, she nodded in approval. As she stepped out of the car, now wearing a snug long-sleeve tee and shorts, she felt more comfortable. She slipped into her flip-flops as she fixed her hair into a ponytail, and headed back to the food trucks with her stomach growling mightily.

She found Del sitting at a picnic table, still in his swim trunks but now with a sweatshirt on. She ignored the strange disappointment of missing his bare torso. Their food was spread out in front of him, and a bottle of water was next to her basket. A wave of calm washed over her. "Thank you," she said and took a seat.

"No problem. Happy birthday."

Lena dug in, the delectable flavor of grilled peppers and onions mingling with lime and cilantro tantalizing her taste buds. Maybe it was the best taco she'd ever had, or maybe it was the overwhelming hunger that had crept up on her, but Lena devoured the first taco in an instant. As she swallowed the last bite and wiped her mouth, she lifted her head and met Del's smiling face.

Her cheeks flushed. "Sorry."

"No, it's cool." He waved her off. "But I'm glad I got you a decent birthday gift." He tilted his head, the grin on his face widening, and the heat in Lena's face grew.

She took a deep breath and opened her water. Although the cold liquid did well to quench her dry throat, it did very little to ease her overheated state. Lena pushed her basket a few inches away, wanting to take a break and not look like a wild animal in front of Del. Why she cared about his judgment, she wasn't sure. He seemed nice enough. Certainly nice enough to look at.

With another big gulp of water, Lena dipped her chin, suddenly embarrassed for her thoughts.

"So, Lena, what do you do?"

Her heart leaped into her throat, but she swallowed it down. "Um, nothing, actually." She reached up to twirl her hair, but it was tied back, so she dropped her hands into her lap and wrung her fingers. "I lost my job a few weeks ago, and I haven't been able to find anything."

Del's face fell. "Sorry to hear that. What were you doing?"

"Interior design." Lena paused when she noticed Del bristle. "I, uh, worked at a firm doing renovations for hotels and office buildings." Lena's shoulders slumped. "I'd been there for almost ten years."

"Wow. And they fired you?"

"More or less."

Del furrowed his eyebrows, pursing his lips as if deep in thought. "Well, maybe my son tipping your canoe was more than an accident."

"What?" Lena crinkled her nose.

"It just so happens I have an employee leaving soon and I'll have an opening." His pursed lips relaxed, spreading into an easy grin.

There's no way this guy owns a design firm. Is there? "And what do you do?"

Del rubbed the back of his neck. "I own a brewery. One of my bartenders is having her baby any day now and wants to be a stay-at-home mom. I'm happy for her, but I'm down one bartender, so if you need a job..."

Lena fought the laugh attempting to burst from her. "You're awfully kind, and I appreciate the offer, but that doesn't sound like my area of expertise."

"I know it's not anything like design, but it pays and has steady hours." His tone held something resembling hope.

"Del, I don't want to feed you some line of crap and tell you I'll think about it, or even keep it in mind, because I won't." She was using her professional tone, not overtly harsh, but not exactly gentle. Lena pressed her lips into a line and softened her voice. "No offense."

He held up his hands. "None taken."

"Besides, I wouldn't know the first thing about working in a brewery. I don't even drink beer."

"Hey, we can train anyone. If they're willing to learn, that is." His eyes flashed with confidence as he arched an eyebrow.

Lena chewed on the inside of her cheek, hesitating to turn down his offer again, but she always held her ground. "Sorry, but it's not for me."

He laughed, hanging his head for a moment, and Lena exhaled with relief. "Okay, fair."

"Hey, Dad. Where's your jet? We're gonna load up." A young guy with shaggy blond hair ran up, patting Del on the back and leaning in toward him.

"Hey, Johnnie. It's over at the west dock." Del pointed behind Lena, but flipped his palm up as he motioned to her. "And I'd like to introduce you to Lena Bouras." He turned his head with a stern look. "The woman whose canoe you flipped."

Johnnie swallowed and gave a sheepish grin. "Sorry."

"Thanks. I managed to survive." Lena chuckled.

"Lena, this is my youngest son, Johnnie."

"Nice to meet you." Johnnie turned back to Del. "Key?"

Del took the key from his pocket to hold it in the air, but snatched his hand away as Johnnie reached for it. "Let Jack back the truck down the ramp."

"Okay, fine." Johnnie rolled his blue eyes that matched Del's, took the key, and ran off to the dock.

Del watched his son disappear down the hill, a one-sided smirk dancing on his lips. "Twenty-one years old, and still such a kid."

"You said he's your youngest. How many kids do you have?"

"Three. All boys. You?"

Lena shook her head vehemently. "None." *And I'm okay with that.*

"Boys? Or kids?" Del asked with a wry look.

Lena laughed. "Neither." She picked up her other taco and took a big bite.

"There's nothing wrong with that." The softness in Del's voice warmed Lena.

When they were both finished with their food, Del wiped his hands on his napkin and tossed it into the empty food crate. "Well," he said, getting up from the table. "I should go supervise to make sure the boys don't drive my truck into the lake. It was nice meeting you, Lena, and I hope you enjoyed your birthday."

Lena nodded, much to her chagrin. Del had been great company. "I did, thank you. I'll have to remember the name of this food truck."

"There's an easy way to remember."

"And what's that?"

"Take the paper in your basket home. It's got their name printed on it." Del nodded toward the table. "Goodbye, Lena. Drive safe."

"Bye." The word came out almost inaudible as Lena's heart sank watching Del walk away. Her eyes dropped to the stylized ocean wave tattoo running the length of the back of his calf.

Oh, I never asked about all his tattoos. She brushed off the thought. *None of my business, anyway.*

The sun kissed the horizon, turning the sky orange and pink, and Lena didn't want to drive home in the dark. She grabbed her basket, preparing to crumple the greasy paper liner, when Del's suggestion echoed in her mind.

She shook her head, but as her eyes fell to the basket in her hand, her breath caught in her throat. There, scribbled on the corner, was a phone number. The words "think about it" were written above the numbers and "Del" was signed underneath. *When did he write this?*

A flutter ran through Lena, but dissolved quickly. Del's kindness and charm didn't negate the fact he wasn't Lena's type. *Besides, he's probably married.*

The thought hadn't struck Lena until then. Sure, there wasn't a ring on his finger, but he'd been on the lake so he probably tucked it away someplace safe. With three kids and looks like his, of course he was married. The phone number was merely in case she changed her mind about the job.

Which she wouldn't.

But would it be such a bad idea to keep it?

Lena swallowed her pride, tore the greased-stained part of the paper away, and tucked Del's phone number into her pocket. Keeping one's options open always made sense, and right now, Del was the only option she had.

Chapter 2

"**W**hat do you mean, you don't have a job yet?" Nicole's voice echoed through the phone speaker so loudly, Lena had to hold the phone away from her ear. "Lena, it's been almost two months."

Lena flopped onto her living room couch. "I know, but I think I need a break from the design world."

"Lena..." Nicole's tone held all the irritation in the world. "You love design, and you're good at it. Why take a break?"

Because I've been made into a fool?

"What happened with all those job postings you told me you applied to?"

Frustration bubbled in Lena's gut, her muscles tensing. "None of those design firms will hire me."

"Really? With your portfolio?"

"None of them have even *looked* at my portfolio. I haven't had a single interview." Lena shut her eyes. The tears were forming, and she didn't want Nicole to know she was crying. Again. "I'm not as good as I thought, I guess."

"Oh, shut up. You only say that because they did you dirty here in L.A. You should've been promoted to senior designer instead of being canned." Nicole paused. "You know I'm right."

Lena opened her mouth, but she couldn't speak. Nicole had always been able to call her out on her true feelings. Even before they were best friends, Nicole had an innate ability to detect Lena's inner workings. She called it her BFI, Best Friend Instinct. A thousand-mile separation couldn't stop her.

Lena and Nicole had known each other for over a decade. They began as coworkers, becoming work besties, and their friendship soon extended outside of the office. Nicole had been there the day Lena lost her job.

"You're a fantastic designer, Lena. Those firms don't know what they're missing. Did they say why they wouldn't interview you?"

"Because they called Hatfield," Lena said through gritted teeth.

"Oh, screw Hatfield. She's nothing but an A-hole." Nicole never cussed. She might have had a smart mouth, but foul language never left her lips, so Lena tried hard not to swear in front of her. "What kind of lies did she say about you?"

Lena tugged on the lightning bolt charm of her necklace, twisting it between her fingers. "That I'm an unreliable, flaky employee who abused her sick time for personal reasons."

"Wow. Just... wow." Nicole sighed several times, as if she couldn't believe Lena's words. "I wish they'd never sold out to that larger firm. If they hadn't, you'd be here in your dream position, and Jennifer Hatfield would be gone."

"I doubt that."

"Oh, please. The senior partners *loathe* her. You know the only reason she got promoted to office director is because her sister, Amelia, bought Designology."

"That can't be the only reason she was promoted. She had to have done something right."

"What? Be a cold-hearted witch? She fired you for using your legitimate PTO. I'm pretty sure that's illegal."

"It's not since I failed to actually fill out the FMLA application. Now I just look like someone who used sick time to take vacations."

Nicole let out a frustrated groan. "I think she could've found an ounce of compassion, considering you were taking care of your dying mother." She paused and heavy silence consumed the air. "How are you holding up, anyway?"

Lena's stomach dropped to her feet. It had been almost two months since her mother passed away at the beginning of April, and the pain was borderline unbearable. She had lost the greatest role model in her life. After being fired, Lena moved back to her childhood home, though the emptiness of her mother's absence haunted her. What she wouldn't have done to hear her mother's laugh one more time.

Lena swallowed, fighting off more tears. "I'm doing okay." Her legs became restless, so she got up from the couch and went to the kitchen. "Can we talk about something else?"

"Sure." Nicole popped her gum. "What's the party scene like out there?"

The kitchen counter caught Lena's weight as she sagged against it, her arms crossed over her middle. "Non-existent. Nicki, this is Aurora, Colorado."

"You're close to Denver, though, right? Isn't there a good scene in that city?"

"I'm sure there is, but I'm not going downtown by myself. I need my wing-woman." Nicole had always been Lena's right-hand, even after Nicole got married.

"You'll have to find a new wing-woman, then. Sorry," Nicole teased.

With a sigh, Lena took out her favorite oversized mug, and dumped a ton of sugar into it. She filled her teapot and put it on the stove to heat. "And how am I supposed to do that? The few people I know here are ones from high school, and I'm only friends with them on Facebook."

"Lena, no one uses Facebook anymore. It's for old people."

"Well, I am forty, you know." She ran her fingers through her long, wavy black hair, pulling at the strands.

"So I guess you'll be using the battery-operated boyfriend I got you for your birthday exclusively, then?"

Lena's mouth hung open. Swear words might not be part of Nicole's vocabulary, but that didn't mean her mouth was clean.

"Okay, you don't have to answer me, but you could just go to a local bar. There has to be hot guys in Aurora."

Lena pressed her fingers into her eyelids. "I'm not desperate."

"How is going to a bar and picking up a guy there, any different from going to a club and taking a guy home here?" When Lena didn't answer, Nicole sighed. "You can't tell me you're still hung up on Ozzie."

Lena bristled. It had been months since she walked in on Ozzie and his receptionist using Lena's bed for a naked rendezvous, but the betrayal still hurt.

Her first serious, long-term relationship since high school and *that's* how it ended. "No, I'm not, but we dated for a year, Nicki. The whole ordeal messed me up."

"I know he was a grade-A jerk, but not all guys are like him."

"Ha, no, but it made me realize I'm a casual kind of woman. I'm not cut out for committed relationships." *Mom always said Ozzie was worthless, anyway.*

"Who said you have to be in a *relationship*? All I was saying is you need to get laid."

"But how do I even find someone for that? I'm *not* using an app. That's how people get kidnapped and murdered." The teapot whistled, and as Lena poured the steaming water into her mug, she recalled meeting Del. A giggle escaped her.

"What's so funny?"

"Nothing. Well, something. Okay, you'll think this is hilarious." The story of Del saving Lena from her overturned canoe came spilling out of her lips. She recounted the wine and the tacos, but left out his impressive physique intentionally. "He even offered me a job."

"What!? And you didn't take it?"

"Because it was for a bartender position at a brewery. What am I going to do at a brewery?"

"Um, make some money? And what do you care? You told me, not two minutes ago, you wanted a break from design. This could be your break."

Lena drained the teabag, then tossed it in the garbage. "Not my scene. Besides, I think Del was interested in more than just hiring me."

"Ooh. Was he hot?"

Del's image popped into Lena's mind. His warm smile beneath his graying beard made her heart flutter, but his body was what made her temperature rise. The way his strong arms held her when she stumbled, the firmness of his chest as she crashed into him. A delicious shiver went up her spine as she thought about it, but she shook it off. "He was a good-looking man. Totally not my type, though."

"Ugh, you and your *type*. Where has that gotten you, huh?"

Lena could picture Nicole rolling her eyes. "Hey, I like what I like."

"You mean thirty-something-year-old, fully-waxed models, who care more about driving a Ferrari than knowing how to spell it?"

Lena clenched her jaw, taking a second to let her frustration ebb. She knew Nicole was right, but Lena didn't need her judgment. "Okay, so the guys I take home aren't rocket scientists. I don't need them to be."

"You just need them to hit all the points on your dumb checklist."

Lena knew Nicole was arching a judgmental eyebrow. "That *dumb* checklist has kept plenty of hot guys in my bed over the years."

"But you said this Del guy is hot, right?"

Lena groaned. "He may be hot, but he's the opposite of everything else on my checklist. He's older than me, has a beard, not only drinks beer, but brews it, and he rides jet skis. The only thing this guy marked off on my list was his tattoos, but that's not even required. It's just a perk."

"But it's a hot perk, and one thing to go on. One check mark is better than none."

Lena paused. Not wanting to let Nicole score this point, she thought hard of how to negate the tattoo aspect. "Oh, and he had a man-bun, for crying out loud."

Nicole's giggle resounded through the speaker. "Still sounds like he could be fun."

"Except he's not the kind of guy I'm attracted to. He's... rugged." Lena lifted her mug to her lips and took a sip, the tea almost hot enough to burn.

"Yeah, I'll never understand you having a type. A penis is a penis; the important thing is how they use it."

Lena nearly spit out her tea. "Nicole!"

"What? All I'm saying is, you should consider stepping out of your box. What was it your mom always used to say? You know, that quote she told you all the time."

A pang of sadness stabbed Lena's heart as she recalled it. "Do something today that your future self will thank you for." She swallowed hard. "But she was referencing my career moves. Working hard today meant my future self would reap the benefits. She wasn't talking about men."

"It could still apply, though. Who knows, this guy, Del, could be a fun fling."

Lena set her mug down and folded her arms. "Not if you want me to take the job he offered. I can't booty-call my boss."

"Why not? It would be like Fifty Shades of Grey."

Lena laughed, picking up her mug again. "Okay, hypothetically speaking, even if I stepped out of my box, he's probably married."

"He gave you his phone number."

"For a job opportunity. He has an opening to fill, that's all."

"You should let him fill your opening," Nicole said under her breath.

Lena threw her free hand up in the air, letting out an exasperated groan. "Okay, thanks for the talk, Nicole. Bye."

"No, Lena. Wait."

"What?"

"In all seriousness, call the guy. Take the job. If anything, to get you out of the house. I mean, eventually, you are going to need income, and any money is better than no money."

Lena rolled her eyes. "Okay, fine."

"Promise?"

"Yeah, I promise."

"Thanks. Talk to you later." Nicole hung up.

Lena stared at her phone for a long minute, her hair wound tightly around her finger. Was Nicole right? Not about needing Del to fill her opening, but about needing the job? And *that* job? Even if the house and her car were paid off, she knew she'd need income sooner or later. Her savings wouldn't last forever.

Yes, it was a hard truth to choke down. Nicole was right.

With leaden steps, Lena went to her purse and fished the crumpled taco truck paper out. She flattened it against her thigh. Del's phone number stared her in the face. As she dialed, she wasn't sure where the butterflies in her stomach came from. Nerves over possibly having a job she knew nothing about? Anxiety about overcoming the defeat of being fired? They certainly weren't about speaking to Del again.

Were they?

Shaking her head, she hit the call button. The anticipation turned into disappointment when a woman answered, "Citadel Brewing. This is Twyla."

Lena smacked her forehead. Of course it was the brewery's number, not Del's. "Oh, um, hi. I'm calling about the opening for a bartender. Is it still available?"

Chapter 3

Staring up at the brewery's sign, Lena gave serious thought to turning around and hightailing it out of there. She knew nothing about beer, other than the fact she hated it, and she had no experience in the food industry. The only thing Lena could list in her accolades for this job was having excellent people skills.

Lena had been a client favorite for years because she knew how to make someone feel important. Listening to a client's wants and needs, while being able to discuss options professionally, was considered an asset in her line of work. Her mother had called it "being conscientious." Nicole called it "schmoozing." Whatever the correct term, it would be her only saving grace for getting this job.

With a deep breath, Lena pulled on the door handle and stepped inside. Her mouth dropped open as she glanced around the large, open room, taking in the décor. Mismatched tables and chairs littered the space, lacy vintage curtains framed the windows, and the floor was covered in an array of area rugs, none of which were in the same design family.

It's like someone was going for shabby-chic, but stopped at the shabby.

"Can I help you?" A young woman's voice sounded from behind the bar.

Lena looked up to find a tattooed, pierced, pixie-cut donning, slender woman wiping the counter. "Hi. I'm here for an interview. My name is Lena Bouras," Lena said, walking to the counter.

"Oh, yeah. Hey." The woman extended her hand to shake Lena's. "Nice to meet you. I'm Twyla. Have a seat, and I'll let Del know you're here."

Lena gave a curt nod as her stomach did a somersault. Taking a seat at the bar, she berated herself. *No stomach flipping. This guy, who's not your type, might become your boss. You can't do casual with your boss.*

Twyla returned moments later with a paper in her hand. "Here," she said, sliding the paper to Lena. "You need to fill this out. Del's on a phone call, but he'll come get you when he's done. You want something to drink while you wait?"

Lena stared at the beer menu. The clever names of the beers put a smile on her face, especially "Peace Out, Brown Stout," but the information below them was like a foreign language. "Water would be great, thanks."

Twyla nodded and filled a glass, setting it in front of Lena before returning to her duties.

Lena set to work on the application. Filling one out on paper was something she hadn't done in years, but it was refreshing not to have to deal with the tiny fields on her phone. When she came to the prior work experience section, Lena had to swallow the lump in her throat. The spot for previous employer phone numbers was like Kryptonite to her pen. She couldn't fill it in.

As she focused on the paper, the room around her faded away. The pop punk music playing in the background melded into Twyla's humming, and a knot formed in Lena's stomach.

"Lena?" Del's voice shot through her thoughts, and she whipped her head up to find him standing in the hall behind the bar. He was dressed in a button-down shirt and jeans; much different from when she'd met him at the lake. Though he still had a beard and wore a man-bun, this professional version of him was surprisingly enticing. Even more so when his mouth ticked up as their gazes met.

Maybe not my type, but there's no harm in appreciating a handsome man.

"Come on back." He jutted his chin toward the hallway.

With a deep exhale, Lena followed Del, though her knotted gut and heavy legs made it difficult not to trudge. She met him at the end of the hall, his arm stretched out toward a door. Passing him with her head ducked, Lena stepped into the small office and took a seat in front of a large, metal desk.

This room was arguably worse than the main room. The only furniture was the metal desk with a padded metal chair, a filing cabinet, and the extremely uncomfortable wicker chair in which Lena sat. Aside from some sort of framed awards, nothing else hung on the walls. No pictures. No artwork. Just blank, forest-green walls, which looked haphazardly painted.

Oh, the things I could do with this space...

"So," Del said, taking a seat behind the desk and steepling his fingers at his chest. "You thought about it."

Lena flipped her hair over her shoulder and nodded. "I did."

"Good." He stared at her for a long minute, his blue eyes boring into her. He blinked and cleared his throat. "Um, can I see your app?"

"Oh, sure." She handed him the paper, and he reached for it with his left hand. It still had no ring on it. Lena ignored the fact that pleased her, and settled back into her chair, adjusting a few times before accepting she'd never be comfortable.

Del's eyes scanned the paper, but stopped almost instantly, and he arched a curious eyebrow. "Your full name's Galena?"

Lena groaned. "Yes. It's a Greek word meaning 'calm'. My mom thought if she named me it, I'd be an easy baby."

"Were you?"

"Not according to her." Lena shared an animated laugh with Del, but hers faded as she thought about the numerous times her mother had complimented Lena about being headstrong from birth. The look of pride in her mother's eyes when Lena chased down her dream career popped into her mind. Would that look still be there if she knew Lena was throwing away her hard work to be a bartender?

"Something wrong?

"Hm?" Lena realized she was staring at her lap, and lifted her head. Del's face was a mess of sympathetic worry. She shook her head. "No, sorry. I'm fine." She pressed her lips together before curling them into a fake smile.

Del narrowed his eyes, then went back to studying Lena's application. After only a few seconds, he asked, "So, how was the rest of your birthday?"

Lena furrowed her eyebrows as she reached up to twist the charm on her necklace. "It was fine, thank you."

Del nodded, glancing at her fidgeting fingers, and silence overtook the room. Other than the hum of the air conditioning, the only sound was faint punk-rock filtering through the door. Moving her fingers couldn't satiate her nerves as she waited for Del to finish looking over her application, so Lena chewed on the inside of her cheek, not wanting to smudge her lipstick.

After a few minutes, he took a breath and sat back in his chair. "Well, this all looks good. Let's talk shop, shall we?"

Lena gave Del her full attention, putting on her most professional face as she folded her hands in her lap.

"First thing's first," Del said, typing something into his computer. He turned the monitor so Lena could see. "This is your pay rate. Does that work for you?"

Lena did some quick math, and panic bubbled in her so fast, she thought she might vomit. The pay was considerably less than she had made in Los Angeles, but this was an entirely different job in an entirely different field. It wasn't terrible, and Aurora, Colorado was cheaper than Los Angeles, but she'd still have to budget better. "It's great." She didn't believe the words, but she hoped Del did.

"Good." He took a breath, turning the monitor back. "You'll make tips, too, so there's that. We're open Monday through Thursday, from eleven to nine, but Fridays and Saturdays, we're open until ten. We're closed every Sunday."

"How do the shifts work?"

"There will be two openers and two closers, plus a manager; either myself or my son, Jack. During the week, we have at least one mid-shift, but on Fridays and Saturdays, we have two or three. I rotate everyone's days off, so you'll get a full weekend every now and then."

"How nice of you."

"I try to accommodate as best I can."

"That's what a good manager does."

His eyes softened, lingering on hers as if he was lost, before he shook himself out of his stupor. "Do you have any questions for me?"

Other than what the hell am I doing here? "Nope, I think you hit all the key points."

"Fantastic. Can you start Monday?"

Lena jerked her head back. Being asked to come in the same afternoon she called about the job surprised her enough, but to be hired practically on the spot downright startled her. "Um, sure. Monday would be great."

Del's lips curled into a warm smile. "Cool. Be here at nine. You'll have two hours before we open to get some shirts, log into the system, and start orientation."

"Okay, sounds good." Lena stood and Del followed suit, holding his arm out toward the office door. They walked down the hall to the main room, where Lena stopped and turned to Del. "Thank you for this. I really appreciate it."

"I'm just glad you thought about it." He winked, and a flutter ran through her. Turning toward the bar, Del shouted over the music, "Twyla! Say hi to your new coworker!" Del raised his arm, turning his hand down to point at Lena.

Twyla's green eyes lit up as she waved enthusiastically.

Del put his hands in his pockets. "See you Monday. Enjoy the rest of your weekend."

"Thanks. You too."

Lena left the brewery feeling rejuvenated, as she practically skipped through the parking lot to her car. She had a job. It wasn't one she'd ever imagined having, but it was a job all the same, and she hadn't had to work very hard at all to get it.

She paused before opening her car door, the keys dangling from her fingers. Why was it so easy to get the job? Del didn't ask any questions pertaining to her work history, or employment in general. He didn't even inquire about the blank spot where her previous employer's contact information should have been. It was as if he'd planned on hiring her with or without an interview.

Lena shook her head. None of that mattered; all that did was she had the job.

Chapter 4

Monday morning, Lena sat in her car, nervously fiddling with her necklace. If her hair wasn't tied up, it would be twisted around her finger tighter than a woven finger trap.

She'd been in the Citadel Brewing parking lot for fifteen minutes. Being early was something she prided herself on, though sometimes she was a bit too early.

Usually, she used this extra time to prepare for her clients. She'd go over last-minute details, flip through her portfolio to ensure it catered to their tastes, and triple-check she'd met the budget if not coming in under the line. It was how she stayed on top of things.

This extra time, though, she used to question everything about taking this job.

I don't belong here. Not only do I know nothing about beer, but I have no experience. Del probably only hired me because he felt bad I lost my job. I should go home.

But what would she do at home? Stare at her computer, not clicking on the links for job postings? That wouldn't get her very far.

With a huff, she let go of her necklace, closed her eyes, and swallowed her anxiety. *You can do this, Lena. So what if you don't drink beer? You can still learn about it.*

She took a second to double check her makeup was on point, and to ensure her hair was secure in the topknot on her head. Climbing out of her car, she straightened her flowy blouse and smoothed her black slacks, taking an extra moment to shake out the heaviness in her legs. Her heels clacked on the pavement as she crossed the parking lot. No sooner did she step onto the sidewalk, the front door swung open with a *WHOOSH.*

Twyla leaned on the handle, half inside the doorway and half out. "Hey there, Lena. Come on in."

"Good morning, Twyla," Lena said, stepping inside the eerily quiet building. Much different from the previous Friday when pop punk music blared through the speakers.

"Hang on a second. I haven't had a chance to set up." Twyla walked behind the bar, disappearing beneath the counter. A few seconds later, music came pouring overhead. Twyla stood, already singing the lyrics to some punk rock song Lena didn't know.

"For crying out loud, Twyla! The Stooges, again?" A guy, the spitting image of Del, complete with a beard, but about twenty years younger with short-cropped blond hair, came from the hall, carrying several trays of pint glasses. "Don't you listen to anything good?" Disdain hung in his words.

Twyla stuck out her tongue, flipped him off, and went back to singing as she rounded the bar and took the trays from him.

With an exasperated sigh, he wiped his hands on his jeans and extended one to Lena. "Hi, I'm Jack. You must be our new bartender." His eyes were the same shade of blue as Del's, but colder.

She nodded as she shook his hand, fighting the urge to shy away under his scrutinizing stare. "I'm Lena. Nice to meet you, Jack."

The handshake was short and stiff. All business. "I'll go let my dad know you're here," he said flatly, then headed down the hallway toward Del's office.

Lena shivered. Between Del and Twyla, she'd received warm welcomes, but Jack didn't seem to harbor the same hospitality.

"Don't let him get to you," Twyla said. "Jack's a good guy. He's just protective of his dad."

"Del needs protecting? From me?"

Twyla gave a knowing look before turning around to stack glasses onto shelves behind the bar.

"Lena, glad you made it." Del's voice sounded from the hall.

She met his gaze, her stomach flipping instantly at those warm, bright blue eyes. "You said nine, so here I am."

His eyes roamed her body up and down. "There you certainly are."

The air changed. Suddenly, it was as if they were the only two people in the room and the world had gone still. Electricity popped within the space between them. They regarded each other for what felt like eternity, and Lena was swept up in the whirlwind moment.

"Earth to Del," Jack said, clapping his father on the back.

Del's body shook as if coming out of a trance, and he shrugged his son's hand off. "What's up, Jack?"

"Lena needs to start orientation. Or do you two wanna finish your staring contest?" The question sounded like a joke, but Jack's tone was accusatory, like he was scolding them for wasting time.

Lena's cheeks flushed, and she ducked her head.

"Smartass." Del cleared his throat. "Lena, can I have your ID, please?"

"Oh, sure." She fished it from her wallet and handed it to Del, who passed it to Jack.

"Her application is on my desk. You can start inputting her into the system." Del turned to Lena as Jack disappeared into the office. "He'll set you up to clock in and out. In the meantime, Twyla can get you a couple shirts, show you around, and familiarize you with what we do here."

"Thank you."

Del raised his hand like he was going to pat her on the back, but stopped and ran his hand over his head instead. With a tight smile, he trotted down the hall to join his son in the office.

The room felt empty without him, which confused Lena to no end. She didn't understand why the butterflies swarmed in his presence, or why she felt flushed when he looked at her. He wasn't her type. Even if he was, he was now her boss, and she couldn't casually date her boss.

Lena deflated as she realized she would have to settle for appreciating his handsomeness from afar.

"Hey. Let's get started," Twyla said, startling Lena. "What size shirt do you wear?"

***

After selecting a few t-shirts to wear as uniforms, Lena was given the ins and outs of serving beer. Twyla explained what beers went with which glasses, and showed Lena how to fill a glass correctly to avoid too much foam on the top.

"When you grab a new glass from the shelf, you always run it through the rinse," Twyla said, turning a pint glass upside down, and setting it on a metal plate. When she pushed the glass down, water sprayed into it. "Or, as I call it, give the glass a shower."

Lena laughed. Despite the obvious almost twenty-year age difference, she and Twyla were getting along splendidly. Twyla was energetic, upbeat, and hilarious in an I-don't-care-what-anyone-thinks-of-me sort of way.

"The used glasses get put in this tray." Twyla pointed to a blue tray, similar to the one Jack had brought out earlier. "Once the tray is full, someone runs it to the back and loads the dishwasher so they can all be sterilized."

"Makes sense."

Twyla let out a breath and leaned onto the bar counter, pursing her lips. "I don't know what's taking Jack so fucking long." She glanced at the clock. It was 9:43 a.m. "I guess we can start getting into the beers. What's your favorite?"

Lena tensed, her spine stiffening. She had been dreading this part. She hadn't drank a beer since college, and it was such an unpleasant experience she didn't even know how to fake her way through this. With a deep swallow, Lena shrugged.

"You've never had any of our beers?"

Lena shook her head, pressing her lips into a flat line.

"Okay. Then what types of beers do you like? We'll start there."

Lena crinkled her nose, grimacing.

Twyla's mouth dropped open, her lip piercing glinting in the light. "You mean to tell me you took a job at a brewery and you don't drink beer?"

"Yes?" Lena dropped her face into her hands. When she finally raised her head, peeking through her fingers, she found Twyla looking at her in sympathy. "I'm clueless."

"Well, clueless, nice to meet you," Twyla said with a teasing smirk.

Lena let out a breathy chuckle, relaxing a bit before she sighed. "I have no idea what I'm doing."

"Lucky for you, I'm here." Twyla turned around and crawled on the counter. She carefully removed each of the beer nameplates before climbing down. Separating them into groups, she explained what each group was. "These are light beers. Some are crisp and refreshing, some are smooth. Also, they're not too hoppy, which is what most beginners tend to enjoy. Then, there are malty beers and the hoppy ones. These last ones are dark beers. They usually sit a little heavier in your stomach."

Lena stared at the nameplates, fifteen in total, and felt a pit form in her gut. "What do I do if someone asks me for a recommendation?"

"Well, most people coming in know what they want, or at least know what kind of beer they like. They're going to say 'I like stouts,' and you'll say 'okay, try this one.'" Twyla points to the Peace Out, Brown Stout nameplate. "Or, they'll say 'the hoppier, the better,' and you'll say, 'then try this.'"

All right, I can handle that. "But what if they want to know *my* favorite?" Being asked about her opinion was commonplace in her world of design, and she had confidence when giving it. Beer was an entirely new universe.

Twyla pursed her lips into an exaggerated duck face as her green eyes lifted to the ceiling. "Well, you can either tell them the truth, which I would not recommend." She dropped her gaze back to Lena's. "Or, you can go with whichever of these beers you think has the best name."

Lena read all the names once more. Some of them were quite clever, like Tis the Saison, and some were just plain silly, like Mister Spock's Bock. The one that kept drawing her eye, though, was one that made her *feel* silly. She pointed at the nameplate. "This one."

"Ah, Love Hops IPA. Good one."

"How did it get its name? All the others are kind of self-explanatory, but that one doesn't really fit."

"Well, it's pretty hoppy, so if someone loves hops, it's the one for them. But Del came up with the name because he said when he drank it the first time, his stomach felt like it was hopping." Twyla gathered the nameplates, but before she turned back to put them away, she locked her eyes on Lena's, giving her a knowing look. "He said it was like being in love."

Lena swallowed, but didn't say anything.

Twyla snorted. "I know. Fucking cheesy, right?" She turned her back to Lena, climbed onto the counter, and replaced the nameplates. When she was finished, she hopped down. Glancing at the clock, she said, "Geez, what is taking Jack so long? We've only got another ten minutes until we open, and you haven't even logged into the damn system."

As if she'd summoned him, Jack came around the corner. "What were you saying, Twyla?" The serious expression on his face, and the harsh tone of his voice, made Lena tense, but Twyla just mockingly sneered at him. He rolled his eyes, turning to hand Lena her ID. "Sorry that took so long. The system was having issues." He checked his watch. "You should try to login before we open. This is your employee number." He handed her a card with a six-digit number on it. "Your password is your birthday, and then you'll be prompted to change it."

"Thank you," Lena said timidly.

With a curt nod, he went back down the hall, and Lena let out a breath.

"'You should try to log in before we open,'" Twyla said in a snotty tone. "He makes it sound like we have people banging on the door to get in."

"Do you guys do a lot of business?"

Twyla tilted her head from side to side. "Decent. We're not the hopping-est brewery in town, but we've got our regulars, and we do pretty well on week-ends."

Lena looked around the poorly decorated space again, letting her eyes wander through the window. A business park across the street caught her eye. "You don't get a lot of business from there?" She jutted her chin toward the tall office buildings.

Twyla shook her head. "Nah, they don't come in here much. Sometimes, later in the evening when they're done with work, but never during the day, and never with clients."

"Hm. I wonder why?" *Drinking beer seems like a good way to schmooze people.*

"I overheard a snooty guy once tell his group he didn't think we looked professional enough." There was annoyance in her voice. "Our décor wasn't up to his impeccable standards, I guess."

Well, that's obvious. Lena opened her mouth to suggest all the things swimming in her mind as to how they could improve the interior look of Citadel Brewing, but snapped it shut. She had to keep telling herself, design wasn't her life anymore.

Chapter 5

The morning flew by. Lena stayed attached to Twyla's hip as she walked Lena through serving and ringing out customers. Lena's biggest snafu was mistaking the mid-shift employee, Marky, for a customer, and as the hours passed, Lena's confidence grew. She began thinking this job wouldn't be so bad.

After the closing team members came in, Twyla suggested she and Lena take their lunches.

"Oh, I hadn't even thought about lunch. What's good around here?" Lena asked.

Before Twyla could answer, Del's voice sounded from the hall. "There's a Mexican place around the corner that has great tacos."

Lena spun around as Del stepped behind the bar. "I do love tacos."

"I know." He leaned onto the counter, resting his forearms on it. "I'm actually pretty hungry myself. Why don't I show you where it is? You know, take the new employee to lunch."

"Sounds good." Lena tipped up on her toes, the start of a bounce, but let her heels down and cemented them to the floor. "Thank you." The excitement bubbling inside her was nothing more than the anticipation of filling her empty stomach. At least, that's what she told herself.

Del's mouth quirked up, his beard shifting with the movement. "Grab your stuff, and I'll meet you out front."

After clocking out, Lena hurried to the break room to get her purse. She eyed the folding chairs. The urge to sit and kick off her heels was strong, but her boss was waiting. She'd have to suffer through the pain of her aching feet.

Once outside, she found Del standing to the side of the front door. He didn't notice her right away, so she paused for a moment to take him in.

His gray button-down shirt looked a bit tight on him from the way it strained around his shoulders, but that wasn't surprising. Lena had seen with her own two eyes his muscular body at the lake. Heat flooded her cheeks as she thought about the what he looked like beneath the shirt.

She bit her lower lip as she watched Del tuck his phone into the back pocket of his jeans before rolling his sleeves up his forearms. Man-bun or not, Del was a fine specimen of a man; Lena couldn't deny it.

You're not looking for a boyfriend. And certainly not with your boss. Lena shook her head, and cleared her throat, making Del look up at her. "Ready?"

He nodded. "It's around the corner. Would you like to walk?"

The notion of walking any farther than her car made Lena's feet hurt even more. She crinkled her nose and glanced down at her designer heels.

"Driving it is. Hang tight, I'll pull my truck around."

A breath of relief blew from Lena's lips, but she quickly sucked it back in as she watched Del walk away. Jeans did the man justice, or his butt, at least.

"Don't stare too hard. You'll burn a hole through him," Twyla whispered as she passed Lena on the sidewalk.

Lena all but yelped, her hand flying to her chest. "For crying out loud, Twyla."

Twyla laughed and walked away with her hand waving in the air.

Moments later, when Del drove up in his shiny, red Ford F-150, he got out and walked Lena around to open her door. She thanked him as he helped her into the cab, and she meant it whole-heartedly. Though the ruggedness of a truck was a stark difference from the sports cars driven by her playboys in L.A., it still felt luxurious. She sank into the plush seat, enjoying the ample leg room, and appreciating Del's refreshing chivalry.

The country music station on the radio was about the only thing making this moment less than perfect.

Del climbed into the driver's seat and pulled the truck away from the curb. "So, you've learned heels aren't appropriate attire for working at a brewery, huh?"

Lena kicked off the heels to rub her feet. "And I learned it quickly."

"Sorry. I should've explained the dress code better."

"No, I should've used my brain. This is my go-to business attire. It's what I'm used to."

Del shot her a sideways glance. "Well, you look nice."

Lena blushed, turning her head to look out the window.

"So, what else have you learned today?"

"Everything." Lena explained how thorough Twyla had been that morning. She gave Del every detail of her first shift, and by the end of her story, they had reached the restaurant.

Del put the truck in park and cut the engine, leaning his forearm onto the steering wheel. "You really came in this morning with no knowledge whatsoever?"

"I told you I didn't drink beer."

Instead of laughing, Del tilted his head to look at her from the corner of his eye. "I won't hold it against you."

"Thanks." Lena shifted in her seat, a question burning on the tip of her tongue. "Why did you hire me?"

"Um, because you needed a job, and I needed a bartender."

"No, I mean, why did you hire me on the spot? You didn't ask about any of my work history, or experience. How did you decide I would be right for the job?"

Del drew in a long breath, a look of embarrassment on his face. "You'll think I'm crazy."

"I already kind of think you're crazy for blindly hiring someone. So, spill it."

His deep chuckle rumbled through the truck's cab. "Your name."

"My name?" If she could be any more confused, Lena's face would be permanently wrinkled. "How did my name make you want to hire me?"

"Well, for one thing, it's prettier than my full name."

Lena stifled a snorted laugh. "And what is your full name?"

Del sighed, hanging his head. "Delbert."

"Delbert?"

"My parents were cruel." He tilted his head up with a smirk on his face, letting Lena know he teased.

"It's not so bad," Lena said gently. She paused, still confused about the legitimacy of him hiring her for her name. "But did you seriously hire me because my name is prettier than yours?"

"No." He sat all the way up, his mouth twitching like he fought a full grin. "Galena is a type of hop."

Lena stared at Del with her mouth open. "You *are* crazy."

His hearty laugh relieved her. "When I found out you needed a job, it was a fantastic coincidence. When you called for an interview, it was a relief. But when I saw your full name on your application, it was like a sign." Del turned his head, his blue eyes sparkling in the sunlight. "Call it a hunch, if you will, but something told me you were the person for the job."

An airy feeling overtook Lena's body, but she couldn't let the flattery get the best of her. "So, you hired me on a hunch? Is that good business practice?"

"You tell me." He winked, and Lena felt a flutter from her stomach to her throat. "Come on, let's get some tacos."

***

Del was right. The Mexican restaurant had fantastic tacos. Lena scarfed down three of them without even thinking. As she sat back, sagging against the booth, she let out a deep breath. "Those were delicious." She reached for her forgotten water glass. The tacos were so good, she hadn't taken a single sip yet.

"Glad you liked them." Del took another bite. "So," he mumbled. "Why do you always order veggie tacos?"

"I'm a vegetarian."

Del stopped before he took another bite, eyeing Lena over his taco. "You are?"

She nodded. "Ever since they made us dissect things in high school science class." Lena stuck out her tongue, feigning a gag.

With a small smile, Del bit into his taco. "Now, I'm intrigued. Tell me more about Galena Bouras."

With a roll of her eyes, Lena took a long draw of her water, swishing it around in her mouth before swallowing. "What else do you want to know?"

"As much as I can get." Del's deep, husky voice gave Lena a delightful chill. "Where were you born?"

"Um, here, actually."

His eyebrows shot up. "Really?"

"Mhm. I lived here all the way through high school."

"So, what happened after that?" Del took another bite.

"I wanted to get out of Colorado. Thought a change of scenery would help me find myself, and figure out what I wanted to do with my life."

"Where did it take you?"

"California."

Del bristled, huffing as he stuffed the last bit of his taco into his mouth.

"You don't like California?"

As he chewed, Del looked at Lena with frustration in his eyes. "I associate it with some negativity in my life."

"Well, it certainly isn't for everyone. Especially L.A., where I lived." Lena picked up her water and swirled the ice with her straw. "I miss it, though. Parts of it, anyway."

"What brought you back to Colorado?"

She took several sips of her water, trying to lubricate the words as if it would help her speak them. "My, uh, mother passed away in April."

"I'm sorry to hear that, Lena. Was it sudden?"

"No. Quite the opposite." Lena wrung her hands in her lap. "She had breast cancer and did chemo for years. Even went into remission, but it came back. The doctors placed her in hospice care in February, so I spent as much time as I could out here with her until the beginning of April when she..."

Silence overtook the air. Lena's watery eyes darted across the tabletop as she waited for Del to speak, but he didn't. She finally lifted her head to find him staring at her, a look of pure compassion on his face. His blue eyes stayed trained on her, but instead of making her squirm, they eased her tension.

Lena gently swiped her lashes, careful not to smudge her eyeliner. "She left everything to me, and I had planned on selling the house, but then I lost my job, so I just moved out here. Seemed easier than dealing with all the shit in Los Angeles." Lena snapped her mouth shut, bringing her hand to her lips. She didn't swear often from being trained by Nicole, and she certainly would never swear in front of her superior, but Del had a way of making her comfortable.

He waved her off like it wasn't a big deal. "What about your father?"

Lena snorted. "I haven't seen him since I was five. He and my mom never got married, which is why when I was born, she gave me her last name. He packed up and left one day, leaving my mom to raise me by herself."

"Well, from what I've seen, she did a fantastic job," Del said, smiling.

"Thanks." Warmth bloomed in Lena's chest at Del's compliment. "I know it wasn't all sunshine and rainbows being a single mom, but her self-discipline and hard work rubbed off on me. She sacrificed a lot, but she was strong." Lena reached up to touch the lightning bolt on her necklace. "This was hers. She said it represented strength and power because Zeus wielded the thunderbolt."

Del arched an eyebrow. "What does Zeus have to do with anything?"

Lena laughed. "My mother got really into Greek mythology at one point. I think being Greek herself made her feel more connected to the stories."

"Ah, I see. And your father, was he Greek, too?"

"Not that my mother ever mentioned. She just said he was a selfish man who couldn't be bothered to give up his dreams to help raise a child, so he left."

"Sounds like my ex-wife," Del said with a tight jaw.

Lena didn't want to be pleased with the word "ex-wife," so she fought the smile crossing her lips. "You were married?"

Del nodded. "Amy and I were high school sweethearts, who got married a year into college because we found out about Jack." He raised his eyebrows with a knowing look.

"Oh."

"Yeah. She decided to put her schooling on hold to be a mom, and I cut back on my credits so I could hold a job to provide for us. Which meant it took me twice as long to graduate."

"But at least you graduated."

Del rubbed the back of his neck. "Which we celebrated in the hospital when our second son, Jameson, was born."

Lena fought a snicker. "What was your degree in?"

"Business. I knew I wanted to run my own, and somewhere in my seven years of college, I developed a passion for brewing beer. So, about two years after I graduated, we had our grand opening of Citadel Brewing." He hung his head, looking up at Lena through his eyelashes. "With two-week-old Johnnie, in tow."

Lena couldn't help it. Even though she felt incredibly rude, she let out a giggle.

Del groaned. "I know. You'd think we'd have figured it out after the first time."

"No, I'm sorry." Lena shook her head, lifting her fingertips to her lips. "I shouldn't have laughed."

"It's all right. We got through it. Some things just took longer than expected, and some" —Del sighed— "never even happened."

"What do you mean?"

He took a deep breath, expanding his chest before leaning against the booth. "Amy put all her dreams on hold to be a mom. I think... I *know* she held some resentment toward me for it because my dreams were coming true, but she also resented the boys."

Lena furrowed her brow. "Why do you think that?"

"Because when Johnnie was three, she filed for divorce, packed up, and left to pursue her career."

What could be more important than your family? "Which was?"

Del licked his lips, biting down hard on the bottom one. "To be a designer to the stars in California." He didn't even try to hide the frustration in his voice.

Lena shrunk in her seat. "Oh."

"Then I was given the dubious honor of being a single dad to my three boys, Jack, Jameson, and Johnnie."

Her mouth quirked up. "That's cute they all start with 'J.'"

Del grunted.

"It's not?"

"It would've been cute if my ex hadn't named them after her favorite whiskeys." He pursed his lips. "She didn't drink beer either."

As Lena's stomach dropped into her feet, nausea consumed her. Her entire body was heavy, and it cemented her to the booth. "Not great odds," she said under her breath.

"What was that?"

Her heart leaped into her throat, but she straightened her posture, swallowing it back down. "I realized I'm three for three with things in common with your ex."

Del furrowed his brow, but remained silent.

"California, design, and disliking beer."

His face fell, the skin around his bright blue eyes crinkling as he smiled warmly. "Lena, you are nothing like my ex. And I would never judge someone based on *her* decisions. Yes, I have some negativity associated with certain things because of her, but it doesn't mean I can't like someone who may have similar interests."

She nodded as goosebumps crept up the back of her neck.

"Now," Del said, laying his napkin on his plate. "I'll get the bill so we can get back to work."

Chapter 6

"Hey, Lena. You wanna come out with me and the girls tonight?" Twyla's question caught Lena off guard as she wiped down tables after closing the following Saturday night.

"Me? With you? Really?"

Twyla shrugged. "Sure, why not? I mean, I know you've only worked here a week, but you seem pretty cool."

And twice your age. "I don't know, Twyla."

"Did you, or did you not tell me about your party days in L.A.?" She rolled her eyes. "It's just us girls looking for the three Ds."

"Three Ds?"

"Dancing, drinking, and dick."

Lena choked on her breath as she let out a hearty laugh.

Twyla grinned. "I'm kidding. I've got a boyfriend, but I still like to dance and drink with my girls. I'll leave the dicks to you all." She picked up the used glass tray. "Think about it," Twyla said as she disappeared down the hall.

Lena pursed her lips as she continued her closing duties. She hadn't been out to party since moving to Colorado, and she missed it immensely. Nicole had said she needed to get out there again, and now she had someone to go with, but should she? These women were all fifteen to twenty years younger than her. Would she be able to keep up with them? Would she look like the old lady surrounded by twenty-something-year-olds? Or worse, would someone mistake her for their mom?

She pressed her lips into a flat line. "Screw it."

"Did you say something?" Twyla asked, coming around the corner.

Lena stood up to face her. "Yes. I'd like to go out with you girls tonight."

"Fuck yeah." Twyla's face lit up. "Let's get finished here and I'll order us an Uber."

"What? I'm not ready to go out." Lena floated her hands down her torso, motioning to her Citadel t-shirt, jeans, and new tennis shoes. She'd learned her lesson after her first day on the job. "I need to go home first."

Twyla waved her off. "Nah, I've got some clothes in my car for emergencies like this." She eyed Lena, as if sizing her up. "You're pretty close to my size. I'm sure I've got a shirt you can wear. What size shoes?"

"Um, eight."

"Perfect. I've got some strappy sandals that'll work."

Lena furrowed her brow. "*You* wear strappy sandals?"

"Ugh, no." Twyla crinkled her nose, waving her hand as if some offensive odor invaded her nostrils. "My mom gave them to me thinking I'd 'grow up' one of these days." The disdain in her voice was palpable. "They live in my car, though, in case I ever need something to throw on. You know, back-up shoes."

Lena laughed, shaking her head. "Okay, I guess I'm game."

***

The thumping of the bass in the club was louder than Lena remembered it being in Los Angeles. The lighting was dimmer too. Masses of bodies crammed together on the dance floor moved like ocean waves. Not the calm, fluid, beautiful waves one sees in vacation ads. No, these waves were those of choppy waters. Like a storm brewed on the horizon, and it would only be a short time before it capsized Lena.

She sat at the table, sipping her fourth cranberry vodka cocktail as she watched Twyla dance with her friends. Lena had offered to keep an eye on their drinks when the alcohol hit her earlier than normal. It may have been the three shots she did prior to the cocktails, but she chalked her lower-than-normal tolerance up to the higher elevation in Denver.

She didn't mind sitting for a while. Besides, this wasn't her song. In fact, Lena didn't even know the song. Only two months out of the game, had she really become so obsolete?

She shook her head, making the room spin. *No way.* Her little break from the clubs and parties was just that, a break. Now she had Twyla to go out with, so she could jump back into the scene and into her old life. Well, the fun parts of her old life.

The job wasn't the same, but it was a job, and a much less demanding one than what she had previously. Her hours were shorter, she was hounded less by the customers, and the atmosphere was pleasantly cooperative. It didn't hurt that she had an attractive boss to ogle either.

Lena sat straight up in her seat, now thankful for the dim lighting hiding her pink cheeks. Del was her *boss*. Nothing more. He wasn't even the type of man Lena was attracted to. He was rugged, outdoorsy, and he drank beer for crying out loud.

Sure, he was refined around the edges. One could even call him polished when he dressed up for work, but underneath, he was different. Lena bit her lip as she imagined what he looked like without the dress clothes. Those broad shoulders that stretched his shirts taut across his chest, and his corded forearms peeking out from the rolled-up sleeves. The way his ass filled out his pants.

Suddenly, Lena was very thirsty, but not for the cocktail sitting in front of her. She downed it nonetheless and scanned the room for a server. As her gaze landed on the bar, a pair of dark brown eyes stared back at her, accompanied by a bright white smile against bronze skin.

Lena smiled back, and the guy slid off his stool to head toward her. He was dressed in a designer suit. Lena could tell from the way the fabric moved with his steps. Cheap suits were stiff, unflattering. This suit moved with him like it had been tailored for his body. He adjusted his shirt cuffs as he reached her, putting his hands on the table and leaning down.

The music faded as he opened his mouth and said, "Hi." His voice was smooth, like satin, and his eyes were like melted chocolate. This was exactly the type of guy Lena usually went for.

"Hi," she replied, leaning closer.

The guy opened his mouth, but the music started again, drowning him out. He pressed his lips into a line and hung his head. When he lifted it, he motioned to Lena's drink and held up a finger as if to ask, "You want another?"

Lena nodded, even though her stomach felt uneasy.

He held up his hand in the "okay" symbol before turning back to the bar.

She watched him intently. He was decently built with a broad frame, and he had terrific posture. He was tall, at least 6'3", but he didn't lumber around. His movements were so smooth, they mesmerized Lena. When he returned to the booth, she scooted in to give him room.

He slid in next to her, leaving hardly any space between them, and handed her drink to her. She mouthed the words, "Thank you," pleased to see a whiskey in his hand instead of a beer.

He leaned in close to her ear. "My name's Darren." He had to speak loudly for her to hear over the music.

As he sat back up, he turned his head and pointed to his own ear. She leaned in. "Lena."

When they faced each other again, he gave an approving nod, as if to say, "Nice to meet you."

They picked up their glasses, clinking them together before taking a sip. The moment would have been awkward, except the music faded into a slow song much less boisterous than the last one.

Darren blew out a breath. "That's better." He turned his body to face her. "Lena, was it?"

She nodded.

"You have a beautiful name."

"Thank you." She blushed as she took another sip.

"Are you here alone tonight?" Darren asked as he looked around the table at the other glasses.

Lena shook her head. "My girlfriends are out there somewhere." The words left her lips as languidly as her hand waving at the dance floor.

Darren didn't even turn to look. He kept his chocolate eyes on her, his stare only wavering when his eyes flicked to her left hand. "Just girlfriends?"

"Mhm."

His mouth ticked up briefly.

"So, Darren, what do you do?"

He threw his arm behind her, resting it on the back of the curved booth. "I'm in finance. My office is around the corner, actually."

A sour taste crept up the back of her tongue, so she took another drink. Ozzie had been in finance. And *in* his receptionist. Lena brushed off the thoughts, but turned on her confidence. "Oh, so you're in here a lot, huh?"

His arm lowered to drape across her shoulders. "Only when there's beautiful women to be found." His fingers grazed the exposed skin of her bicep, and Lena stifled a nervous shiver.

It had been a long time since a man had touched her, with the exception of Del at the lake, but that was different. Del had been saving her from falling into the water. It didn't matter that his chest was firm, or that his embrace gave her a sense of safety, or that his eyes were soft and□

"Lena?" Darren's voice interrupted her thoughts. "You okay?" His fingers were actively brushing her arm now and he was sitting close enough for their thighs to touch.

She shook her head to clear it before nodding.

A sly smirk crossed Darren's face. "Look, I don't normally do this, but..." He leaned over to put his mouth to her ear. "Would you like to get out of here? I don't live far."

Her breath caught in her throat. This is what she was used to; being taken home by a hot guy in a club, when they both knew it was for nothing more but the night. Darren was young, early to mid-thirties, and his eyes were full of lust. Exactly what Lena wanted.

But when she turned to say, "yes," the word stuck to her tongue. Images of her and Darren tangled in his bed sheets, slobbering over one another until the sun came up flashed in her mind. The thought of which left an emptiness in her chest. She should have been elated, or at the very least, turned on, but she wasn't.

Feeling deflated, she shook her head. "No, thank you."

"What?" Darren's head jerked back, a crease forming between his perfectly sculpted eyebrows.

"No, Darren. I won't be going home with you tonight." As drunk as she was, Lena still couldn't believe the words as she said them, though they felt right leaving her lips.

"Bitch," Darren derided and stormed off.

Lena let out a sigh and sagged against the booth, surprisingly unbothered by his absence. What happened? In Los Angeles, she met a new guy every weekend and never had any qualms with the one-night-stand arrangements. Was this what middle age would be like? Losing the happy-go-lucky parts of yourself and vying for stability? If so, Lena wasn't prepared for it.

She huffed a breath and gulped her drink down, the room spinning more as she finished.

"Heeyyyyy!" Tywla sang as she slipped into the opposite side of the booth. The other girls followed, all scooting around to file in.

Lena smiled, trying to hide her defeat. "Having fun?"

They all nodded as they sucked down their waters before picking up their cocktails.

"You should come dance since you're done with your drink," Twyla said.

Lena twirled her glass on the table. "Actually, I think I'm going to call it a night. I'm pretty wiped out from work today." She stood up, sliding her hands into the back pockets of her jeans.

"What? No! Stay!" Twyla begged.

"No, I'm ready for bed." The music picked up, so Lena wiggled her fingers in the air and the girls all waved back. As Lena turned to leave, she tapped her phone screen to order an Uber.

What a waste of a night.

Chapter 7

Lena groaned heavily as she poured herself another cup of English breakfast tea. This would make her third of the day and it wasn't even 10 a.m. She massaged her temple, leaning onto the counter and over the mug so the steam wafted into her face.

"How am I *this* hungover?" Her voice broke through the usually uncomfortable quiet of the room. Right now, though, she was thankful for it.

She picked up the mug and shuffled to her living room. After carefully setting her tea on the coffee table, she flopped onto the couch, flinging her arm over her face. The events of the night replayed behind her closed eyelids.

Too many shots. Maybe one too many cocktails. I shouldn't have taken the drink from... what was his name? Damon? She shook her head. *No. Darren. What a jerk.*

Frustration bubbled in her gut. He had been right up her alley. A perfect way for Lena to not only release some pent-up tension, but also to take back her life. A one-night stand was exactly what she needed to feel like her old self again.

But she threw it away.

For what, though? Darren was young, hot, charming. Sure, he was probably only interested in seeing her for the night, but that was all Lena wanted. Wasn't it?

With a groan, she pulled her phone from her bathrobe pocket to call Nicole, but her mouth dropped open when she glimpsed her reflection in the screen. She looked feral. Her hair sat in a tangled mess on top of her head while her eye makeup was smeared down her cheek. Lipstick strayed dangerously outside her lip liner like a Picasso painting.

She jumped from the couch to head into the bathroom, where she splashed water on her face and finger-combed her hair. *Thank goodness I woke up alone.*

The thought gave her pause. While she certainly considered herself lucky to be unattached, she'd never viewed an empty bed the same. Waking up next to a gorgeous naked man was a phenomenal way to begin a day. She'd done it several times over the years.

Why, then, was she content to be alone now?

"It's just a bump in the road," she spoke to her reflection in the bathroom mirror as if it would respond with validation. "I've had a rough couple months, and I deserve a little me-time. I'll get back on the party bus at some point, but there's no rush."

The words made sense, but unease settled in her stomach. She brushed it off as part of the hangover. Sitting down on the couch, Lena took a sip of her tea. The hot liquid ran down her throat, chasing away the quiver in her gut, and her body sagged into the cushions.

"Just a bump in the road," she repeated, closing her eyes to let the darkness ease her headache.

***

Two weeks later, Lena was well on her way to job confidence. She had learned the little things, like how to fill a pint glass properly and how to manage serving multiple tables, but she also had become a pro at trouble shooting the computer system. Several times, she fixed an issue without calling the IT company. She'd always been a quick learner, and experience was the best teacher.

Which made the easiest part of the job getting to know the regulars.

Her previous line of work was all about knowing the client and their needs. Lena knew how to listen actively while tucking information into her brain for future use. This skill proved handy at Citadel Brewing, too.

"Thanks, Leen," one of their regulars said as he tossed a few dollars on the bar.

"No problem, Sam. Tell Mona I hope she feels better."

He waved as he ambled out the door, and Lena grabbed her tip, wiping the counter after she did. She stuffed her money into her pocket, and deposited the used glass into the tray as she mentally patted herself on the back for a job well done.

"Well, Beth's officially not coming in today," Marky said, snark in his tone as he leaned against the counter. Lena had met all the employees at this point, and every one of them welcomed her. Jack was the only one still distant. "I overheard Jack talking to her. Something's wrong with her car."

Lena glanced at the clock; it was almost 5:30 p.m. The morning crew would be leaving soon. "I was starting to wonder if she'd ever show up, but that sucks about her car." Lena whipped her head up. "Wait. She's supposed to close with me tonight."

Marky waved her off. "Oh honey, Jack will probably ask me to stay and knock the extra time off another day."

Like clockwork, Jack appeared from the back office. "Hey, Marky. Can you stay tonight and help close up? You can take a long lunch or something another day?"

Marky shot Lena a knowing look before turning to Jack and nodding. "Sure thing, boss man." He saluted Jack, standing at attention like a soldier.

Jack rolled his eyes and went back to the office.

Lena giggled. "I don't think he appreciates your humor."

"Whatever." Marky ran his hand over his perfectly gelled dark hair. He grabbed the used glass tray. "I'll go load the washer."

Being a Thursday, the brewery wasn't very busy, so Lena and Marky were able to handle the evening. A little after 7 p.m., Del came in looking much more casual than usual. He still wore his jeans, but donned a t-shirt instead of a button-down, and it was stretched tight across his chest.

Lena pepped up as he walked through the door, her stomach fluttering. "Hey, Del." His name rolled off her tongue easily; a little too easily.

As their eyes met, a light flashed in his and his features softened. "Hey, Lena." He walked to the counter, leaning onto it. "How's it going?"

"It's been fine. Even without Beth, Marky and I have handled everything."

Del furrowed his brow. "Where's Beth?"

"She was having car issues, so Jack asked Marky to stay and cut his extra hours somewhere else."

Del's brow remained furrowed, but he also pursed his lips. "Is Jack in the office?"

Lena nodded, jutting her chin toward the hall.

He stood upright, taking a deep breath. "Excuse me. I'll be right back." Del not-so-lightly walked down the hall to the office. A few minutes and a rather loud conversation later, Jack stormed into the tasting room and out the front door.

Del appeared moments after, running his hands over his hair to tighten his bun. He caught Lena's confused expression, and opened his mouth, but before he could speak, Marky came around the corner. "Hey, Del. What's up?"

Del sighed, but composed himself. "Marky, what time are you supposed to be off?"

"Um, in, like, twenty minutes."

"Well, I appreciate you agreeing to stay and help Lena close up, but you go home when you're off. I'll stay and close."

A flutter of excitement shot through Lena. Other than their lunch on her first day, she hadn't spent any time alone with Del. She enjoyed his company, and as much as she hated to admit it, she was looking forward to the eye candy.

"You sure, Del?" Marky scratched his clean-shaven chin. "I don't mind."

Del shook his head. "Jack is the assistant manager. He should be the one stepping in to help, not you." His tone was laced with annoyance.

"Okay. I'll, uh, go wipe down the tables." Marky grabbed a dish cloth, and sashayed away from the bar.

Del stood for several moments, rubbing his eyes and groaning.

"Everything okay, Del?" Lena asked.

When he looked at her, all the frustration melted from his face. "Yes. It's fine. Jack needed to be reminded about his place as a manager."

I wonder if Jack just didn't want to be closing alone with me? "Well, it goes to show how dedicated you are to your business, and your employees. It's admirable."

Lena swore Del's cheeks tinged pink beneath the beard, but he nodded and walked away too quickly for her to confirm.

The rest of the evening trudged along. The only customer to come in after Marky left was another regular, Megan; a single mom who worked at the Chili's across the street. She would come in after her shift during the weeks her kids were with their dad. Megan was the first regular Lena had met.

The two women nodded at each other as Megan came in the door. She took a seat at the bar as Lena finished filling up a pint of *What the Helles?* "Long night?" Lena asked.

Megan nodded. "We were short two servers, so I had three sections to myself."

"Oof. Rough." Lena set the glass down in front of Megan, and leaned onto the counter. "How are the kids?"

They talked until closing time came. Megan paid her tab, thanking Lena for listening to her complaints, and went home. After Lena followed Megan to the door to lock it, she lingered, staring at the handle and smiling to herself as pride filled her. Megan had left in a considerably better mood, and Lena knew it had been her doing.

"How did you do that?" Del's voice startled Lena, making her yelp and spin around. When he saw her surprise, he threw his hands up. "Sorry. Didn't mean to scare you."

"It's okay," Lena said in a breath. "How did I do what?"

"Learn so much about our customers in three weeks. You and Megan talked like you were old friends. You knew details about her kids that I didn't know, and she's been a regular here since before those kids were born."

Lena put on a smug face. "It's part of who I am. I learned a long time ago how important it is to make not only clients, but people in general, feel special.

Listening to them and remembering things about their lives is the best way to do so."

Del's eyes softened. Appreciation poured from his bright irises as he stared at her. Lena stood taller, pride swelling inside her, but then, the moment changed. Del's eyes darkened, and his features became serious. The appreciation melted away, absorbed by something more heated, more passionate.

Lena cleared her throat. "I'll, uh, start cleaning." She stepped past Del to grab the cleaning supplies and headed off to sweep. She heard Del sigh as he shut down the register, taking the till to count. It wasn't until she heard the money room door close that she let herself breathe.

When the sweeping and mopping were done, she cleaned the bar. As she wiped the counters, Del came back. He went to the register, inspecting it inside and out.

"Missing something?" Lena asked.

"Mhm. A receipt." He tucked his ink pen behind his ear. "Sometimes they get lodged under the tray and stick to the back of the drawer," he said, reaching his arm into the empty register tray, his beautiful bicep tattoo peeking out from under his shirt sleeve. He grunted and twisted his arm, but it was too muscular to get all the way in.

Lena chuckled and shook her head. "Here, let me." She slid her slender forearm into the drawer easily, and after a moment, withdrew it, the missing receipt in her hand. "Easy peasy."

"Thank you. I'm glad you're here." The huskiness was back in his voice, and Lena's mouth ran dry.

As she handed him the receipt, their fingers grazed, and a shock wave rushed through her. Del's touch was like a lightning bolt. Everything tingled from her fingertips to her toes. It was so startling, she flinched and dropped the cleaning rag from her other hand.

Del smirked as he leaned over to pick it up. He rose back up slowly, as if dragging his gaze up her body. When he finally came back to standing upright, he held up the rag. "You dropped this."

Lena's heart hammered in her chest. She didn't mean to, but her eyes flicked to Del's lips, the urge to know what they felt like on her own gnawed at her. When she looked up at him again, he tilted his head and leaned in. Lena thought her heart would burst from her ribcage.

The pen tucked behind Del's ear fell to the counter, the clack breaking the intense silence in the room.

They jumped apart, both instinctively reaching for the pen before it rolled off the edge. Lena got to it first with Del right behind. His large, warm palm covered hers, but he didn't move it away. Lena took a big breath, trailing her eyes up his muscular arm to his face, where his blue eyes were fixed on her.

Everything inside Lena screamed for her to kiss him. Her lips tingled with anticipation and desire settled low in her belly. She hadn't felt this kind of draw toward someone in a long time. Never mind the fact Del was the opposite of everything she looked for in a man. And her boss.

MY BOSS!?

Lena yanked her hand from Del's. "Um, I should finish up so we can get out of here." She turned away, grabbing the used glass tray and heading toward the back room to load the dishwasher.

Once she was safely in the back, Lena set the tray down more forcefully than she meant to, the glasses clinking. She pressed her clammy palm to her forehead. "What the hell was that?" she whispered.

Del was her boss. She was his employee. Why on Earth would she think he would kiss her? It would be wildly inappropriate, especially in the workplace. The bigger question for Lena was why did she *want* him to kiss her?

Chapter 8

"**Y**ou have to come!" Twyla shouted, even though Lena stood right next to her. "It's my birthday!" She and Lena were in the middle of serving the Saturday mid-afternoon rush.

"I'm closing tonight." Lena handed a pint over the counter to a customer.

"So is Marky, and he's coming."

"Jack's closing, too. Is he going?" Lena arched an eyebrow.

Twyla snorted and shook her head. "Just come when you get off."

Lena groaned. "Where?"

"At The Landing Pad down the street." Twyla took a customer's order, pausing to look at Lena before filling their glass. "Even Del will be there."

Lena jerked her head back. *Why would she specify that to me?* Lena hadn't seen Del since their tense Thursday night closing, and the idea of seeing him again made both her heart and her stomach flutter. One out of excitement, and the other from dread.

Pretending to ignore Twyla and her insinuations, Lena cleared the bar of customers in no time. She sagged against the counter and let out a breath. Her eyes found the tray of used glasses. It was full.

Lena grabbed it, but before she could pick it up, Twyla put her hand on top. "Come, Lena. Please? For me?" Twyla made puppy dog eyes.

With a laugh, Lena tugged on the tray, carrying it to the back room. "Okay, fine."

Six months ago, Lena wouldn't have thought twice about going to a bar. That had been her life outside of work. She drank, she danced, and she partied until the cows came home. It's what she did, especially after big design galas. She may not have been privy to the lavish Hollywood parties where there were movie stars left and right, but she helped design elite restaurants and hotel banquet halls. There were always huge names in attendance whenever those reveals happened. It's how she met most of the men she dated.

Like Ozzie.

Lena shrugged off the heaviness settling within her, and headed back to the tasting room. Marky and Twyla were handling the crowd easily, so Lena made the rounds to all the tables to check on the patrons. Saturdays bustled with business, so every table had customers. She kept herself busy by gathering empty glasses, taking refill orders, and wiping tables after customers left.

Before she knew it, the morning crew, including Twyla, had all gone home, and the mid-shift employees were on their way out. The seconds of the final business hour ticked by. At closing, Lena finalized the remaining customers' tabs, and set to work on her after-hours duties.

Jack made an appearance to collect the register till, saying nothing as he disappeared back down the hall.

"Mister Business finally came out of his hovel, huh?" Marky said quietly into Lena's ear as he passed her while sweeping.

Lena laughed, but felt guilty for it. Jack hadn't done anything wrong; he just wasn't as friendly as the other employees. Nothing like his father.

Del. The thought of his name sent a delightful shiver down Lena's spine.

The three employees left Citadel Brewing, with Jack locking the door behind them. Marky offered to drive Lena, but she wanted to have her car in case she needed to leave. She wasn't going to get drunk. The old Lena would have been drowning in shots, but the new Lena Bouras was enjoying her tamer life. Especially after the hangover she had from clubbing a few weeks ago. A glass or two of wine would be all for her.

As she pulled up to The Landing Pad, Lena furrowed her eyebrows. "A dive bar?" She reeled inside.

Chipped paint, warped siding, and cracked sidewalks were not welcome mats for her. Upscale bars and clubs were her scene in Los Angeles. She'd never be caught dead in what was most certainly going to be a dark, dirty, and dingy place. With a roll of her eyes, Lena swallowed her judgment, and went inside.

She was pleasantly surprised.

The Landing Pad may have looked disheveled on the outside, but the inside wasn't so bad. Airplane décor littered the place. Posters of old advertisements for airlines hung on the walls, model airplanes dangled from the ceiling, and the epoxied bar counter top looked like a runway. It certainly was a nice change of pace from Citadel's drab interior, but not what Lena would have expected for Twyla's birthday.

I wonder if some sort of theme like this would suit Citadel? Certainly couldn't make its décor any worse.

"Eeeee!" Twyla squealed as she threw her arms around Lena's neck. "You made it!" She swayed their bodies from side to side.

"Yeah," Lena choked out. "I see you've been having fun."

Twyla let go and stepped back. Her eyes were glossy and her cheeks pink, but she had a smile plastered to her face. "Of course I am! It's my birthday!" She hugged Lena again.

Lena patted Twyla on the back as her eyes roamed the room. Disappointment filtered through her when she noted Del's absence. "This is a nice bar, but not what I was expecting. Why did you choose this place?"

"Oh, my boyfriend works here." Twyla let go, but grabbed Lena's hand, dragging her to the bar. "Hey, babe! We need some drinks!" Twyla shouted.

A tall, blond guy turned around with an amused smirk on his face. Even without any facial hair, he looked exactly like what Del probably looked like in his twenties, aside from his gauged earlobes. He even donned a man-bun. He sauntered over, leaning his tattooed forearms onto the counter, and putting his face directly in front of Twyla's. "What's the magic word?"

"Pretty please?" With a pout, she batted her eyelashes.

"You know I can't resist that look. Come here," he said, then laid his lips on hers. As they separated, he winked before turning to Lena. "Hey, I'm Jameson." He held out his hand.

Lena took it, giving a firm shake. "Nice to meet you. I'm Lena."

Jameson's eyes widened briefly, like something connected in his brain. "So, what do you ladies want to drink?"

Before Lena could speak, Twyla yelled, "Shots! Tequila! Two of them!"

Lena's eyebrows shot to the sky. "What? No. No way, Twyla."

"Oh, come on! Just one? For my birthday?" Twyla whined.

Lena groaned, letting her head fall back. "Okay. *One* shot."

Twyla squealed again, making Lena press her finger into her ear.

"Okay, here you go. Two top-shelf tequila shots for my girl," Jameson said, setting two salt-rimmed shot glasses and two limes down before laying another kiss on Twyla.

Twyla wasted no time downing her shot and stuffing the lime into her mouth. "Come on, Lena!" she mumbled.

Lena took a breath, shut her eyes, and threw back the shot. She hated tequila, even if it was top-shelf. The shots she normally took were fun shots like Kamikazes or Washington Apples. Straight tequila was the worst. After a harsh exhale, Lena shoved the lime in her mouth, but it didn't make things much better.

"More!" Twyla shouted again, bouncing in her seat.

"If you keep drinking like that, Jameson will have to carry you home." Del's voice sounded behind Lena, and suddenly, the warmth in her chest wasn't alcohol induced anymore. He took a seat on the stool next to Lena, locking his blue eyes on hers. "Don't let her bully you into drinking."

"Shut up, Del," Twyla said as she got off her stool to hug him. "Jamie! A shot for your dad!"

Jameson's head whipped up, a mischievous smirk on his face. He poured a shot of clear alcohol into a glass, and set it in front of Del. "Here you go, old man. Bottoms up."

Del shook his head, downed the shot without issue, and set the glass down firmly on the counter. "No more of those for me," he said hoarsely.

Everyone shared a laugh. Jameson stepped away to check on other customers while Twyla scooted off to socialize with her other party guests. Then Lena was left alone with Del.

She twirled a piece of stray hair around her finger before tucking it behind her ear. "So, you don't like shots either?"

Del winced. "Too much low-end vodka in college." He waved for Jameson to come over. "Would you like something else?"

"A glass of red wine, please. Pinot Noir, if they have it."

"Sure thing." Del turned to Jameson as he reached the counter. "I'll have a Dos Equis, and Lena will have a glass of Pinot Noir. Whichever one's the most expensive."

Jameson nodded, turning to fill the order.

"He's your second oldest?" Lena asked, jutting her chin at Jameson.

"Yep. And it's true what everyone says about second born, middle children."

Lena arched an eyebrow in question.

"They're rebellious."

She chuckled, watching as Jameson leaned over the counter to kiss Twyla between pouring the drinks. "He seems like a good man, though."

"He is." Del took a deep breath, sighing as he released it. "At least I know I got something right."

"Why doesn't he work at Citadel?"

"He did for a while. He met Twyla there." Del's eyes softened as he watched his son playfully flirting. "They're kindred spirits, those two."

"So why doesn't he work there, anymore?"

"Jameson went to bartending school, so he wanted to branch out. Working at a brewery, you really only pour one type of drink, and I think he wanted to utilize his skills. It worked out, because now Twyla has somewhere to celebrate her birthday."

Lena furrowed her eyebrows as she studied Jameson. He certainly had a zest for life displayed in his mannerisms. Between his personality and his general energy, Lena could see why Twyla was drawn to him. Not to mention, his tattoos. They spread from his wrists to slip under his t-shirt sleeves and peeked out of the collar.

Glancing at Del, she pictured the tattoos she'd glimpsed a few weeks ago. Two of them she knew; the ocean wave on his muscular calf, and the word written in elegant script on his bicep. There were at least three more she hadn't seen clearly. Since that day at the lake, Del was always fully clothed, and Lena had almost forgotten about the tattoos completely. She worked harder to conjure the images, but instead, Del's sculpted torso made an appearance in her mind.

His firm tattooed pec she crashed into, his broad shoulders draped in ink. How she longed to run her fingers down his ribs where she recalled layers of green cascading down his side.

Heat rushed to her cheeks. She wished Jameson would bring her drink; at least then she could blame her red face on the alcohol. "You know, you didn't have to specify the most expensive. I can drink whatever's available."

"Not after having to shoot tequila. Besides, you deserve the best," he said, a softness to his voice.

"Well, as long as you're buying."

Del laughed as Jameson set their drinks down. He took out his wallet and tossed some bills on the counter, swiveling to face Lena. "Cheers," he said, clinking his already sweating bottle against her glass.

"Cheers." Lena sipped her wine. It was strong, but smooth, coating her tongue in a delectable mix of alluring berry notes, and ending on the savory side. It went down easily. "Good call on the expensive one."

"Glad you like it," Del said, wiping his hand on his pants.

Lena furrowed her eyebrows. "Do you ever wear anything other than jeans?"

He jerked his head back. "Why? What's wrong with jeans?"

"Nothing," Lena said shyly, lifting a shoulder to her ear. "I've just never seen you in anything else."

"Not true." He picked up his drink, tilting the bottle to his flirtatious smirk as he leaned his forearm against the counter. "You saw me in my swim trunks at the lake."

The delicious image of shirtless Del crept into her mind for the hundredth time, and Lena had to take a breath to keep her composure. As he turned to sip his drink, Lena studied him. His physique had her mouth watering that day at the lake, but working with him made her realize how gorgeous he was. Both inside and out.

When she didn't stop staring, he gave her a sideways look. "What?"

She blinked, realizing she'd been caught ogling him, so she reached up to twirl a lock of hair. "You look like the guy from those Dos Equis ads. You know, 'The Most Interesting Man in the World?'"

Del snorted. "It's the gray hair, isn't it?"

Lena ducked her head, giggling. "No. Well, yes, I guess. You have that distinguished, handsome guy look. Even if you have a man-bun." She said the last part out of the corner of her mouth before taking another drink of wine.

His mouth quirked up, and he leaned closer. "You think I'm handsome?" The question rolled off his lips low, husky.

Lena's cheeks flushed. Apparently, she shouldn't do shots, ever. She swallowed deep, lifting her glass to her mouth and staring at the counter.

Del sat upright, taking another drink of his beer. "And what's wrong with my man-bun? I'm only forty-seven. I can still have fun hair," he teased.

Lena opened her mouth, but was interrupted by Jameson making his rounds. "You need anything else, Dad?"

"Not just yet, son. Lena did compliment the wine, though. You'll have to keep that one in stock."

"I'll text you a picture of the bottle. Hold on." Jameson walked to the wine shelf, and a few seconds later, Del's phone chimed.

He rolled his eyes. "Kids," Del said as he took his phone from his back pocket.

Jameson returned, leaning his hip against the counter. "Did you get it?"

Del nodded.

"Good. Now you have a reason to ask for Lena's phone number." Jameson winked, then walked away.

Del cleared his throat, sitting straighter, and taking a sip of his beer.

They sat in silence for a few minutes, each sipping their drinks and avoiding eye contact. As the clock hit 10 p.m., the music grew louder. Even if they had been talking, Lena wouldn't have been able to hear Del over the speakers. She could hardly hear herself think.

Del tapped his fingers on the bar in Lena's line of sight. She turned and watched his mouth move, but she couldn't hear what he said. Shaking her head, she gave him a confused look. He grimaced, and tried again. She still couldn't make out the words, so she shook her head and pointed to her ear. Del rolled his eyes, grabbed her wrist, and led her toward the patio.

The cool night air floated over Lena as they stepped outside. She took a deep breath, letting it fill her lungs.

Del shut the door behind him. "There. That's better," he said over the soft din of music pouring from the outdoor speakers. "Sorry."

"It's okay. It's what you deal with at bars."

"Which is why I don't own a bar."

With a smirk, Lena ducked her head, unable to look Del in the eye as a comfortable silence fell between them. There was still one thing on her mind, though. "What were you trying to say inside?"

"That I'm glad you came tonight." His voice oozed confidence.

"Me too." She watched her feet as she dragged the toe of her shoe across the pavement. "Even more so when you showed up."

Del reached down and gently took her hand, his warm palm enveloping hers. "Well, when I heard you'd be here, I couldn't stay away."

Lena's breath stuck in her throat as her heart raced beneath her ribs. She raised her head to meet Del's gaze. Shining under the patio lights like diamonds, his bright blue eyes were locked on hers. When she licked her lips, his eyes flicked to her mouth, and Lena's checklist blew away with the breeze, as did her self-control.

She crashed her mouth to his, throwing her hand around his head and twisting her fingers into his hair. As she pulled him closer, his beard tickled her face, but she didn't care. The feeling of his lips on hers was exhilarating. Lena's entire body burned with desire on contact.

Del's strong hands ran up her arms to land on her shoulders. He drew her to him, their chests pressing together, and he deepened the kiss for the briefest of moments before he abruptly pushed away.

Lena stared up at him, breathless, but confused.

"I'm... I'm sorry," he muttered, then quickly stepped back inside.

Lena gaped after him. Did she dream it all? Was Del not flirting with her? She dropped her face into her palm, her cheeks burning and her eyes tearing up with embarrassment. What a fool she was to kiss her boss. Her *boss*, of all people.

With a deep breath, Lena decided against going back inside; she'd endured enough awkwardness for one night. With a happy birthday text to Twyla, Lena left through the patio gate, skulking to her car and all the way home in utter defeat.

Chapter 9

Sunday morning, Lena laid in bed, sulking. The events of the previous night weighed heavy on her mind, but none so heavy as her utter disappointment. She'd been turned away, dumped, and even cheated on, but none of those instances were as hard to accept as Del's rejection.

Which made no sense.

With a groan, she rolled over to grab her phone. She dialed Nicole's number, and drummed her fingers as she waited for her to pick up.

"Uh, hello?" Nicole sounded groggy.

Lena checked the time. It was only 8 a.m., which meant it was only 7 a.m. in California. *Oops.* "Hey, girl."

"Lena? Do you know what time it is?"

"Yeah, sorry. I didn't even look at the clock until just now."

Nicole yawned. "This better be an emergency."

"You were right. My checklist is crap."

"Mmm," Nicole hummed in satisfaction. "Well, I'm glad you finally accepted that, but did you have to do it so early?"

"I actually figured it out last night. When I did something stupid."

"I'm all ears," Nicole said, her voice perking up.

Lena wound her hair around several of her fingers. "I kissed my boss."

"What!?" Nicole was wide awake now.

Burying her face in her pillow, Lena left enough room for her mouth so she could recount the story to Nicole. She explained the bar, the drinks, and what she thought had been Del's obvious flirting. "Then, I don't know, I couldn't help myself anymore. So, I kissed him."

"And? How was it?"

Lena melted into the mattress thinking about how Del's soft lips felt on hers. "Magical."

"Eee!" Nicole squealed, and Lena heard a man's groan through the phone.

"Sorry Jayce," she said loudly.

"Oh, don't mind him." The sound of a kiss and a mumbled "good morning" came from Nicole before she asked Lena, "How adorable is it that his kiss made you toss out your ridiculous checklist?"

"It wasn't just the kiss, though. He's been dismantling my checklist from day one."

"Awww. Okay, explain yourself."

Lena laughed as she pictured Nicole sitting cross-legged in bed, at complete attention. "Well, there's the obvious first point; his age. I always thought younger guys were the hot, muscular ones, but Del proved me wrong on that front the moment I saw him."

"Sorry to interrupt, but I'm going to need a picture at some point if he's as hot as you say. Okay, continue."

Lena flipped onto her back and shook her head, smiling. "I don't need to go through the whole list, Nicki. He's the opposite of everything I thought I wanted in a guy, right down to the beard, which wasn't bad, to be honest." She sighed. "But there is one thing I can't completely toss out the window."

"The man-bun?"

Lena laughed outright. "No. That has actually grown on me. I find it kind of... sexy."

Another squeal from Nicole had Lena holding the phone away from her ear. "Oh, girl. This is good stuff. Okay, so what can't you get over?"

Lena chewed on her lip, her eyes darting across the ceiling. "Del being more than a fling."

"Lena..." Nicole's excitement deflated.

"It's just... Ozzie was the first real relationship I'd had since high school. *High school*, Nicki. I thought I was ready to settle down, and then he ripped my heart out. I don't think I can handle it again."

"Do you think Del is that kind of guy?"

"No. He certainly doesn't seem like it, but I thought the same about Ozzie." Lena paused, a knot in her stomach forming as she thought about Del rejecting her the previous night. "He pushed me away last night."

"He *pushed* you?"

"No, not like that. He broke off the kiss, said 'sorry,' and went back inside." Lena waited for Nicole to respond, but she was silent. "Are you still there?"

"Yeah, yeah, I'm here. I'm thinking. What did you do after he went inside?"

"I left." The defeated tone in her voice sounded pathetic even to herself.

"So, you didn't get an explanation, then?"

Lena groaned, flopping her arm over her face. "No."

"But you're going to get one tomorrow, right?"

Bile crept up Lena's throat. She hadn't even thought about how awkward it was going to be at work. "Ugh, what am I going to do?"

"Nothing."

"What?

"You're not going to do a darn thing. He's the one who pushed you away and he needs to explain himself."

"That seems childish. Shouldn't I apologize? I mean, I assaulted him, Nicole."

"Oh, please." Lena could almost hear Nicole's eye-roll through the phone. "From what you told me, he wanted the kiss as much as you did. So, don't go crawling back to him with an apology, because you didn't do anything wrong. The ball's in his court."

Lena mulled over Nicole's words. Although waiting for him to make a move would test Lena's patience, Nicole had a point about it being Del's turn. "Okay, I'll let him come to me. Thanks, Nicki."

"No problem." A long yawn sounded from the phone speaker. "You've worn me out. I'm going back to bed."

Lena said her goodbye and hung up the phone. She rolled out of bed, padding her way downstairs to make some tea. As she waited for the water to heat, she glanced around her kitchen and living room.

She'd officially moved into the house two months ago, but it still didn't feel like home. Yes, she'd grown up there, so she had many fond memories, but Los Angeles had been her home for close to twenty years. Everything encompassing Lena was out there. Her own apartment, her job, her friends. Colorado still felt like a foreign country sometimes.

But this place is still my own, and I have a job. Plus, I've made some friends. An image of Twyla's face popped into Lena's head, easing her mind, but her breath was stolen when Del's image found its way in.

Del.

Lena groaned as the teapot whistled. The frustration of the entire situation sat heavy in her gut. She had finally let go of what she now knew to be ridiculous requirements for men, and the first guy she found interest in rejected her.

Maybe it was for the best. Del was her boss, which didn't leave room for a casual hook-up. The only way to go would be a full-on relationship, and she wasn't ready. Was she?

Lena poured the water into her mug, and absentmindedly watched the tea bag float as she thought.

When Ozzie had asked Lena to dinner instead of back to his apartment that night, she'd felt respected. A new feeling for her, since all she'd known were temporary sleeping arrangements. She thought he could have been someone to go the distance with, but a couple of weeks later, when he asked her to be his steady girlfriend, it didn't feel right. She blamed it on not having a long-term relationship since high school. "Jitters" she had called it, and brushed it off.

Now, she kicked herself for not listening to her instincts.

She had been wrong about Ozzie, so was she wrong about Del, too?

***

Lena had a closing shift on Monday. Which meant she had the entire morning and early afternoon to fret about seeing Del in person. She'd spent Sunday coming to terms with Nicole's plan of acting like nothing happened, but doubt still gnawed at her from the recesses of her mind. So much so, she couldn't keep her thoughts straight.

She became so frazzled from the what-if questions, she didn't even put on makeup. For the first time since college, Lena Bouras went to work au natural.

It didn't bother her, though. She slunk through the Citadel Brewing door, not caring one bit about her plain face. What did it matter, anyway? Del wasn't interested in her, and no one else remotely tripped her radar.

Marky was at the front counter, serving customers, and Twyla was waiting on a table in the far corner. Lena quickly made her way to the break room to unload her stuff. She wasn't in there but a few seconds when the door swung open.

"What the fuck happened to you Saturday night?" Twyla's voice called from the door, making Lena even more tense. "One minute, you were there, and the next, you were gone. What gives?"

Lena turned around, an apology spread across her face. "Sorry. Shots and wine don't mix well. I needed to get home."

Twyla put her hands on her hips, scrutinizing Lena's response. "Hm. Well, Del disappeared, too. I thought something had happened."

"Nope," Lena said, popping the "P" as she turned to her locker, trying to swallow down her thumping heart. "Speaking of Del, is he here?"

"Nah. He came in early this morning, but left a little while ago. He said he had some things to take care of and wouldn't be back today."

A breath of relief bled through Lena's lips. At least there wouldn't be any issues during her shift.

The rest of the week went by without issue as well. Lena didn't see Del once. If she worked late, he came in early and left before she arrived. If she had an opening shift, he either came in after she was gone, or didn't come in at all. He hardly made any appearances at Citadel all week. Except for Wednesday when she was off, and he apparently was there all day.

It didn't take a rocket scientist to know Del was avoiding her.

At first, Lena felt relieved. His avoidance meant she wouldn't have to endure the awkwardness of bringing up their kiss. As the week went on, though, Lena realized she missed Del's presence. The emptiness she felt without him around weighed heavy in her gut, and she worried she'd never see him again.

Until Saturday, when Del strode through the doors in the late afternoon. As soon as she laid eyes on him, all the anxiety, worry, and doubt melted away. He was like a breath of fresh air filling her lungs and loosening her constricted chest. It wasn't what she had expected to feel when she saw him, but she certainly welcomed it. Time seemed to move in slow motion as she watched him pass the bar where she stood.

Her heart sank when he gave a tight, half-smile with a sideways glance, and disappeared to his office. Lena slumped against the counter.

"Hey, what's up?" Twyla asked after finishing with a customer. For a Saturday afternoon, it was strangely slow.

"Nothing. Just a long week."

Twyla nodded as she wiped the counter. "Any plans this weekend?"

"Nope. Sitting around." *Wallowing in the confusion of my love life.*

"You want to come out with me and Jamie? We're going to a concert tonight, but you could meet us downtown afterward to bar hop."

Lena's mouth quirked up, but she shook her head. "Thanks, but I'll pass." With a deep breath, she pushed off the counter. "I'll go load the dishwasher."

The last hour of Lena's shift was excruciatingly slow. There were hardly any customers, which left Lena with too much time to think about Del. She kept anxiously watching the hall for him. She made excuses to go to the back room so she could pass his office in hopes he'd come out. She even stayed an extra fifteen minutes past the end of her shift thinking he'd come out if he thought she had left.

No such luck.

Utterly defeated, Lena clocked out, gathered her things, and slunk away to her car. *At least it's Saturday,* she thought. She would have an entire day away from Citadel to lick her wounds. Or maybe drown them in wine.

That sounded like a better plan.

Dark clouds were coming in from the west, which meant rain. Perfect weather for curling up on the couch in her pajamas, and staying there all night. She wished Nicole was there. Talking on the phone sufficed, but face-to-face girl time was irreplaceable. The idea of hanging out with Twyla crossed her mind briefly, but this instance called for Lena's best friend.

With a sigh, she fished her keys from her purse, but as she was about to click the unlock button, someone called her name. Lena whipped around to see Del trotting across the parking lot in her direction. Her heart raced, and her stomach knotted.

"Hey, Del," she said, the high pitch in her voice betraying her nonchalance as he reached her car.

His chest heaved. "Hey. I wanted to catch you before you left."

"Well, you're lucky I left late, then."

"Do you have a minute? I'm not keeping you from anything, am I?"

Lena shook her head. "Some Chinese takeout, a bottle of wine, and a romantic comedy that's been in my queue for a month." Warmth spread through her at Del's chuckle. "What do you need?"

As his laugh faded, he shoved his hands in his pockets, dropping his head slightly. "I, uh, want to talk to you about last weekend."

Lena steeled herself. The onslaught of rejection reasons had her insides twisting and churning. "Okay, what about it?"

"I need to apologize." He lifted his head to look at her through his lashes, his blue eyes apologetic, but also sad. "You had been drinking, and I took advantage of your inebriation. I'm sorry."

That's what he's worried about? Lena's heart slowed to a normal beat and her stomach untwisted. "Thank you, Del. It's admirable of you, but you don't have to apologize. I wasn't even drunk."

"Drunk. Tipsy. Doesn't matter. It was wrong of me not to ask first."

"Del..." Lena teasingly scolded. "*I* kissed you. And I wouldn't have if I hadn't wanted to."

He pepped up, his face brightening, but it fell. "I feel like I led you into it by flirting. I never intended for our first kiss to be a drunken impulse."

"You've given thought to our first kiss?" Lena couldn't help the warm fuzzies building her chest.

Del blushed beneath his beard. "Well, I, uh... I hoped it would happen one day, but not like that."

"Del," Lena said quietly, stepping forward to put her hand on his forearm. "I wasn't drunk, by any means. Sure, the alcohol may have stiffened my spine a bit, but I still would've kissed you without the drinks."

"Yeah?" His eyes lit up, the blueness sparkling even under the cloudy sky.

Lena nodded, before letting out a breath. "I wish you had said something. I've been going crazy all week thinking you weren't into me."

"Oh, no. Quite the opposite." He swallowed hard, his Adam's apple bobbing. "I can't get you out of my head. Your kiss burned itself into my memory, and it's all I can think about."

It was Lena's turn to blush. "So, does that mean you want to do it again?"

"Absolutely." The sparkle in his eyes changed to a fiery longing. "But I'd like to take you to dinner first. Treat you properly before I swoop in."

"I'd like that."

Del finally took his hands out of his pockets, his muscles noticeably relaxing. "Good. How about tonight?"

"Tonight?" Lena's eyebrows shot to the sky.

"Yeah. Unless you had your sights set on Chinese takeout?"

Lena laughed, dropping her eyes to her sneakers before lifting her head. "Oh, um, can you give me, like, an hour? I need to shower and change clothes." She motioned to her work attire and lopsided bun on top of her head. "I'm not even wearing makeup."

"Sure thing." Del leaned in close. "But for the record, you always look beautiful."

"Thanks." Heat crept up the back of Lena's neck as she ran her fingers through the strands of hair that had fallen loose, twisting one around her finger.

"Can I pick you up at seven?"

She nodded. "You know, you never got my phone number last weekend."

Del smirked. "I guess I need to remedy that, then."

Chapter 10

After a quick text to Del, giving him her address, Lena drove all the way home with an ear-to-ear grin. It stayed put through her shower and a short phone call to Nicole to catch her up. Even as she applied her makeup, Lena couldn't stop smiling.

Getting ready for her date took almost exactly an hour, so Lena didn't have to wait long for Del to show up. When the doorbell rang, she flew to the front door, a light skip in her step. Her heart raced as she fluffed her perfectly curled hair one more time before opening the door.

Del stood on her front porch, also freshly showered, and Lena drank him in.

Even with his hair still in a bun, he looked so different than what she was used to. His gray button-down shirt peeked out from behind a dark suit jacket, the sleeves rolled down to his wrists. A plain black tie stretched down his chest. But the biggest surprise came when Lena realized he wasn't wearing his normal jeans. Tonight, he donned a pair of black slacks. The sophisticated casual guy with a hint of rugged outdoorsman was gone, and a sleek, refined gentleman stood in his place.

Everything about Del had been the opposite of the men she dated before. They were always younger than her, by at least five years, though Ozzie had been ten, and they were party boys. They dressed in designer clothes, their hair gelled until it was cemented in place.

Del was different. He was refreshing, but tonight it seemed like he was trying to be someone he wasn't, and Lena felt a twinge of disappointment.

"Hey," he said quietly, his blue eyes trailing her body up and down. "You look nice."

"Thanks." Lena nervously ran her hands down her pink sundress, smoothing it out. "I haven't had a reason to wear this yet, so I thought why not tonight?"

Del's eyes fixed on hers, desire burning behind the sparkle. "I'm a lucky man." He held out his hand. "Shall we?"

"Sure, but can I ask you something?"

"Shoot." Del tucked his hand into his pocket.

"What happened to your jeans?"

Del's face reddened. "Well, someone once gave me a hard time for always wearing them, so I thought I'd change it up. I thought this would impress her."

Guilt settled heavy in Lena's chest. "Del, I didn't mean to criticize." She reached up to twirl her hair around her finger. "I like the jeans. In fact, I like the way you dress. It suits you."

Del blew out a relieved breath, loosening the tie. "Good, because I'm horribly uncomfortable." He removed the tie and jacket, and rolled his shirt sleeves up to reveal his corded forearms. "And I'm giving these pants away." They shared a laugh before he extended his hand once more. "Ready to go?"

Lena nodded and took his hand. As soon as her fingers brushed his palm, a jolt ran through her. Instead of flinching, though, she embraced it. Savored it. This sort of reaction to a man's touch wasn't familiar. Sure, some level of excitement went with any romantic encounter, but this was different. This was electric, and it was exhilarating.

Del opened the truck door for her, helping her inside before shutting it, and hopping into the driver's seat. "Where to?"

Lena' eyebrows furrowed. "Um, you don't have a plan?"

He shook his head. "My only plan was you. I didn't think much ahead." He stared at Lena for a long while, not moving a muscle until laughter erupted between both of them. "I'm kidding. Of course I have a plan." He backed out of the driveway.

As Del navigated his way through the neighborhood, the din of country music filled the cab. Lena's adrenaline ran high, so she stayed quiet, keeping her gaze out the window to avoid saying something stupid. With her hands in her lap, she watched the dark clouds overhead. They rolled across the plains as she looked east, lightning flashing in the distance. She thought surely it would rain, but Colorado was finicky about its weather. It always did the opposite of what was expected.

Lena's head whipped over as Del took her hand in his and moved them to rest on the center console. Her heart slowed at his soft caress, the adrenaline pumping through her veins ceased, and her muscles melted against the seat.

Feeling more relaxed, Lena started talking. "So, you like country music?"

"It's better than the crap Twyla and Jameson listen to."

Lena laughed, but nodded in agreement.

"Why? You don't?"

She shrugged. "It's not my favorite. I'd rather listen to Ed Sheeran or Adele."

"I can honestly say I don't know any of their songs. You can change the station if you'd like."

"No, it's your truck, so you get to pick the music." She reached up to play with the charm on her necklace. "And I don't *hate* country, it's just not my first pick."

Del pursed his lips, but said nothing.

Great, Lena thought. *I've offended him.* Wrapping the chain of her necklace tight around her finger, she fought for a change of subject. "Why did you wait to ask for my phone number?"

Del glanced at her, then back at the road. "Uh, because I wanted to make sure you were interested. Asking a woman for her number can be quite nerve-wracking, let alone a female employee of yours."

"No." Lena shook her head, pinching the bridge of her nose. "I mean, why even ask? Don't you have my number on file from my application?"

"Well, yes, I do." He gave her a sideways glance with an arched eyebrow. "But wouldn't you have been a little freaked out if I called you out of the blue without you giving me your number in the first place?"

Lena pursed her lips. "I guess it would've been weird if you called to ask me out instead of something work related."

"Exactly. I didn't want to be creepy on top of being embarrassed if you said no."

"I wouldn't have said no." She squeezed his hand.

Del kept his eyes on the road, but took a deep breath, squeezing her hand in return. "So, how do you feel about pizza?"

***

When Del had mentioned pizza earlier, Lena felt a little discontent. Pizza was casual. The cop-out of date dinners. There wasn't anything fancy about the cheese-covered pie, and while Lena hadn't expected Del to take her to a five-star restaurant, she at least thought they'd go somewhere that required silverware.

So, when Lena walked into Enzo's Bistro, she was pleasantly surprised.

The ambiance was to die for. Traditional, red-checkered cloths covered the tables, classic Italian music poured through the overhead speakers, and mouth-watering aromas filled the air. Each table had a single candle surrounded by delicate greenery, and strands of twinkle lights hung across the ceiling.

A woman wearing a white blouse, black slacks, and a green apron greeted Lena and Del. She showed them to a table and took their drink order, returning quickly with two water glasses before scooting off to the bar.

"Del," Lena said in a breath. "This place is adorable."

He smiled. "I hoped you'd like it. I've been coming here for years, though it's usually me alone, or with the boys." The smile faded, not disappearing, but changing into something resembling gratitude. "I'm glad I get to share it with you."

"Me too." Lena's heart sped up with every second his blue eyes stayed on hers.

It was becoming too much until Del cleared his throat. "Do you want to split a pie?" he asked, picking up his menu.

Before Lena could answer, their server came back, setting a glass of Pinot Noir in front of Lena, and a pint of beer in front of Del. When she asked if they were ready to order, they requested a few more minutes.

Del picked up his glass, clinking it against Lena's. "Cheers."

"Cheers," Lena said quietly, lifting her glass to her lips. As she eyed Del over the rim, she was reminded he was a beer drinker, and she wasn't. Her mind then spiraled through all the commonalities she shared with his ex-wife, instead of him.

"Lena?" Del's voice lured her back to the present. "Would you like to split something?"

"Um, sure, but remember, I'm a vegetarian." *One more thing to divide us, I'm sure.*

"Of course, I remember. I was actually going to suggest this pizza, here." Del leaned forward, laying the menu on the table and pointing to a specialty item. "It's called the 'Veg-Out' and it's my favorite. They use a garlic butter sauce instead of red sauce, and the veggies are all seasoned before they're roasted. Though, I order it without mushrooms."

Lena snapped her head up, a crinkle in her brow. "I hate mushrooms."

"Me too."

Lena's chest filled with warmth. It was a morsel. A grain of sand. A small something to connect them outside of their ages, but it breathed hope back into her. She had to test him. "Sun-dried tomatoes?"

Del stuck out his tongue. "Bleh."

"Celery."

"Not without cream cheese or peanut butter."

A smile now accompanied the warmth. "Asparagus."

"Ah, there's where I have to disagree. I love asparagus."

"So do I. That one was a test." Lena giggled.

Del gaped at her. "Sneaky." He took a sip of his beer. "Okay. Enough about what we hate. Tell me something you love to eat. What's your favorite dish in the world?"

"My favorite?" Lena pursed her lips, tapping her nails on the table. "You'll think I'm silly."

Del drug his finger across his chest in an "X" as he shook his head.

"Grilled cheese sandwiches."

"Seriously?"

Lena scoffed. "See? I told you it was silly."

"No. You said *I'd* think you were silly. For the record, I don't. It just wasn't what I would've guessed in a million years."

"What about you? What's your favorite?" Lena picked up her glass, leaning back in her chair. As she sipped her wine, her worries from a minute ago slowly melted away.

"Mine's also a little silly." Del tilted his head from side to side. "Chicago style hot dogs."

Lena went to bite her lip, but stopped when she remembered she was wearing lipstick. "Well, to make this conversation even more absurd, what does 'Chicago style' mean?"

Del furrowed his brows before arching them in understanding. "Right. Vegetarian." He sat his glass on the table, before animatedly using his hands while he spoke. "It's a hot dog with certain toppings. Mustard, onions, relish, pickled peppers, tomatoes—"

"Not sun-dried."

"No, certainly not, but it's topped with a full pickle spear. The boys and I used to get them at ball games when they were younger." Del's hands fell to the table, his eyes following the motion with a wistful gleam. "I haven't had one in a *long* time."

"How long?"

Del took a breath, rubbing his beard with his fingers. "The last time I took the boys to a Rockies game was for Jack's eighteenth birthday, so almost a decade ago."

"Are you ready to order?" the server asked as she returned to the table.

Lena and Del ordered their single pizza, sans mushrooms, and enjoyed a fabulous evening getting to know each other better. Del's recommendation on the pizza was spot on. The garlic mingled with the seasoning on the vegetables perfectly, and it complimented Lena's wine as well. Things were moving along smoothly. The conversation was lighthearted, not heavy, and Lena was thankful personal history never came up.

When the pizza was completely gone, Lena picked at the leftover vegetable pieces on the tray as Del watched her every move. "So, it was good, then?" he asked with an arched eyebrow.

Lena stopped mid-lick of her finger. "Uh huh." She noticed Del's eyes fix onto her mouth where her finger sat between her lips, so she took her time sucking the last bit of garlic sauce off. She slid her fingertip from her mouth slowly, dragging it across her bottom lip.

Del shivered, but recovered quickly as he downed the last of his beer. He flagged the server over to the table. "Check, please."

The drive home was not as lighthearted as dinner. The tension in the air was thick. Not with anger or anxiety, but anticipation. She chose to chew on the inside of her cheek because Del would see her knee bobbing, and he'd certainly know if she was playing with her hair since he was holding her hand.

Would she invite him into her home? If she did, would he expect something? The biggest question, though, was if *she* expected something. Whether or not Del thought he was going to get some action, he was enough of a gentleman to abide by her wishes if she said no. It was her decision, and at the moment, she didn't know what she wanted.

Her heart tugged her toward Del. He was everything she wanted in all the boys she dated in California, because that's what they were, boys. Del was a man. A fine specimen, at that. In the short time she had known him, he treated her with more respect than any other man in her life. He was warm and affectionate, charismatic, and she melted every time their eyes met.

He was unfamiliar territory, though, and her skepticism reared its ugly head. Attraction to a man was one thing, this electric allure of Del's was entirely another. Lena couldn't help herself when they were in the same space. She'd been growing used to having him around at work, and after their date tonight, she wanted him around a lot more.

But could this thing between them be casual? And did she want it to be?

She wanted things with Del to be different, that much she knew. On some level, she needed him to be only hers. The thought of him seeing other women pricked her like a bee sting, but commitment was like diving naked into the hive.

"We're here," Del said as he parked in her driveway.

Lena blinked, turning to him with a forced smile to show she wasn't reeling inside. As soon as she laid her eyes on his, her worry evaporated. She felt at ease, like she was right where she should be.

The pull toward him manifested again. Lena leaned over the console, ready to feel his lips on hers, but he slipped his hand away, and cut the engine.

He cleared his throat. "I'll, uh, walk you to the door." He hopped out of the cab, leaving Lena in utter confusion. When he opened her door, he extended his hand to help her down.

Feeling defeated, Lena laid her hand in his. The electric shock of skin-to-skin contact struck her once more, and she knew for a fact something existed between them.

Once on her front porch, Lena stood on the top step, which put her eye to eye with Del. "Thank you for a lovely dinner. It was perfect."

"You made it perfect." His tone was warm and soft.

Lena blushed, but was still confused. Del gave all the signs of having interest, even signs he wanted more than just dinner, but he hesitated when the time was right. Yet, here he was, flirting again. It made no sense.

Del shoved his hands in his pockets. "Lena, I want to ask you something, and it's absolutely fine if you say no."

Her heart raced as she nodded.

"I don't want to repeat what happened last weekend, so I need to make sure it's okay this time." He locked his blue eyes on hers, a timidness swirling in them. "May I kiss you goodnight?"

Lena's laugh shook out of her. "I thought you'd never ask."

The timidness gave way to longing as Del's gaze flicked to her mouth. He took a step, closing the gap between them. One hand wrapped around her waist, and the other around the back of her head, pulling her close. He tilted her head and pressed their lips together.

Forget electricity, this was straight up lightning.

Lena fell into him, throwing her arms around his neck and deepening the kiss. She didn't care about his beard being itchy, or her having garlic breath, or being on her front porch for her neighbors to gawk at. All that mattered was the intense passion coursing through her.

Del's tongue slipped between her lips, begging for entrance, which she happily granted. With their tongues dancing, the fire inside Lena grew. Desire pooled low in her belly. Her fingers twisted into his shirt as she tried to draw him closer.

As his chest pressed against hers, his thigh working its way between her legs, Lena moaned into Del's mouth, and he pulled away. They both stood breathless, their rib cages heaving in the cool night air.

Lena looked up at him through her lashes. "Do you want to come in?"

A heated desire to say yes flashed in Del's eyes, but he took a breath and ran his hand over his hair. "Lena," he said, his voice quaking. "I don't want you to think that's all I'm after, and while I'd love nothing more," □he winked□ "this is very new. Let's not rush things, okay?"

She nodded, a strange warring of emotions inside her. On the one hand, she was disheartened she'd still be alone in the house tonight, but on the other, Del's genuine respect for her made everything all right.

He slid his knuckle under her chin, tilting her head up. "Goodnight," he whispered before brushing his lips against hers once more.

Chapter 11

The chiming of her phone woke Lena from a blissful slumber. All night she'd been dreaming about Del and his intense, searing kiss. So, with the help of her birthday gift from Nicole, she dealt with the unreleased tension easily.

With a groan, Lena lifted her head to look at her clock. It was only 7:30 a.m. Smacking her lips, she rolled over to swipe the screen of her phone. She tapped the messages icon, and through her bleary, sleepy eyes, she saw a new message. From Del.

DEL: *Good morning. I hope I didn't wake you. Just wanted to say I had a great time last night, and I can't wait to do it again.*

His message was accompanied by a winking emoji.

An airy feeling filled her chest, and she thought she might float away as the previous night replayed in Lena's mind. Everything from the moment she opened the front door had been perfect. Dinner was delicious. The conversations flowed naturally. Even the quiet drive had exceeded her expectations.

And let's not forget about our goodnight kiss. Heat bloomed within Lena as the memory of Del's lips still burned on her own. *I certainly can't wait to do that again.*

Her heart sank, yanking her back down to Earth, and her phone slid from her hand. "Is that what Del meant, too?" she whispered.

Was he only interested in seeing her again so they could continue the kiss? Or take the kiss even further?

She shook her head. *No.*

Lena knew how men acted if all they wanted was sex; she'd met plenty of them in Los Angeles. Men who kept the drinks plentiful, but never bought dinner. Men who kept the conversation short, and the flirting shameless. They never asked about her personal life beyond work, never bothered to ask before they kissed or touched her, and never stayed the entire night. They were always gone before she woke up.

And it's how Lena liked it. Or, she thought she did.

Del wasn't like them. He had given her a taste of what being treated with the utmost respect was like. Opening doors for her, helping her to and from the truck, taking her into consideration when ordering food; he did everything right. He even made it a point to tell her he was interested in more than sex. Time and time again, Del had proven himself to be a genuine person.

And he was like that before we went out. Shit, he was like that before he became my boss.

Lena sat straight up in bed, her mouth agape and her eyes wide. "MY BOSS?!"

Could she date her boss? What were the rules? She picked up her phone so fast, it nearly flew out of her hands. After a minute of Google searching, Lena's heart slowed to a normal pace. There wasn't anything illegal about dating one's superior, it was simply frowned upon.

A relieved breath bled through her lips as Lena sank back into her pillow, but she quickly began chewing on her lip. Even if it wasn't illegal to date Del, there were other issues which could arise. What if Del started giving Lena preferential treatment? What if she suddenly got all the good shifts, or the easier tasks? There would certainly be some animosity from her coworkers if that was the case.

She didn't expect preferential treatment, and hoped she had the correct impression of Del as a manager. He seemed to be fair. He treated everyone the same, and Lena would be no exception, but she had to make sure her coworkers were okay with her dating the boss.

***

Citadel Brewing was abnormally slow Monday afternoon when Lena arrived for her closing shift. She expected to see at least two or three of their regulars, but there wasn't a single customer in the tasting room. Lena had been noticing a slight decline in business over the past few weeks, but this was bad, even for a Monday.

Twyla and Beth chatted behind the bar, but as soon as she saw Lena, Twyla followed her into the break room. "Hey, girl. How's it going?"

"Hey. I'm good." Lena put her things into her locker as she watched Twyla from the corner of her eye. "How about you? How was the concert on Saturday?"

Twyla bounced on her toes. "Fucking amazing!" She slid onto a table, swinging her feet in the air. "I was there for the opening band. They're a local group I've been following for a while, so it was cool to see them playing an actual gig."

"Nice."

"What about you? What did you end up doing Saturday?"

Lena swallowed the lump in her throat. "Can you keep a secret?"

"Ooh." Twyla wiggled her butt on the table, settling in like she was about to hear the story of the century. "Of course, I can."

"Well…" Lena finger combed her hair. "Del and I went on a date," she whispered.

Twyla's curious expression fell. "Oh, yeah. We all knew that already."

"What do you mean?" Lena's eyebrows furrowed.

"Come on, Lena." Twyla rolled her green eyes. "Even if Del hadn't been talking about you from the day you met, it's super obvious he's into you."

Lena's cheeks flushed. "He's been talking about me?"

Twyla nodded. "Ever since Johnnie tipped your canoe. And it's only gotten worse since you took this job." She sighed, drumming her fingers on the table. "After he asked you out on Saturday, he came right back in here with the biggest shit-eating grin on his face, and we were all stoked you said yes."

"Wait." Lena braced herself on the back of a chair, and pinched the bridge of her nose. "Everyone *wants* me and Del to be together?"

"Mhm."

"Why?"

Twyla licked her lips, and her fingers stopped drumming. "Lena, I've worked here for two years, and I can count on one hand, the number of dates I've seen Del go on, and they never ended well. Whatever happened between him and Jamie's mom fucked him up. So, when he got all gaga over you, well, it was exciting."

Lena covered her mouth with her hand briefly before letting out a breath. "What a relief. I was afraid us dating would cause issues. I didn't want anyone thinking I was getting preferential treatment."

"Pffft. First of all, we all know Del. He's a good person and a great boss, and he wouldn't run his business that way." A knowing smirk played on Twyla's face. "But even if he gave you all the good shifts, we'd know it was because he wanted to spend time with you, and we wouldn't give a shit. All we want is for Del to be happy."

Lena's features softened as she appreciated not only Twyla's honesty, but also her love for Del. It was like she spoke about her own father. *Father.* Lena's stomach dropped. "Even Jack?"

Twyla pressed her lips into a flat line. "I wouldn't worry too much about him. I mean, he *is* the reason Jamie doesn't work here anymore, but..."

"What? Del said Jameson wanted to utilize his bartending degree."

"That's what Jamie told him, but it was really Jack. Jamie loved working here, but when we got serious, Jack expressed his very strong opinion about coworkers dating." Twyla's shoulders went slack. "I think Jack was really gunning for *me* to quit, but Jamie had his bartender certification, and he knew it would be easier for him to find another job than me."

Lena tightened her grip on the back of the chair.

"If you're really worried about it, you should talk to Del." Twyla arched her eyebrows with a pointed look.

Pushing off the chair, Lena ran her hand through her loose curls again, this time twirling one around her finger. "Yeah. Yeah, you're right."

"It'll be okay." Twyla hopped off the table, putting her arm around Lena. "But are you ready to get to work? I'd like to take my lunch."

Chapter 12

The rest of the afternoon scooted by surprisingly quick for as slow as business was. Lena, Twyla, and Beth spent most of the time talking and ignoring their duties other than waiting on the few customers that wandered in. When 4:30 p.m. rolled around, Lena was about to head to her lunch break as Del waltzed through the door.

As soon as his eyes met hers, they lit up. He honed in on her, making a beeline for the bar.

"Hey, Del," Beth said, pretending to be busy wiping the counter.

"Hey." Del didn't take his eyes off Lena.

"I didn't think you were coming in today." Twyla chimed in as she sorted receipts next to the register.

"I wasn't, but I remembered someone special was closing, and I thought I'd come see if she had plans for her lunch hour."

"My lunch was hours ago," Twyla said with a snicker.

Del turned his head with a sarcastic expression, blinking his eyes slowly. "Jameson should be the one taking *you* to lunch." With a shake of his head, his eyes softened. "So, how about it? Mexican?"

The smile and nod were automatic as an excited flutter ran through Lena. She clocked out, grabbed her things, and met Del outside in the heat of official summer. Colorado hadn't wasted a single day of June warming things up. Luckily, a breeze kept the temperature in the shade at bearable levels, but when Del suggested walking, Lena knew she wouldn't be cool for long.

Thankfully, the Mexican restaurant wasn't far, but time dragged under the baking sun. Lena was already sweating, but a delicious chill ran up her spine when Del reached down to take her hand. The squeeze he gave made it even more delectable. She inched closer to him, and melted into his side as if she were made of chocolate, resting her head against his shoulder.

"That's an awfully precarious position for as hot as it is," he said with a chuckle.

"Are you complaining?" She tilted her head up, arching an eyebrow.

"No, ma'am." He squeezed her hand again. "But I am sorry I suggested we walk. I didn't realize what a difference riding in an air-conditioned truck made."

"It's okay. I'm just glad I wore my tan Citadel shirt today, and skipped the makeup. My eyeliner would probably be running down my face right now."

Del leaned down to study her face. "Well, like I said the other night, you always look beautiful. Makeup or not." He pursed his lips as he narrowed his eyes like he was picturing what she described. "But it is a good idea you went without makeup today. I don't think Alice Cooper would be a good look for you." He dragged his finger down his cheek, tracing an invisible line as if to say Lena's eyeliner would be melting.

They shared a hearty laugh which settled into comfortable silence. Strolling along, Lena enjoyed holding Del's hand and soaked up his presence.

When they reached their lunch destination, frigid, air-conditioned air blasted through the door as Del opened it. Relief from the heat hit Lena in the form of goosebumps rising on her skin. As hot as it was outside, she'd adjusted to it during the walk, and she shivered as she slid onto the cool vinyl booth.

Del stood at the end of the table, his eyes narrowed. He pursed his lips, then turned to the hostess who seated them. "Is the patio open?"

She nodded and motioned for them to follow her.

Del extended his arm, as if presenting the path to the patio. "Can't have you freezing."

"Thank you," she said, and slid from the booth.

The patio seating was perfect. The sun, now low enough to be mostly hidden by the building, still kept Lena enveloped in a blanket of warmth. As soon as their server set their waters down, Lena and Del ordered their meals.

"So," Del said after the server had left to put in their orders. "How are you?"

"Fine. You?"

"I'm good." He picked up his glass and swirled it. "I'm sorry if I bothered you yesterday."

Lena furrowed her brow. "What do you mean?"

"Well, I thought maybe I made you mad by texting too early, or something." Del's gaze stayed fixed on his water. "You never responded." The defeated tone of his voice made Lena's heart sink.

"Del…" Lena shut her eyes for a moment, almost wincing as a heaviness settled in her gut. "I'm sorry. It wasn't intentional, I just forgot. I got in my head about things and let it carry me away."

He lifted his head, curiosity swirling in his irises behind the hurt. "What carried you away?"

"Well, at first, your message had me happily reliving our date." Lena bit her lower lip, fighting the urge to look at Del's mouth. "But, then reality struck, and there were things I hadn't taken into consideration when I agreed to go out with you."

"Like what?"

Lena shifted in her chair. She hadn't planned on having this conversation yet, but there was no time like the present. A breath blew through her lips. "You're my boss."

Del's forehead wrinkled. "Yes, I know."

"And I don't want you treating me any different than the other employees just because we're…" Lena leaned back in her chair, folding her arms. "Romantically involved."

His mouth ticked up as his posture straightened.

"I'm still a Citadel employee. I don't expect you to make exceptions for me or treat me any differently than you have been."

Del nodded softly. "Lena, I appreciate your concern on the matter. Really, I do. I promise I won't change anything about our relationship at work." His eyes darkened, intensity flashing in them. "Unless there's no one looking." His low, husky tone made Lena's heart race.

She cleared her throat. "Thank you."

He settled back in his chair. "What else is on your mind?"

"Well," Lena said as she tugged on her necklace, twisting the lightning bolt between her fingers. "I'm worried there might be someone at work who won't condone us dating."

Del perked up, his posture straightening as he lifted his chin. "We're dating?"

Lena rolled her eyes, but smirked. "What would you say?"

"I'd say I'd like that."

She ran her hand over her hair as if to smooth it out. "But are you worried about anyone being upset over us being together?"

"You mean, Jack?"

Lena crinkled her nose and nodded.

Del took a breath, lifting his water to take a long drink. "The thing about Jack is□"

"Here you go," the server said as he placed their meals in front of them. "Please be careful. The plates are very hot. Enjoy!"

Lena used her napkin to adjust her plate on the table. "You were saying?"

"Um, I know Jack can be a little standoffish."

"A little?" Lena stopped mid-bite to arch her eyebrows.

Del let out a one-note chuckle before sighing. "He's just protective of his old man, that's all."

"But why?"

"Because he was old enough to remember when his mother and I split up." Del absentmindedly pushed his food around his plate with his fork. "Jack was ten when Amy left, so he remembers all the fights, the yelling, the nights of me sleeping on the couch and the nights when his mom would leave and not come back until the next day."

Lena laid her fork down, giving Del rapt attention. "That would be tough for such a young kid. What about Jameson and Johnnie?"

"Jameson was four and Johnnie was three. They don't remember much about that time, but Jack does. Not only everything before the divorce, but afterward too."

Lena sat quietly, waiting for Del to reel in his emotions enough to continue. The fact he wasn't looking at her told her how difficult this was for him.

He took a breath, still playing with his food instead of eating. "After the divorce was finalized, Amy moved to California. She gave up all her parental rights, granting me sole custody, and left without even telling the boys good-bye." Del swiped at his nose, sniffling. "There were a lot of tears on the nights when Johnnie and Jameson wanted their mom to tuck them in. They may not remember it now, but it was the most upset I've ever seen either of them."

Lena's heart broke in two as she watched Del wipe a tear from his eye.

"Try explaining to a three-year-old why his mom isn't there to kiss him goodnight. It's heart-wrenching."

"I can only imagine," Lena said quietly. "And what about Jack? Where was he through all this?"

"He was right there trying to help me." Del took a deep breath, a sad smile curling across his face. "If it weren't for Jack, I don't know what I would've done."

"So, he became more of a parent than a sibling?"

Del nodded. "It wasn't fair, but it was the hand he was dealt. The hand all of us were dealt."

Lena licked her lips, taking her bottom one between her teeth. Her eyes darted across the table as she contemplated extending the conversation. "Is that why Jack is so protective of you? Because of what his mom did?"

"Mostly."

"Did something else happen?"

Del tilted his head from side to side. "He also saw what a mess I was after the divorce. He's the only one of my boys who's seen his old man cry."

A sympathetic sigh escaped Lena.

"But if it wasn't for Jack, I wouldn't have ever tried dating again. He set me up on my first date after the divorce... with his sixth-grade science teacher."

Lena giggled. "How adorable."

"Yes, it was. Especially because she wasn't single."

Lena crinkled her nose. "What?"

"When we finally met at conferences, she told me she was married. She didn't have the heart to break the news to Jack since he'd worked so hard to get us together. We told him we went on a date, but all I did was go to the lake for an hour and a half, then we told him we wanted to be friends." Del shrugged. "It seemed to make him happy."

"What a good father. And son, also."

"He's good to his dad, that's for sure. But after seeing what the divorce did to me, and the struggles I went through with dating, he developed this sense of protection over me. I guess he didn't want to see my heart broken anymore."

Lena took a drink, swishing the water around in her mouth. "Makes sense why he doesn't like me, then."

"Lena," Del said, reaching across the table to take her hand, his thumb softly stroking her skin. "It's not that he doesn't like you; he just doesn't know you yet. Give him some time and he'll see you for the wonderful person you are."

"How do you know I'm wonderful? You haven't known me very long, either." Lena pursed her lips and arched an eyebrow.

Del's eyes flicked between the two of hers, his hand tightening around hers. "I just feel it."

Lena blushed, ducking her head.

"And, it doesn't matter if Jack likes you. *I* like you." Del locked his shining blue eyes on hers. "He may have strong opinions on dating in the workplace, but it isn't illegal, and he'll be professional, even if he's seething on the inside." His mouth quirked up on one side. "Besides, I'm his father, and I don't think he'll be lecturing me any time soon."

Between Del's hand on hers, the devoted look in his eyes, and the confidence in his voice, Lena felt at ease with the idea of them being involved. She had expressed her concerns, and he had addressed them. They were both adults who could act as such, so there was no reason they shouldn't be together.

Except for one thing...

"Anything else you need to get off your chest?" Del's cheeks flushed as he spoke the words and his eyes briefly flicked south.

Lena bit her lip again. "One more thing." She swallowed deep. "I don't want to get into the details right now, but I want you to know my last relationship ended almost six months ago, and it left me with a pretty hefty scar."

"Lena," Del whispered. "I told you on Saturday, I don't want to rush things. We can go as fast or slow as you're ready for. It's been a long time for me too, and I'm perfectly fine easing into things."

A comforting warmth bloomed in Lena's chest. "Okay."

"Now, for the love of tortilla chips, let's eat our food before it molds."

Chapter 13

Del and Lena had lunch every day that week. Whether Lena opened, closed, or was off completely, Del made it a point to ask about her lunch plans. He chose different places, each one as good as the last. Maybe because Lena had never been to them. Or, maybe it was solely because she shared the time with Del. Whatever the reason, she found herself anxiously awaiting their next lunch date.

On Saturday, Del took her to a little bistro inside one of the office buildings across the street. As soon as they walked through the door, the décor dazzled Lena. Stylish wallpaper covered the walls from floor to ceiling, leading her eyes to a cluster of crystal chandeliers hanging above an elegant seating area outside the bistro. It resembled the offices she designed in Los Angeles, though it lacked the familiar clack of her high heels on the marble floor.

She missed design immensely, but Del being at her side muted the pain.

"Do you have any plans for tomorrow?" Del asked, taking a bite of his shrimp scampi.

Lena shook her head.

"The boys and I are going to the reservoir. Would you like to come?"

She whipped her head up as she chewed and swallowed her mouthful of grilled vegetable panini. "You want me to come hang out with you and your boys?"

"Sure. I mean, why not?"

Lena took a long drink of her water. She hadn't ever spent time with Del and all three of his sons in one sitting. She'd only met Johnnie once, and she'd spoken to Jameson at Twyla's birthday and occasionally if he came to see her at Citadel.

Jack was the only one she saw on a regular basis, but they didn't exactly hang out.

Her throat constricted as she tugged at her necklace. There wasn't a good reason why she shouldn't go, but Jack was the one reason she didn't *want* to go. If it were only her and Del, the answer would have been a resounding "yes." Throwing the boys into the mix complicated things.

"You don't have to, if you don't want to." Palpable disappointment hung in his tone.

"What? No, I want to go."

"Really? Because that" —he pointed at the delicate chain wound around her finger— "tells me you're nervous about it."

She quickly untangled her fingers and dropped her hands to her lap. "What are you talking about?"

"I've noticed you either play with your hair or your necklace when you're anxious."

Lena stared at Del in amazement. She knew about her nervous ticks, but hardly paid attention to them anymore. Apparently, Del did. "I didn't want to be the fifth wheel if you were spending time with your kids."

Del shook his head. "You won't be a fifth wheel. If anything, you'll be there to save me from all the trendy lingo I don't understand and the mimis, or whatever."

"Do you mean memes?"

With a sharp nod, Del snapped his fingers. "Yes!"

Lena laughed. "I think you're beyond any help I can give."

"Please?" Del made the most adorable puppy dog face, his eyes shimmering in the late afternoon sun. "Don't leave me alone with those youngins."

Lena feigned an annoyed huff. "Fine. I'll come."

Del's puppy dog expression faded into a pleased smile. "Thank you. I'll pick you up around nine, if that's okay?"

Lena nodded. "Perfect."

***

"Are you crazy? I am *not* getting on that thing." Lena stood on the beach with her arms crossed.

Del's entire body sagged, the life vest in his hand lowering to his feet. "It's perfectly safe, Lena." He patted the handle of the jet ski.

She shook her head. "Nope. No way."

"Why not?"

"*That's* why not." Lena pointed out to the reservoir, where Del's three boys did daredevil stunts, giving Lena a heart attack every time she looked at them. Aside from their polite greetings that morning, they'd been on the lake since arriving two hours ago.

A smirk pulled at Del's mouth. "I promise we won't do anything crazy. And I'll take you over there, so we won't be in the boys' path." He pointed across the lake to an open area, his arm extended so his bicep was on full display, the word "Stratton" tattooed across it in script.

Lena traced the delicate lines with her eyes, losing herself for a moment in their beauty, but shook her head. Now was not the time for wonderment. She had an argument to win. "I'm not dressed for it." Her hands floated down her torso, presenting her shorts and tank top.

"Don't you have your swimsuit on under those?"

Lena folded her arms across her chest once more. "Yes."

"Then lose the clothes and come with me."

Her bottom lip worked its way between her teeth. "Del..." She let her arms fall to her sides, but quickly began wringing her hands. "I'm not... a good swimmer."

Sympathy spread across Del's features. "I'll take care of you." He held out his hand. "I promise."

Even though every rational part of her screamed to keep her feet on dry land, Lena took Del's hand. As soon as her fingers grazed his skin, she eased. Sure, the electricity was there, but it held a safety she couldn't explain.

Del showed Lena the jet ski, explaining all the parts and how it worked. He made sure she knew all about it, which eased her anxiety even more. It wasn't as scary once she knew the ins and outs.

As he backed the jet ski into the water, Lena undressed on the beach. She laid her clothes on her camping chair, and double checked the knots on her black bikini. Her fingers ran along the edges to ensure all her sensitive parts would be safely covered. As she adjusted the top, she heard a throat clear.

Her head whipped up to find Del staring, a very obvious struggle happening in his eyes. "Please stop doing that, or I won't be able to drive." His voice was strained, like he was fighting to keep his composure.

"Sorry," Lena said through a giggle. She picked up her life vest, sliding her arms in, which was the easy part. Once she clasped it, she realized it was too loose. Not wanting to relive the discomfort of her last dip in the lake, Lena fiddled with the buckles, but couldn't get the straps to tighten.

"Here, let me," Del said, motioning for her to come to him.

Reluctantly, Lena stepped toward the lake. She slipped into the cool water, the waves lapping at her ankles as her feet sank into the saturated sand. Wading out to where the water hit her knees, she stood before Del, arms at her sides.

He started with the bottom strap, taking his time to adjust each one and checking with her for comfort. When he came to the top strap, Del forcefully tugged her to him. Lena's breath shook. Their vests practically touched as mere centimeters separated their faces. A smug smirk sat on Del's lips as his eyes drifted down to watch his hands adjust the top strap. When he finished, he brushed his fingers along the exposed skin of her chest up to her chin where he cupped her cheek.

A path of fire followed his touch, but sent a delicious shiver up her spine. Lena wished they had a private beach.

He leaned in to put his lips next to her ear. "Just wanted you to feel what I felt a minute ago."

Lena turned her head slightly, and if she had been quicker, their lips would have met. But Del hopped on the jet ski. Lena sighed, running a hand over her hair, and saddled up behind him.

"Hold on to me," Del said, and Lena gratefully obliged.

She pressed the front of her life vest into Del's back so tightly, there wasn't a millimeter of space between them. Her inner thighs framed his outer thighs, and her knees tucked into the backs of his. If it weren't for the panic bubbling in her gut, this would have been quite the intimate event, but when she brought her arms around him, and her hands couldn't meet, her heart leaped into her throat.

Her fingers fidgeted uncontrollably as she tried to find a way to clasp her hands together. A rumble of dread rolled through her. Fear took hold, but its clutch loosened when she realized the rumble was Del's laugh.

He gently took her hands in his, caressing her skin with his thumbs, and moved them to the buckles of his life vest.

When her hands were secure, Lena exhaled and laid her cheek against his back.

"I told you I'd take care of you," he said, promise in his voice. "Now, hold on."

As Del started the jet ski, the engine roared to life, making Lena's heart race. Slowly, Del inched away from the beach, waiting until they were a good distance away to give it some gas. He was true to his word.

They glided across the lake, creating small, diamond-encrusted ripples on the surface. Lena's muscles eased with each passing minute. The more she realized Del meant what he said, the more her trust in him grew, and the less tense she became. Her hold on him never wavered, but her anxiety did.

He zoomed around the lake, avoiding the large waves caused by his sons, and made sure to check with her before he punched the throttle. It was shaping up to be a very enjoyable first jet ski ride.

Until Johnnie came barreling across the lake. He whistled and whooped as he sped by, making a sharp turn back in their direction.

Lena felt Del's muscles tense, and she shut her eyes tight.

"Don't even think about it, Johnnie," Del said gruffly.

The next thing Lena heard was something resembling a war-cry followed by the very distinct sound of water sloshing. A string of swear words erupted from Del right before what felt like a waterfall landed on him and Lena. She yelped, going rigid. When she finally opened her eyes, she saw Johnnie racing away toward his brothers, animatedly pumping his fist into the air.

Del vigorously shook his head, his sopping wet man-bun flopping around and spraying Lena with more water. "Are you okay?" he asked.

She snorted and ran her hand down her face. "Yes, I'm fine."

"I'll make sure he pays for his antics," Del said, and turned the jet ski back toward the beach.

As they passed by the boys, they all hollered like they'd accomplished some daring feat, even Jack. Despite being soaking wet, and not happy about it, Lena had to laugh.

Del beached the jet ski and helped Lena off, walking her up the beach to her chair. "If you're okay here, I'm going back out. Someone out there needs to be taught a lesson," he said with a low, steady tone.

Lena undid her life vest straps. "I'm great right here. I'm going to lay out and let the sun dry me." As she tore off the life vest, her bikini top moved with it, coming dangerously close to exposing her nipples, which she quickly covered with her arm. She turned to see Del's Adam's apple bob with his deep swallow.

"I won't be long." He leaned in to give her a quick peck on the lips before trotting down the beach.

Lena pressed her fingertips to her mouth briefly as she watched Del walk away. Even a small brush of his lips set hers on fire.

After patting herself dry, Lena spread the towel on the sand, grabbed her sunglasses, and laid back to absorb some rays. Soon, the sun warmed her. The balance of her heated skin against her wet bikini made for a comfortable temperature, and she relaxed enough to close her eyes.

All the sounds around her melded together. Her mind quieted and all Lena focused on was the blackness behind her eyelids. As her breathing came easier, she felt herself slipping into a slumber, when the roar of a jet ski and shouting hit her ears.

Lena jumped to sit, ripping off her sunglasses and scouring the lake for the commotion. Her heart pounded in her chest as she found it. Del stood on his jet ski, arms raised in the air in victory as all three boys bobbed in the water. They scrambled to their jets and gave Del some spirited hand motions.

Lena let out breath, which became a hearty laugh as she watched their shenanigans. The laugh caught in her throat when Del, Jameson, and Johnnie took off across the lake while Jack headed to the shore. She watched as he beached his jet ski, leaving his life vest on the seat, and stalked through the sand toward her. Lena tucked her knees to her chest.

Jack went directly to his chair and toweled off before taking a seat, huffing as he did.

Lena cleared her throat. "Your dad took revenge on you and Jameson too, huh?"

Jack grunted.

She chewed on the inside of her cheek. Del said Jack didn't hate her, that he just didn't know her, but how was he supposed to get to know her if they didn't talk? A sigh escaped her as she rested her chin on her knees. Her gaze floated out across the lake, watching the waves gently lapping at the shoreline.

"He was avenging you." Jack's voice startled Lena.

She swallowed. "I know, and I appreciate him for it."

"He likes you. A lot."

"I know that too, and I like him." A smile pulled at her lips. "*A lot.*"

Jack took an extremely long, deep breath, folding his hands in his lap but kept staring at the lake.

"I know you don't condone us dating, Jack." She watched him bristle from the corner of her eye. "But we're adults and we can act accordingly at work."

"It's not work I'm worried about," Jack said, low and gruff. He pushed up from his chair and stalked back to the shore, where he slid into his life jacket and climbed onto his jet ski.

Lena's heart sank watching him speed across the lake to his family. Winning him over wouldn't be an easy task.

She pushed the thoughts aside as Del came back to the beach. As he strode toward her, sans life vest, the tattoo on his pec came into focus. Three tiny footprints walked along his muscle, each one a different shade of blue, and each with a name written in script below.

"Were you watching?" he asked as he toweled off.

"I wasn't, but I heard it and saw the aftermath." Lena placed her hand on her heart, batting her eyelashes. "My hero."

Del spread his towel out next to hers, then plopped down on his side. "Anything for you," he whispered before brushing his lips against hers.

A lightness settled in Lena's chest. She felt truly happy to have him by her side again.

As he pulled away, her eyes dropped to his tattoo again, and she lifted her fingers to trace the names; Jack, Jameson, and Johnnie. "How many tattoos do you have?"

Del cocked an eyebrow.

"It's just... I saw them the day we met, but didn't get a good look. Honestly, I kind of forgot they were there since they're always covered."

"I have four, but this one started them all." He covered her hand with his. "I knew as soon as I held Jack the first time, I wanted to have him branded on me forever."

Lena melted at Del's words.

"Do you have any?" he asked.

She shook her head. "I've never had the urge to get one."

"Good." He gave her a pointed look. "Don't start. They're addictive."

With a giggle, Lena asked, "Then why do you only have four?"

"Because the ones I have are not only fairly large, but colored, which makes them more expensive. Plus, it's not something I do without consideration."

Lena pressed her palm firmly into Del's pec. "So, they all have meaning?"

"Mhm. Remind me to show them all to you sometime." He winked, and Lena blushed, but her stomach ruined the moment when it rumbled.

"Hungry?" he asked.

She nodded, looking past Del at the food trucks in the parking lot. "Think the taco one is back?"

"Only one way to find out." He helped her up from the ground and they walked, hand-in-hand, all the way up the hill.

The taco truck was indeed there, and they ordered the same thing as on the day they met. This time, they each picked up a taco and pretended to cheers, with Lena laughing throughout the action.

After lunch, the day flew by. Lena spent the rest of the afternoon on dry land, telling Del she'd endured enough jet ski excitement for the day. He and the boys, on the other hand, were relentless on the lake. They did crazy turns, splashing each other and trying to knock one another into the water. It gave Lena terrible anxiety to watch, so she grabbed her phone.

"Ugh," she groaned, holding up her phone in different directions. "No service out here."

Luckily, she'd brought a book just in case. She wasn't a hefty reader, but she always carried a book or magazine with her. It was a habit she'd formed in L.A. When she met clients outside the office, she discovered people were more receptive to her if they found her reading instead of playing games on her phone.

Before she knew it, the day came to an end. Not quite sunset, but the sun lowered and an evening breeze came with it. Del and his sons loaded the jet skis onto the trailer, and one-by-one, they left.

Then, Lena and Del were alone.

"Would you mind if we stop by my house to drop off the jets before taking you home?" Del asked as they stood beside his truck. "So I can avoid driving through town with the trailer, and can get them unloaded before dark."

"Sure, no problem."

"Thank you." He kissed her cheek before opening her door.

Chapter 14

"This is your house?" Lena's wide eyes took in the almost palatial estate as Del pulled the truck up the circular driveway.

"Yep. I've lived here a few years now."

"By yourself?" Lena asked, because the house, while a ranch-style one-level home, was big enough to fit two full families inside. It was adobe plastered, with two wings branching out from each end, and had a huge detached garage set back from the house. Beautiful flowers and shrubs lined the front, and trees surrounded it, rising over the roof from the backyard.

"Johnnie lived here for a year, but as soon as he was legally able, he got his own place." Del sounded sadly proud about that fact.

"It's so... big."

Del tilted his head to meet his rising shoulder. "My father died before the divorce, leaving me a big sum of money. I knew spending it wasn't the right way to go, so I invested it. I must have picked the right stocks."

"But why such a big place?"

"Well, when Amy and I divorced, I had nowhere to go for support. Both my parents had passed away, and I had three kids to look after. I promised myself right then and there, I would always have somewhere for my kids to come if they fell on hard times. This place is big enough for all four of us to live, if need be." Del scratched at his beard. "And, in the off chance I actually get grandkids, I want to have a place big enough to house everyone for holidays and things."

Lena's heart melted. "What an adorable reason to have such a big house."

"Thanks." Del blushed, rubbing the back of his neck. "Well, I'll let you inside while I unload the skis."

"You don't need help?"

He shook his head. "Nah. I'll back the trailer into the garage and lock up. I'll make one of the boys come help me clean them tomorrow."

Lena followed Del into his house. As she stepped through the doorway, she marveled at the vaulted ceilings, simple but elegant paint scheme, and beautiful wood flooring. The spacious main room included a luxurious wrap-around couch, two recliners, a fully stocked entertainment center, and an entire wall of windows from floor to ceiling. The only division was a half-wall between the living room and kitchen.

Words wouldn't form in Lena's mouth as she gaped at the space.

"Do you want to actually come in?" Del asked, a teasing tone in his voice.

Lena shook herself out of her stupor and followed Del farther inside the room. "This is breathtaking. I love the décor and color scheme. It's... so different from Citadel." An image popped into her mind of how different the brewery would look with some simple changes, but she shook it away.

Del snorted. "Well, contrary to popular belief, I don't live at Citadel." He led Lena around the couch. "Make yourself at home while I put the jets away. Remotes are there, and you're welcome to anything in the kitchen. I won't be long." He planted a kiss on her cheek before disappearing outside.

This man keeps surprising me, Lena thought as she plopped onto the cushy couch, sinking into it. A shiver ran through her from the stark contrast of air-conditioning compared to the warm summer air. She grabbed a throw blanket, equally as soft as the couch, and snuggled in it, leaning her head onto the armrest. *I could get used to this.*

Closing her eyes, Lena replayed the day at the lake. Aside from Jack's saltiness, it had been enjoyable. Johnnie and Jameson had seemed to accept her into their father's life, so why couldn't Jack?

Lena decided against stewing over it, and instead, floated away with thoughts of Del.

"You look like you belong here." Del's voice was like velvet as he said the words.

Lena blinked her eyes open to find him standing over her, staring down with the utmost affection pouring from his blue irises. She stretched her legs. "I must've fallen asleep. What time is it?"

"Almost seven."

She groaned and tilted her head from side to side. "I guess you should take me home." Even as the words left her mouth, they tasted wrong. She didn't want to go home, but the thought of asking Del to stay the night made her gut roil. She scooted across the cushion to get up, but Del stood in her way, shifting back and forth on his feet.

"Would you like to have dinner first?"

Lena bit down on her lip, but it didn't stop the smile from spreading. "I don't think I can eat any more tacos."

He chuckled. "I was actually thinking I could make something here. Maybe pasta and sauce? Plus, I've got some veggies which need to be eaten, so I could grill those real quick."

"That sounds delicious, but I want to help."

"Lena..."

She put her hand up. "Nope. You said to make myself at home, and the only way I can is to act like I live here." She shucked the blanket and rose to her feet. "Now, show me where this pasta is."

***

Del's fingers gently brushed the skin of Lena's bicep as they snuggled on his patio after dinner. Lena was stuffed, and feeling extremely relaxed after two glasses of wine. A warm breeze filtered through the trees, rustling the leaves to create the most wonderful white noise.

Lena hummed through closed lips.

"Relaxed?" Del asked.

"Mhm."

"Good."

They sat like that for several more minutes, each enjoying their third drink of the evening. The sun was setting behind the mountains in the most spectacular sunset Lena had seen yet. The color scheme of the sky and clouds rivaled an impressionist painting. Soft pulls of orange and pink strewn with purples and blues as the eastern sky faded to black; it was picture perfect.

"Should I take you home?"

The idea weighed her down, so Lena shook her head. "I close tomorrow, and I don't have to be home for any reason." She turned to look at Del. "I don't want to go yet."

His eyes scanned her face, falling to her lips. "And I don't want you to." He put his mouth to hers in a gentle kiss. "But what should we do?"

Lena pursed her lips, and Del quickly pecked them. She mockingly scoffed.

"They were teasing me."

She giggled. "We could watch a movie."

"More snuggling? Sounds good to me." Del led Lena inside, where they situated themselves on the couch in a similar position as they were outside. He grabbed the remote. "Now, what do we watch?"

They agreed on a quiet drama. Nothing too sad or sappy, but also not filled with explosions and mayhem. The perfect ending to a perfect day.

Lena snuggled against Del's side as her fingers absentmindedly drew circles on his thigh. She felt him shiver slightly, so she turned her head up to look at him. "Are you cold?"

He sucked in a breath. "No. It's just the feeling of your fingers on my leg is... distracting."

"Oh." Lena pressed her lips together to keep from smiling as she lifted her hand from his thigh. "Sorry."

"It's perfectly fine. Please, don't stop." He tilted his head down. "I like you touching me."

Lena's heart picked up speed. "And I like touching you," she said in a shaky voice, taking her lower lip between her teeth.

Del's eyes flicked to her lips momentarily before he crashed his mouth to hers. The kiss was fiery, passionate. Different than the quick and tender kisses she had received throughout the week, this was more like their post-date kiss last weekend. Del claimed her with his lips, and Lena let him.

Her hands wrapped around him, one behind his head where she played with the loose strands of his hair, the other gripped his muscular shoulder. When he ran his tongue along her lips, she opened her mouth to deepen the kiss. Passion ignited in Lena's core, like a fire, and she lost herself in Del's embrace.

His strong arms held her chest against his as his fingers dug into her waist. One of his hands ran up her spine to tangle in her hair, giving her goosebumps, and he laid her onto her back. Leaning to one side so he didn't crush her small frame with his weight, Del tucked his knee between hers, entwining their legs. His free hand had begun roaming.

At first, Lena relished the feeling of Del's gentle touch. She moaned into his mouth as his fingertips brushed down her side and hip, coming around and up the top of her thigh. It was like a sensual tickle. When he continued up her stomach to her ribs, though, Lena's heart rate spiked.

She hadn't been touched like this in six months, and the last time it happened was a week before she caught Ozzie cheating. Casually dating Del kept Lena's heart safe, but would this moment turn their relationship into something more serious? Adrenaline coursed through her, partly from anticipation, but mostly from uncertainty. Which is why, when Del's warm palm cupped her breast, Lena flinched.

Del immediately retracted his hand, breaking the kiss with the motion. "Sorry."

"No, don't be," Lena said, breathlessly. "I didn't mean—"

"You didn't do anything wrong." He brushed his knuckles across her cheek. "I got carried away."

"We both did."

Del ran his finger along her lips. "It's easy to do with you." He cleared his throat, sitting up and bringing her with him. "Should we finish the movie?"

"I think we missed a lot."

"I can rewind." With a wink, Del lifted his arm to invite Lena back into his side.

She nodded, snuggling against him once more, but stayed very much aware of what her hands were doing and where they were.

Chapter 15

When Lena awoke the next morning, she yawned and stretched. Her arms extended over her head as her toes reached for the end of her mattress. Smacking her lips, she blinked slowly, but her eyelids popped wide open when she realized she wasn't in her room.

Out of instinct, and with a racing heart, she sat straight up, clutching the blanket to her chest. There was no need, though, as she was still fully clothed in what she wore yesterday. Her flip flops and purse were tucked under the sideboard beneath the window. She turned to find the rest of the bed empty, the blankets still pulled up.

With furrowed eyebrows, Lena surveyed the room. The queen bed she lay in was centered on the wall adjacent to a large window covered in peach-colored light-filtering curtains. A chair-rail lined the entire room with white paint above and cream paint below. Minimal furniture adorned the room; the bed, sideboard, dresser, and two side tables.

This obviously isn't the main bedroom, Lena thought as her eyes found a piece of paper on the side table next to her. She picked it up, and almost instantly, a smile crept across her face.

Good morning,

I hope you don't mind, but you were sleeping so well last night, I didn't have the heart to wake you. You have your own bathroom, so if you want to shower, you can. Otherwise, I'll be waiting in the kitchen with coffee.

-Del

Her heart swelled. She'd never been treated with such respect before. If this had been one of her party boys in L.A., she would have woken up in *his* bed with nothing on but her underwear. He would've claimed he wanted her to be more comfortable, but he wouldn't have asked. He certainly wouldn't have taken kindly to Lena refusing his touch.

This was a whole new ballgame for her.

Del was not only incredibly understanding when she abruptly ended their make-out session, but he never pressed her for more. Not even when she fell asleep on him...

Lena thought very hard about the previous night. She remembered snuggling with Del after her freak-out. He rewound the movie to the spot they had left off on, but she didn't remember how the movie ended. She must have fallen asleep fairly quickly.

Del carried me in here?

Happy tears pricked her eyes as the warmth of appreciation filled her. She needed to thank Del properly. Lena leaped from the bed, bouncing to gather her things. She stepped into the bathroom to freshen up, and found toiletries laid out for her. Not only the essentials like shampoo, conditioner, and body wash, but also toothpaste and an unopened toothbrush.

She bounced on her toes the entire time she brushed her teeth.

Before leaving the bedroom, she turned down the blankets so Del would remember to wash the linens.

In the kitchen, Lena found him with a mug of coffee in his hand, like his note said. What the note failed to mention was he'd be wearing a tight t-shirt and jogging shorts that showed off his muscular limbs. Her mouth ran dry as she eyed him from his toned calves to his taut chest and up to meet his gorgeous blue eyes.

A knowing grin spread across his face. "Good morning."

"Morning," Lena choked out before stepping onto the cool tile floor.

"Did you sleep okay?"

She nodded. "I slept great. Thank you for letting me stay."

"Well, I figured by the time I got you up and home, you'd be wide awake. This way, you got to sleep. I hope I didn't overstep."

"Not at all." She walked to him, placing her hand on his forearm, and tipped up onto her toes to place a kiss on his cheek. "You did everything right."

Lena saw Del blush beneath his beard, but he turned to set his mug on the counter. "Would you like some coffee?"

"I actually don't drink coffee."

He turned to her, eyebrows furrowed. "Really?"

"Really." She crinkled her nose. "I'm a tea person."

"Oh, well, in that case, follow me." Del crossed the kitchen to a set of French doors. When he opened them to reveal a spacious pantry, he motioned to a shelf holding several different boxes of teas. "Help yourself. I'll put on some water." He kissed her temple and left to fill the teapot.

Lena eyed the array of tea boxes in front of her. She loved tea, but usually only kept three or four types at any given time. Del had at least ten different boxes sitting on the shelf. Some she knew and loved, like Earl Grey, but others had never tried, like Oolong.

She decided to stick with a safe bet and went with English breakfast tea. Made sense, since it wasn't even eight o'clock yet.

Del lifted his coffee mug to his smiling lips as she met him at the counter once more. "What did you pick?"

"English breakfast. It's always a winner."

"Mmm," Del hummed before swallowing his sip of coffee. "Mugs are in the cabinet behind you. The one next to the stove."

Lena turned around and opened the cabinet. Inside she found the entire bottom shelf filled with mugs of different sizes and shapes. "Why so many?"

"The boys all enjoy coffee. Sometimes, depending on how long they stay when they come over, we'll go through two or three pots. Having so many mugs saves us from washing one every time we brew more."

Lena laughed, shaking her head. Spotting a rather large, green and blue swirled mug, she reached for it as the teapot whistled. In the moment the high-pitched screech of the kettle ebbed, Del's arm snaked around her middle and he eased her into his side. His chin rested on her shoulder, his bearded cheek pressed to hers. He removed the teapot from the stove and poured the hot water into her mug, all without relinquishing her from his embrace.

"Thanks," Lena whispered as she tore the package open and dipped the bag into the mug, watching the clear water turn brown.

"Do you want sugar or cream?" Del's deep voice rumbled through her.

She shook her head. "I like mine black."

"Suit yourself." Del reached up to place his hand on hers, helping her dip the teabag in and out of the water.

The silence between them was noticeable, but not ominous. It consumed Lena. Not in a bad way, though. She was comfortable not speaking and simply existing in this moment with Del. There was no need to fill the void because there wasn't one. She leaned into his embrace, dropping the string of the teabag and turning her palm up to entwine her fingers with Del's.

He lifted their hands to press the back of hers to his lips, making her skin tingle. "I'm glad I didn't take you home." His voice was low, gruff.

She nuzzled her cheek harder against his, the scruff of his beard rubbing her skin. "Me too."

When he moved, she turned her head, and Del planted his lips on hers. The kiss was gentle, affectionate, but there was passion behind it. It gave Lena pause. After the previous night, she didn't want to get hot and heavy, only to push Del away again. She kissed him long enough to show she enjoyed it, but broke it off with a sweet smile before it became a make-out session.

Inching out of his embrace, she grabbed her mug and blew across the top of it. "What's for breakfast?"

***

After stuffing herself full of Del's delicious homemade pancakes, Lena let him drive her home. She almost took him up on his offer to shower there, but the last thing she needed was to be naked and wet in Del's house.

On the drive, they both relished their time together. Their hands rested on the center console, entwined tightly. Every so often, Del would lift their hands to kiss the back of hers, and Lena's heart skipped a beat every time he did.

When they arrived at her house, Del walked Lena to her front door. On the top step, she turned to him. "You have to do this every time you drop me off now."

"I wouldn't have started if I'd intended to stop." He stepped forward, closing the gap between them, and pressed his lips to hers.

Lena's eyes fluttered closed as she lost herself in the gentle kiss.

Del didn't deepen it this time. He kissed her soundly, but kept it soft and affectionate before inching back. "Now, go in and get ready. I don't want you to be late for work." He brushed his knuckles down her cheek. "I'll see you later for your lunch hour."

Chapter 16

On Wednesday, when Lena arrived at work, she saw Del's truck in the parking lot and a burst of excitement flitted through her. Their shifts didn't always align, sometimes only overlapping for a few hours, but sometimes, they worked the whole day together. Lena hoped this was one of those days.

Working at Citadel had been fairly relaxed so far, but Del always made things better. It was so easy to be around him, so effortless. Lena naturally relaxed in his presence, aside from the ache between her thighs, but she wasn't quite ready to tackle that.

Not wanting to work herself up, she shook off the rising sexual tension and skipped through the door, waving at Marky behind the bar. On her way to the break room, she paused when she looked down the hall to see Del's office door cracked open. The thought of saying hi before clocking in hopped into her mind, but before she even reached his office, she stopped.

Del's voice traveled through the air, but it was far from the gentle tone she knew. His words were heated, frustrated. He sounded angry.

Who is he talking to that has him so upset?

Then, Lena heard Jack speak. The harshness of his tone matched his father's. Whatever they were arguing about had them both up in arms, and it didn't sound like either one was about to back down. Lena thought it best to leave them alone, so she slunk back to the break room, twisting a lock of hair around her finger.

What were they fighting about? And why was it so heated?

Lena tried her hardest not to let her mind make it about her, but she kept circling back to the idea that Jack hated her, and was condemning her relationship with Del. It would make perfect sense. It was something both Jack and Del felt strongly about, though they had opposing opinions on the matter. That would make for an intense argument.

Lena stood at her locker, staring into it like it was a vast, dark abyss holding the answer she sought. When she finally took a breath, she shut the locker. There was no sense in dwelling on the unknown. If Del and Jack were arguing about her, Del would talk to her.

Wouldn't he?

As she opened the break room door, she was almost sideswiped by Jack storming down the hall. The gust of air from his movement nearly knocked her backward. Lena steadied herself and turned her head toward Del's office. The door was still cracked. After checking to see if Marky needed any help, Lena crept down the hall and knocked on Del's door.

"Yeah?" he asked in an exasperated breath.

She pushed the door open to find Del hunched over his desk, his head resting in his hand. He looked defeated, like he was about to collapse, but when he saw Lena, his eyes lit up. His posture straightened, chest inflated, and the shell of a smile spread across his lips.

"Can I come in?"

Del nodded and motioned for her to sit.

"I, uh, saw Jack leave." Lena stepped inside and took a seat. "He looked upset. Is everything okay?"

Del's mouth tightened. "Of course. Everything's fine."

"Are you sure?"

He held her gaze, though it looked to be a struggle. With a heavy sigh, he finally shook his head. "I can't lie to you."

"Del, what's wrong?" She wrung her hands in her lap. "What were you and Jack arguing about?"

He furrowed his brow.

"I could hear you two from the break room." It was a stretch of the truth, but she didn't want Del to think she had eavesdropped.

He rubbed the back of his neck, dropping his chin. "We were arguing about Citadel."

The knot in her stomach disappeared. "What about Citadel?"

"Jack's worried about our financials. We've had a significant dip in sales over the last few months, and he doesn't think we're going to stay afloat."

Lena dipped her head to look Del in the eye. "And you don't agree?"

When their eyes met, it was like life was breathed back into Del. The heaviness of the conversation melted away, and Lena saw peace. "I told him it's a low point. All businesses have ups and downs. We've had them before, and we'll come out of it like always. Everything will be all right."

Del would have been convincing if it weren't for the shake in his voice. Pursing her lips, she leaned back into her chair and folded her arms. "Why is Jack so worried, then? What makes this low different than any of the others?"

A sly smirk spread across his face. "Nothing gets past you, huh?" He took a deep breath, running his hand over his hair. "This low is lower than any other we've had. It's also lasted the longest."

"Do you know why?"

"I think it's a combination of things. We used to have events here during the week. Trivia nights, live music, things like that. Since those have stopped, we've seen a significant decline in new customers. We have our regulars, but we don't see as many new people coming through the door as we used to."

"Why did you stop all the events?"

"We didn't stop doing them. They just fizzled out, then everything sort of snowballed from there." Del shrugged. "The guys that did our trivia quit, and we never replaced them. It became too hard to tamp down live musical acts, and when those went away, so did the music fans. When our customer base declined, it was harder to get food trucks to host a night here, and when there's no food, there's even less people."

Lena gaped at him. This lackluster, no-motivation version of Del sitting in front of her, was not how she knew him. "Have you tried setting any of these events back up?"

"We have done a few here and there, and they work great. For a few days. Then, the crowd thins back out. We might gain a new regular customer or two, but apparently it's not been enough."

"I wonder what it is that people aren't connecting with. There has to be something about Citadel that they're not drawn in by." She tapped her finger on her chin. "Do you think it's the beer?"

Del vehemently shook his head. "There's no way. We've won too many awards for our beer, and I don't think we'd have so many regulars if our beer wasn't fantastic."

"Then what could it be?" Lena chewed on the inside of her cheek as she contemplated. Suddenly, the conversation with Twyla from weeks ago came streaming into her mind. The businessmen from across the street had said Citadel didn't look professional enough. Lena grinned. "Del, have you ever considered redecorating?"

He furrowed his brow. "Why?"

Excitement bubbled inside Lena as she shifted in her chair. "I might have an idea to attract new clients. Just hear me out, okay?"

Del nodded, but kept his brow furrowed.

"What if we gave Citadel a glow-up?"

"Glow-up?

"A facelift. You know, redo the design to make it more cohesive, more inviting."

Del leaned back in his chair and folded his arms. "What's wrong with the design we have now?"

"Well," Lena said, crinkling her nose. "I don't want to be rude, but this place isn't exactly easy on the eyes." When Del didn't respond, she broke eye contact briefly, and continued. "When I walked into Citadel for the first time, I remember thinking it looked like someone had been going for shabby-chic, but stopped at the shabby."

Del's features softened and a grin spread across his lips. "That someone would be me."

Lena's heart leaped into her throat. "Oh, sorry. I didn't mean□"

"Lena, it's okay. I'm not offended." His grin fell slightly. "When we first opened Citadel, Amy decorated the whole place. She liked to do it and she was good at it, so it became her duty." He leaned forward, resting his forearms on the desk and folding his hands together. "After the divorce, I couldn't stand to look at this place, so I slapped some new paint on the walls, bought new furniture, and hung different pictures and stuff. I didn't realize it looked so bad."

Lena's heart ached to reach out for him, to hold him and never let him go. But they were at work, and they were talking business. She straightened her posture and cleared her throat. "Del, I get where you were coming from, but that was a long time ago, and even if your design wasn't... um..."

"Horrible?" he asked with a teasing tone.

She rolled her eyes. "Yes. Even if that wasn't the case, it could be time for a change anyway."

Del drew in a long, deep breath. He leaned back in his chair, rubbing his beard and studying Lena with narrowed eyes. The look on his face made her squirm, but then he smiled, and she relaxed. "Tell me your idea."

Lena bloomed with nervous excitement. On the one hand, this was her element and she'd been out of it too long. On the other, the idea of designing made her nauseous. Being fired had shaken her, but being bad-mouthed by her former boss all but drained her confidence and she wasn't sure she would be up for the task.

Design was in her blood, though.

She took a steadying breath. "Well, you said you have a few new beers almost ready to be tapped, right?"

"Yes. We'll have three ready in a few weeks."

"Okay. So, what if we redecorate Citadel, and have a beer release slash come-see-our-new-look party?" She hiked her shoulders to her ears, giving Del a pleading look.

Del pursed his lips as his gaze floated around the room. He began nodding, an easy grin spreading across his face as he looked at Lena once more. "I love it. You'll have to come up with all the design ideas, though."

"I already have several in my mind."

"Of course you do." Del chuckled, but it sounded nervous. "How soon do we start?"

"I can have everything ready by the weekend."

Del's eyes widened. "Really? That quickly?"

She nodded. "When I have an idea, things move fast. I can bring it all in on Saturday."

"No. Saturdays are too busy. You'll be needed elsewhere. Jack will have a conniption fit if we're back here instead of on the floor." Del rolled his eyes. "Plus, I don't want him to know anything about this until we have a solid execution plan."

"Well, I open on Saturday. I can bring everything to your place after work."

He shook his head. "I don't want you to have to cart stuff around. I'll come to your house, if that's okay?"

Lena's chest warmed, her pulse fluttering. Del hadn't been past her front porch thus far, and now he'd be inside her home, on a Saturday night when neither of them had to work the next day. She swallowed hard. "Sure," she said, her voice shaking.

Del gave her a sidelong look. "All right. Text when you're ready for me, and I'll come."

Her breath caught in her throat at the double entendre, but she righted herself and nodded. "Okay. I guess I should get out to the floor. Marky is probably cursing me right now."

Lena rose from her chair, but didn't make it quite to the door before Del stood too. "Wait a second." He rounded his desk to join her on the other side, embracing her in his arms. His rich scent filled her nose, melting her core with delicious notes of juniper. He tucked his knuckle under her chin and lifted her head. "I need to thank you for your help." Del planted his lips on hers in a sweet, affectionate kiss. "Thank you," he whispered against her mouth.

"Mmm," Lena hummed. She didn't want Del to let go, but he did, and she immediately missed his warmth. It was time for her to get to work, but her heart was already working overtime.

Chapter 17

"He'll be here any minute, Nicole. I don't have time for that." Lena rolled her eyes as she paced her living room. Her presentation materials were laid out on the coffee table, ready for Del to scrutinize, but she was more worried about him scrutinizing her.

"I'm just saying, breaking out that battery-operated bad boy might help you relax a little." Nicole snickered through the phone.

Lena sighed. "What if he hates all these ideas? It'll make me look like a fool."

"You're not a fool." Nicole's tone was rock solid. "The pics you sent of those designs are spectacular. He's going to love them."

"Yeah, maybe." Lena tucked her fingernail between her teeth. "What do I do after we go over them, though?"

Nicole was silent.

"Hello? Nicki, are you still there?"

"Yeah, I'm here. Just wondering what the heck happened to L.A. Lena who had confidence coming out of her wazoo, and always had an idea of what to do with a man after dark?"

Lena could picture the look on Nicole's face. A saucy eyebrow arched, slight sneer on her plump lips, and all the judgment pouring from her eyes. She groaned. "This is so new for me. I've never been with someone like Del."

"I thought you chucked your list out the window? Lena, this—"

"No, it's not about that." Lena licked her lips. "Del is by far the most respectful man I've ever been with. I'm used to guys who take control and drag me along for the ride. This is totally different."

"And it sounds totally perfect."

"I don't know how to conduct myself." Lena ran her hand through her hair. "Party boys and one-night stands are all I've really known. I can count the number of actual relationships I've had on one hand, and I don't want to mess this up by treating it like a fling."

"First of all, Lena, those days of casual hookups are so far behind you. I mean, you broke up with Ozzie, like, six months ago, and you were faithful to the scumbag for a year. You're out of the fling phase."

Nicole's words rang true in Lena's ears. The heaviness lifted from her chest, allowing her to breathe a little easier.

"Are you in love with this guy, or something?"

No longer feeling light, Lena's heart jumped into her throat. She swallowed it down. "What? No. How can you even ask that? We've been dating for two weeks."

"I know, but I've never heard you this uptight about a guy before."

"I just explained it all." Lena pinched the bridge of her nose. "It's new and scary because I've never been with a man like Del."

"Is it that, or is it because you've never had a man give you these kinds of feelings, like Del?"

Lena's hand fell to her side as her eyes scanned the floor, searching for an answer. Her mouth opened and shut, but no words came out.

Luckily, there was no time for Nicole to continue pressing the issue, because the doorbell rang, and Lena's stomach flipped. "He's here. I'll talk to you later, Nicole." Lena hung up the phone and trotted to the front door. She opened it to reveal a handsomely dressed Del, holding a pizza in one hand and a bottle of Pinot Noir in the other. "Hi," she said quietly.

"Hi," his deep voice rumbled. "May I come in?"

"Oh, yes. Sorry." Lena stepped aside to give him space, tucking a piece of hair behind her ear as she did.

Del leaned down and kissed her cheek. "You look lovely. Hope you're hungry."

Lena skipped after him as he walked into the kitchen. "You want to look over my designs first? I have everything ready in the living room." She motioned to the binders on the coffee table.

"With all due respect, I'm starving and I think it's better to eat before it gets cold." He sat the pizza on the counter, turning to take Lena's hand. "Don't get me wrong, I'm very excited to see your ideas, but I want to be able to give you my full attention, and I can't if my stomach is growling at me."

She nodded, trying to hide her disappointment. "Fair. I'll grab some plates."

Dinner was quick. Del hadn't been lying about being starving. Of the whole medium pizza, Lena got three pieces. He devoured the rest. Then, they opened the wine to sip while they went over Lena's designs.

"Show me what you've got," Del said as he sat next to her on the couch, his posture rigid.

Lena licked a drop of wine from her lips. "Well, I have three options. Each is not only distinct in its elements, but also has a dynamic different from the others." She waited for Del to nod before continuing. "This first one" —she picked up the light-blue binder— "has the most extensive changes." She opened it across her lap, and Del scooted closer, taking a long draw of his wine as she flipped the pages. "It involves painting, new décor, and all new furnishings."

"You mean all the tables and chairs?"

"Mhm. We would replace all of them with matching sets for a more uniform look."

Del hummed through his closed lips as he eyed the pages. "I like the color scheme you've got here, but replacing *all* the furniture and décor seems extreme. Can't we use some of it, at least?"

Lena grinned and sat the binder down. She picked up the green one. "That is what my other options include." She flipped through the pages depicting rooms in a sage green and dark cream color scheme with watercolor and airbrushed artwork. "This option still involves painting and new décor, but will allow us to use some of the tables and chairs. I took inventory of how many matching sets we have, and there's about half we can use."

"I like this one. It feels very relaxed, comfy." Del ran his finger along a picture before taking another large sip of his wine.

"I like it too. I might be biased, though. Green is my favorite color."

Del tilted his head, his eyes scanning her face, as if committing new information to his memory. "Good to know." He laid his hand on her knee, sending a thrill through Lena, but before the air between them could change, he turned back to the coffee table. "What about the last one?"

Lena cleared her throat before picking up the red binder. "This one is the fun one. I put together a more modern look while still harnessing the Citadel image." As she flipped the pages, Del's eyes gleamed, making her fingers tingle with anticipation to keep going. "This one incorporates some of the existing furniture, not as much as the last option, though. But it also doesn't involve replacing all the décor. We can keep some of the artwork. Mainly the logos and branding ones you have, but they'd have to be re-matted and framed."

"Still have to paint." Del smirked, arching an eyebrow.

"Yes, they all involve a new paint scheme."

Del downed the rest of his wine. "Well, I like them all." He leaned back into the couch, folding his arms behind his head. "But how do we budget for each of them? Jack's going to ask that first thing."

Lena bristled. She knew Jack was going to be an obstacle, but she didn't like being reminded of it at that moment. "I'd have to do some shopping around. In L.A., I had certain things memorized. Like paint, for instance." She drank her remaining wine. "I know how much we need for a certain square footage, and I knew the prices out there. They might be different here, though." Setting her glass on the coffee table, she leaned back into the couch beside him. "And I had an 'in' with some furniture suppliers. I got discounts depending on how much we ordered. I don't have any of those connections here."

"Maybe tomorrow, you and I can get some preliminary numbers. Put together some basic costs, at least." He leaned forward, picking up her glass. "More wine?"

She nodded. "Thank you." As Del walked to the kitchen, Lena leaned on the arm of the couch to watch him amble about her house. He seemed like he belonged there. Moving around the room as if he'd lived there his whole life, Del not only refilled their wineglasses, but he also filled two tumblers with water and carried everything back to the coffee table without spilling. The man may have been burly, but he was graceful at the same time.

"So, how do we pick which option to go with? Like I said, I think they're all great."

Lena thought as she sipped her full wineglass. "What if we had an employee vote?"

"I'm listening."

"We could post the options in the break room and have everyone cast their votes, and the one with the most votes wins. We keep everyone involved, but we don't have to make the decision ourselves."

"I like the way you think." Del clinked his glass against hers before taking two large gulps.

The look on Lena's face was surely an awkward one. She was fighting the prideful smile attempting to break through, but also trying not to seem concerned with how fast and how much Del drank. She cleared her throat. "We could also invite the employees to help paint to save some money."

"What do you mean, 'invite' them?"

"A painting party. After the new design is chosen, we buy the paint and everyone comes in on a Sunday to help."

"I'd have to pay them. I can't ask employees to volunteer time."

"Okay, well, what if they sign up for a four- or five-hour painting shift, and then everyone cuts an hour off each shift during the week?"

Del pursed his lips before taking another drink. "That could work. Still volunteering, but they're getting paid and getting shorter days. Hm." He rubbed his chin. "I think you've got a plan here, Lena."

She grinned. "Thanks." She took a small sip as she watched Del finish off his second glass.

"More?" he asked.

Lena shook her head, setting her glass on the coffee table. "I didn't think you were a big wine person."

"Just because I prefer beer doesn't mean I can't enjoy a robust Pinot Noir." He smirked, but it looked forced.

Lena shifted in her seat. "Del, is everything okay? You've been acting a little off ever since we spoke about the redecorating. Do you not want to do it?"

"It's not that." He sighed, twirling his empty glass on his leg. "This is bringing up a lot of memories. I did all this with Amy years ago, and now it's like I'm reliving the past. Not in a good way."

"Oh." Lena shrunk back.

"No, Lena." He grabbed her hand. "It's not you. You have done a fantastic job here. But when I look at all these designs, all I can think about is how I should've given more effort when Amy brought me her ideas." He sighed, letting go of her hand to run it over his hair. "Amy had several designs in mind too. I was so absorbed in everything else going on, like, the loans, inspections, codes, that I picked the first one she brought to me."

Lena watched as Del's hand tightened into a fist. "And then, opening night, whenever anyone complimented our décor, I said, 'Thanks, we worked hard.'" His fist went slack, as if he'd been defeated. "I didn't give Amy the credit she deserved."

"Del, all that stuff you were dealing with all those years ago were legitimate issues. Opening a business is a lot of work, and yes, you probably should've shown more of an interest in what your wife was working on, but you were handling a multitude of other things. She should've been able to see the stress you were under."

His head shot up, and he locked his bright, albeit sad, blue eyes on hers. "That's what I told myself. I blamed her for a long time for leaving us, but one day, I had to own up to the fact that I pushed her away. She gave up on her life to be a mom and wife while I got to live out my dream. It wasn't fair of me."

Lena scooted close to him and placed her hand on his.

He set his glass down, covering their hands with his free one. "Which is why I want to do this with you. We'll do this together, I promise, because I *am* interested in your ideas, and I do appreciate your help. I don't want to lose you too."

Strong words for a two-week-old relationship. "You're not going to lose me." She squeezed his hand. "Is that why you're so dead-set on doing everything for me? Why you're so attentive?"

Del watched his thumb stroke the back of her hand. "I'm so scared of making the same mistake." His voice was barely above a whisper.

Lena reached up to cup his cheek and put her forehead to his. "You're so far from making that mistake, you have nothing to worry about."

"Lena," he breathed her name as he brushed his lips against hers.

Del kissed her soundly. It was full of affection and passion, but was forceful. He ran his hand down Lena's arm, taking her wineglass and setting it on the table, all without breaking the kiss. It was impressive. His hand returned, but landed on her waist and pulled her close.

They slunk down so Lena was on her back and Del hovered above her. The weight of his body enveloped her like a warm cocoon of safety as he deepened the kiss. He nudged his knee between her legs, weaving them together, and Lena felt an all-too familiar ache between her thighs.

Her breath shook. She wanted this. She wanted him, but so many thoughts raced through her head. Was she ready to dive in? If so, how far was she willing to go? Sex seemed like a huge gauntlet to run, but she couldn't keep Del at arm's length forever. Sooner or later, he'd get frustrated.

The many questions were getting the best of Lena when Del let out a moan and pressed himself against her. His generous erection against her hip jolted Lena out of her head. She didn't mean to, but she flinched, and Del instantly retracted.

"Sorry. I'm sorry," he said gruffly as he put several inches between their bodies.

Lena smacked her palm over her face. "No. I'm sorry, Del. I didn't mean to... It was an involuntary reaction."

"Hey," he whispered, nudging her hand from her face. "I told you I'm not trying to rush things. It's been a long time for both of us, and I know we□"

"It's not only that."

Del furrowed his brow. "Then what is it?"

Lena groaned. "There's something I need to tell you." She took a deep breath, releasing it slowly. "My last boyfriend cheated on me." The last words came out almost inaudible.

Del's grip tightened around her hand.

"I caught him with his receptionist after a visit with my mom. I went back to L.A. early because we signed a huge client at work, and I wanted to get a head start on proposals." With a huff, she scooted herself up to sit, a tightness forming in her chest. "When I walked into my apartment, he was in the kitchen, cooking in his underwear, and I thought he was there to surprise me."

Del cleared his throat, but said nothing.

"His receptionist, Shannon, came out of my bedroom in her lingerie before I even had time to put my bags down. That's how I found out they'd been sleeping together for a few weeks." She raised her head to find nothing but sympathy in Del's features.

"Lena," he said quietly as he brushed his knuckles down her cheek, turning his hand over to cup her face. "I am so sorry that happened to you. If you'll give me this guy's name and address, I'll go teach him a lesson on respect."

She covered his hand with hers, kissing his palm. "He's not worthy of your time, or mine. I needed you to know what happened because it... hurt me. A lot."

"Something like that would hurt anyone. Thank you for telling me." He kissed her forehead. "But like I said, I'm not here to push you into anything you're not ready for, and I'm certainly not going to judge you for wanting to go slow."

A warmth of appreciation bloomed inside her, but she kept her eyes on Del's. "I appreciate it, but I feel like I'm leading you on by not letting things progress." She ran her palms down her legs to her knees and back up. "The idea of jumping into bed, though, has me overthinking."

"Well, we can do other things besides sex."

Lena didn't appreciate the tone in his voice that made him sound like he was talking to a child, so she decided to have a little fun. She plastered on her best deer-in-headlights look before locking her eyes on his. "Really? Like what?"

Del jerked his head back. "Oh, um. Well, we could..."

She laughed. "Del, I'm forty years old. I know about all the things we can do besides sex."

"You scared me there for a minute." He let out a breath, composing himself. "So, what if we did some of those other things to ease you into the idea of us being together?"

"I'm not sure I follow."

"Well, from the looks of things"—he dropped his gaze to his strained jeans, clearing his throat, and Lena giggled—"I'll be ready to move things ahead when you are. So, what if we have some fun, but *you* get to be the center of the festivities? Let me make you feel good. We can do as much or as little as you want. You have complete control."

Lena squirmed. She wanted him. She wanted him so badly her muscles ached and her fingers burned with the desire to feel him, so what he was proposing made perfect sense.

She took her bottom lip between her teeth. "What would we start with?"

A sly smirk spread across Del's face. "Why don't we pick up where we left off a minute ago? I'll let you know what I'm thinking of doing, and you can either approve or deny. I won't be offended either way."

Lena nodded, reaching for him. She pulled him closer, and their mouths reconnected. Del did, in fact, pick up where he left off. The kiss was the exact same as it had been; not too eager, but no hesitation in it, and the passion grew with each second.

Del shifted his body. "Ready for contact?" he whispered against her lips.

"Mhm," Lena hummed, so Del pressed himself to her. This time, when his erection nudged her, Lena didn't flinch. Instead, she moaned louder into his mouth.

They stayed like that for several minutes, simply enjoying the taste of each other, until Del's hand ran over her hair and down to the nape of her neck. "May I feel you, Lena?"

"Yes," she breathed.

As his tongue found hers once more, Del's hand lowered to cup her breast. She sucked in a breath at his touch, though it was gentle. His large hand massaged and caressed as his fingers traced the subtle ridge of her pebbled nipple through her clothes. She arched her back to press her breast firmly into his palm, eliciting a strong moan from Del.

"More?" he asked quietly.

A slight nod was all it took for Del's hand to find the hem of her shirt and dive underneath it. The moment his fingers hit her bare skin, Lena was on fire. Each touch was like a lightning strike, hot and searing, and made her heart race. When his fingers slid her bra aside to pinch her nipple, hers dug into him, and she felt him smile against her mouth.

He moved his lips from hers to trail kisses down her jaw and neck. "I'd like to kiss you elsewhere, if it's okay?"

All Lena did was moan.

It was enough of an answer for Del. He pushed her shirt all the way up, kissing his way to her breast. His tongue traced the edges of her hardened nipple, flicking and twirling around the sensitive skin before sucking it into his mouth.

Lena's fingers dove into his hair, loosening his bun, and she gasped. She rolled her hips to meet Del's and hooked her calf around his. Desire pooled low in her belly as she rubbed her leg along his erection. She needed friction. Now.

"Del." His name rolled off her tongue in a breathy whisper.

"Say the word, Lena, and I'll do it," he said with her nipple between his teeth. "Touch me."

Without taking his mouth from her breast, Del ran his hand down her abdomen to the fly of her shorts. He undid the button, unzipping them slowly. His fingers skimmed the rim of her panties, tickling her skin and giving her goosebumps.

It was an agonizingly slow process, so Lena bucked her hips.

Del chuckled. "All right, all right." And with that, his hand dipped into her underwear, his fingers going farther south until they slid along her wetness. It was his turn to gasp.

Even lost in her ecstasy, Lena swelled with pride. When it came to sex, she never had trouble in the arousal department, and Del was learning firsthand how much he'd turned her on.

He took a moment to compose himself before slipping his fingers inside her, and a loud moan emanated from his throat. As his tongue laved her nipple, his thumb circled her clit. He quickened the pace of his pulsing fingers.

Lena writhed beneath his weight. Her ragged breath blew from her lips in short bursts as the pressure built within. The crest was upon her, but she didn't want the moment to end. Del's touch was exhilarating. Sensual and passionate, he stroked her tenderly until the precipice of release teased her. She shifted her thigh between his, dragging it along his hard length, and with a few hearty moans, she not only found her own release, but so did Del.

Their bodies shuddered together, though Del kept his fingers moving inside her until her orgasm was complete. It was the most attentive any man had ever been with her. He took care to ensure she came, even though she never touched his cock, and when it was all over, he kissed her tenderly. He held her in his arms. He made her feel safe, cared for.

Dare she say, "loved?"

Chapter 18

"Will you stay the night?" Lena asked as she ran her fingers through the loose strands of Del's hair. He lay next to her on the couch, his head resting on her chest.

"The whole night?" He feigned a wince when she playfully tugged at his hair. "Of course I will. Let me go get my bag from the truck."

Lena cocked a scrutinizing eyebrow. "You keep an overnight bag in your truck?"

His eyes widened for a second. "It's not what you think. Just an emergency pack. A few things to get me through a night if I find myself in a tight spot." He tilted his head up to kiss her. "I'll be right back."

As she watched Del disappear through the front door, Lena let out a contented sigh. He wasn't like any man she'd ever been with. Sure, she'd had plenty of orgasms, but there had always been the caveat of her returning the favor. It was never one-sided. Unless that one side favored the guy.

A twinge of guilt ran through her. Should she offer to take care of Del the way he'd done for her? He'd already met his release, but the night still held plenty of time. How should she do it? By hand? Mouth? She'd already proved she could do it with only her leg, but he deserved more. He deserved to know how much she appreciated him.

The front door closed, snapping Lena to attention. As Del stepped into the living room, he dropped his bag and crossed the space. Sitting down, he slid his arms around her, kissing her temple.

Lena leaned into him. Their bodies fit together perfectly. It was as if he was built to snuggle her, and had no qualms about doing so.

"What's on your mind?" he asked quietly against her ear.

"Hm?"

"You're chewing on your lip and your fingers are twirling *my* hair. You've got something going on in there." He tapped her forehead. "What is it?"

She released her bite on her lip, and dropped her hands to her lap, folding them together. "I was thinking about how much I appreciate what you did for me tonight."

"Say no more. I'm happy you enjoyed it." He nipped at her earlobe. "And I'm happy to do it whenever you want."

A delightful shiver ran up her spine. "Thank you. I'll keep that in mind." Her lip worked its way between her teeth again. "But I want to repay you..."

"Lena." Del's tone was stern but supportive as he put his knuckle under her chin and tilted her head up. "I didn't do it because I wanted something in return. I did it because I wanted to make you feel good. I want you to be comfortable with me and the idea of me giving you that kind of pleasure."

Lena hummed through closed lips, dragging her foot along his calf. "I'm getting used to the idea."

Del let out a strained groan, but shook it off. "Well, until you're one hundred percent ready, I'll wait. No strings attached, okay? Obviously, I can enjoy your satisfaction without even being touched."

Lena giggled, reaching up to cup his bearded cheek. "I know, and it's extremely flattering, but it feels selfish."

"Look, whenever you're ready, I'll let you do whatever you want to me, but until that time comes" —he winked, lifting her hand to kiss it— "I'll be right here."

Lena's heart was so full, she thought it might burst from her chest. Del's words were enough to make her want to jump on him, but she refrained. She knew he was right. Waiting for her to be completely ready was the best choice. Executing it would be another thing.

***

Waking up snuggled against Del's firm chest, surrounded by his muscular arms, was nothing short of bliss. His warm, steady breath trickled down her neck as his beard brushed her skin with each inhale. The way his legs entwined with hers felt so natural; she didn't know where she began and he ended. The entire position was perfection.

Of course, his hard length pressing against the small of her back wasn't a bad feeling either.

Lena bit her lower lip. The idea of reaching behind her to give him a good morning hand job flicked into her mind. It would certainly get his day started right. She giggled as she thought about his reaction.

He stirred, and she went stock still.

A small groan escaped him before he yawned and smacked his lips. "Good morning," he said into her ear, his voice husky with sleep.

"Good morning indeed," she replied, arching her back to press her ass into him.

Del immediately scooted away. "Sorry. Can't help it."

Lena rolled over to face him. "It's all right. I'm well aware of what happens to men in the morning."

"Well, it doesn't help anything waking up with the sexiest woman next to me."

She blushed. "Sexy? Even with bedhead and morning breath?"

Tucking his knuckle under her chin, he tilted her head so their mouths aligned. "Always sexy." He pressed his lips to hers. A gentle kiss at first, but within seconds, he deepened it. His tongue ran along her lips, begging for entrance, which she happily granted.

She inched closer to him and ran her hand down his side until she reached his hip. Her fingers trailed the rim of his boxers, dipping under the waistband.

Del sucked in a breath, and Lena giggled. "I'm glad you slept in your underwear last night."

"Really? Why?"

She bit his lower lip while simultaneously sliding her hand into his boxers. "Easy access," she whispered, and took his hard length in her hand.

Del tensed, but quickly relaxed as she began pumping him. He was bigger than she'd imagined. In fact, he was bigger than any man she'd been with. The idea of how he'd feel inside of her made her thighs clench. The friction. The pressure. The movement. It was enough to break her resolve right then and there.

She pushed the thought out of her mind, though. He was her focus.

With a deep groan, Del's hands roamed all over her body. One slid under her t-shirt to find her hardened nipple, and the other settled on her ass, fingers dipping under the hem of her panties. He groped her like some kind of horny teenager.

It made Lena's heart race.

"Lena," he growled. "Please?"

"I want this to be about you," she said between breaths.

"Then let me touch you. It's what I want."

Her answer was to moan and plunge her tongue deep into his mouth.

He took that as a "yes," promptly sliding her panties aside and slipping his fingers inside her. It was his turn to moan. He pushed her onto her back so he could lean over and take her nipple in his mouth.

"Del," Lena breathed.

He pushed his fingers deeper. "Don't stop, Lena."

She gripped him harder, pumped him faster, and soon his cock was slick with precum. Her hand slid up and down his shaft with ease, making him grunt as he moved his hips. This is what she was used to; making a man come before she did. Which is why she wasn't at all surprised for him to finish before her.

What did surprise her, was after Del emptied himself into her hand, he took a moment to compose himself before continuing to finger her. His tongue worked more furiously than before, making laps around her nipples. When his thumb found her clit, it circled the sensitive nub.

Lena didn't have much time to relish the fact he was taking care of her, because before she knew it, her crest found her. She arched her back and dug her nails into his shoulders as his name rolled off her lips in deep moans. The wave crashed over her entire body, and Del rode it out until she finished.

With one last kiss of her nipple, he pushed off the bed and headed to the bathroom. He returned with a handful of tissues, and cleaned her hand. As he wiped, he stole glances at her face, but said nothing.

He tossed the tissues into the wastebasket beside the bed, then crawled in to snuggle Lena. "Thank you," he whispered before kissing her temple.

"Mmm. Thank you too."

They sighed in unison, content to hold each other for several moments until Del took a breath. "So, do we really have to go shopping today?"

Lena giggled. "Yes, Del. For pricing, at the very least."

"Okay, fine," he groaned, playfully nudging her with his elbow. "Can we at least have breakfast first? I'm not used to such strenuous physical exertion first thing in the morning."

***

"What do you think about these tables?" Lena asked, running her hand around the edge of a round glass-top table. "They would work with a good number of the chairs we already have, so we would only have to find a few more sets."

Del frowned, picking up the pricing signage. "They're twice as much as the other ones."

"Yes, but the other ones will only work with one set of chairs. We'd have to buy all new ones, which..." She used her phone to do some quick math. "Will only end up saving us one or two hundred dollars. You have to decide what is more important, a little bit of money or a lot of convenience."

"Money." Del's answer was curt. He didn't even look up from the pricing signage before walking away.

A frustrated sigh escaped her, and she skipped to catch up to him. "This isn't some Band-Aid we're using to cover a wound, Del. This is something Citadel will be branded with for years."

"I know that." His words were clipped.

Lena stopped in her tracks, putting her hands on her hips in frustration. "Then don't make a decision because you want to save some money. I know the budget is tight, but we can make concessions elsewhere."

He groaned, tilting his head back as he turned around. Folding his arms, he leaned against a buffet. "I'm sorry, Lena. I don't mean to be difficult."

"Hey," she said quietly as she walked to him and placed her hand on his forearm. "I know this is hard for you, but I have to say how much I appreciate you doing it with me. Usually, I did this stuff alone."

"Really? Your clients didn't go with you?"

She shook her head. "They'd give me a budget, a style, and a list of things to avoid, then I had to compile profiles based on those. Sometimes it was nice, because I could go do my thing and I didn't have anyone to second guess me, but that wasn't always the case." Lena shrunk back as she thought about the numerous times she was yelled at because the given instruction was so vague, she couldn't produce unique presentations. She'd either improvised, choosing generic styles which were safe, or went with her gut and put together a profile of her own tastes. It didn't always work out in her favor.

"Lena?" Del's voice stopped her from falling into her own self-pity.

She straightened her posture. "But that's all behind me, now. I'm here with you, and we're going to do this together. Okay?"

Del nodded, taking her hand.

"So, no more sulking. For either of us. We've got a schedule to keep if we want everything to fall into place."

"You're really good at this design stuff. And not just the aesthetics, you've got the planning and scheduling down too." Del relaxed. The frustration radiating off of him ebbed, soon replaced with pride. "I can tell you enjoy the hell out of it."

"I do. It's exciting to see the visions in your head come to life, you know?" Lena shrugged. "And even though I had some difficult clients, most of them loved my work. The way their eyes lit up when they saw my final product, that was the most rewarding part."

Del's eyes focused on hers, a deep, longing residing in his irises. "I have a pretty good reward for you, too." He tugged her to him, kissing her deeply.

Chapter 19

Lena spent her non-working hours on Monday and Tuesday preparing her presentations for the employee vote. Armed with updated versions of the binders she had shown Del, they now included options of the tables and chairs they saw on Sunday while shopping. Each design was also accompanied by a budget and a list of vendors and artists to be used for art commissions.

Her nerves rattled when she thought about stepping into the role of decorator again, but she felt confident in her designs. After all, it really wasn't the vote she worried about. It was one employee in particular.

Jack.

The one person she couldn't get a read on, and his opinion weighed heavier than anyone else's. Ultimately, it was Del's decision, but Jack excelled at voicing his side. Lena worried about the other employees agreeing with Jack out of sheer fear of the man. If he opposed her ideas, others would surely follow.

Wednesday was the day. Del scheduled everyone for an employee meeting at 8 a.m. to present the idea for the beer release event, and so Lena could show her designs. As she sat in her car, her foot shook uncontrollably while her hands tangled in her hair, both twisting pieces around her fingers.

"Ugh, this won't do." She untwisted her fingers, and frantically scoured her glovebox for an extra hair tie.

She came up empty, but at 7:55, Del's truck pulled into the parking spot next to her, and Lena's entire body relaxed. Her foot stopped wiggling and her breath returned to normal. She stepped out of her car to meet him at the trunk.

Slipping an arm around her waist, he kissed her gently. . "Good morning, beautiful. Ready?"

"As ready as I'll ever be, I suppose." Her voice shook.

"Hey." Del squeezed her until her splitting nerves reconnected. "You're going to do fine. Everyone will love your work and will be on board with the changes. You'll see." He kissed her cheek. "Now, let's go set up."

As they worked, the employees arrived, with Jack being the last. He strode through the door, wading through the others to settle behind the group. With a huff, he leaned against the wall, folding his arms across his chest.

Lena's muscles instantly tensed. Frustrated with herself, she closed her eyes and took a deep breath. *Don't let him ruin this for you.* Another few breaths had Lena's tension ebbing, so she put the finishing touches on her display, and promised herself not to let Jack's grumpiness crush her excitement.

When everyone arrived and had taken a seat, Del began speaking. "I'm glad you all decided to show up." A collective laugh rose from the group. "Seriously, though, I appreciate you all coming on such short notice. I know this meeting was called last minute and out of sequence for our regular staff meetings, so thank you."

He cleared his throat and continued. "I'm going to start with some honesty. Citadel has been seeing some rough times. Our general business is down, lower than it's ever been, and we need to make some changes before it's too late to reconcile our losses."

The employees grumbled, a few shifting in their chairs.

"It's been brought to my attention," he said, glancing at Lena, "that Citadel could use a face-lift. It seems our décor is lacking in the style department."

Another chuckle from the group, but it sounded like they tried to hide it.

Del licked his lips in an exaggerated manner. "That being said, Lena has come up with an idea to drum up some business. Hopefully recurring customers." He turned toward her, extending his arm. "Lena, your turn."

Lena flicked her gaze toward the group, but quickly refocused on the floor. She didn't want to chance a look at Jack in case his expression held anything remotely resembling distaste. She had been true to her earlier promise about not letting him get to her, and hadn't looked at him once. With only a few more minutes to go, she raised her chin and walked around the bar.

As she approached, Del ran his hand up and down her back, his touch comforting her. "Well, Del used much nicer words than I did when he spoke about Citadel's décor." Lena eased at the laugh from the employees. "But he's right. Citadel needs a change, and I've got some ideas." She picked up one of her foam-board displays. "I've put together a few different options on how we can improve the look of this place. Each one has its own perks, its own budget, and different options on décor."

Lena's gaze floated across the room, finding blank stares, and she had to take a deep breath. "As you all know, Del has a few new beers in the works. They'll be ready in a couple weeks, at which time, Del plans to have a release event. What I'm proposing is we give Citadel its much needed makeover and showcase it during said event. We can advertise the new beers with the added bonus of coming to see our updates."

"How do we know it'll increase business?" one of the employees asked.

"Well..." Lena trailed off, unsure of how to answer.

Del stepped in. "We know from experience that beer releases attract people. We're hoping they'll not only come that night, but will also continue coming once they see our improvements." The grin he gave Lena raised her confidnce. "Plus, we've been talking about starting up our weekly events again. Trivia, live music, food trucks; those will draw in more customers as well."

"You really think people will care what this place looks like?" Beth asked, sitting with her arms folded and legs extended out.

Lena was about to respond, when Twyla cut her off. "Oh, come on, Beth. Look at this place. It's damn ugly." She turned to Del. "No offense." When he dipped his chin in response, she continued. "And I heard firsthand from the suits across the street that, even though we have great beer, they'd never bring clients in here because it was so shabby." She locked eyes with Lena, her green irises sparkling. "I think it's a great idea."

Lena beamed and nodded at Twyla. "And you are all included in the decision. We're going to post the boards in the break room and you all will have the opportunity to vote on which design we go with. The board with the most votes wins."

The air in the room lightened a bit at the idea. Getting a say in the changes to be made must have resonated with the staff. Lena felt even more at ease.

"Where are we getting the funding for this?" Jack's harsh voice echoed over the din of the other employees, destroying Lena's peace of mind.

Del narrowed his eyes at his son, his jaw tightening. "Each design has a budget attached. Lena and I have gone over the numbers and each one is well within our means." He cleared his throat. "But we have an opportunity to save *some* money. With the help of all of you, that is."

Grumbling accompanied confused faces from the group as Del continued. "Once the design has been chosen, we will purchase the necessary paint and will be hosting a painting party this Sunday. I am asking for volunteers to come in for a few hours throughout the day. You'll be paid for your time and can knock off the extra hours during the week."

"Is it required?" Marky asked.

Del shook his head. "Strictly volunteer basis. I know we're throwing this at you with little notice, so don't feel obligated, by any means. Only come in if you can. There will be a signup sheet in the break room next to the design voting."

The rest of the meeting went as such. Some questions from the employees, answers from Del and Lena, but overall, the staff received Lena's idea well. When the meeting was finished, and all but the opening employees had left, Lena began packing up the displays to move them into the break room. She noticed Del and Jack still talking in the corner.

They'd been huddled there for several minutes, arms folded, but with their postures relaxed, and their voices low enough so Lena couldn't hear what they were saying. She took it as a good sign. It meant whatever they were talking about wasn't a hot topic and their conversation was civil.

Relief flooded her. She thought maybe Jack was coming around. Maybe he would see her as more than a temporary part of Del's life. The tightness in her chest loosened a bit, but constricted once again when Jack shot her an icy glance. The distrust in his eyes was plain to see.

Lena's body suddenly grew heavy, the defeat crushing her, so she plopped onto a stool at the bar. With her chin in her hand, she rested her elbow on the counter, sighing as she traced the woodgrain lines.

"Well, I just cast my vote," Twyla said, coming around the corner from the hall. "Those designs were fucking good, Lena. How did you come up with them?"

Lena said nothing as she kept her eyes on the countertop.

"Hey, what's up?" Twyla leaned on the bar, ducking her head to meet Lena's eyes.

"I thought my idea to revamp this place had merit." Leaning back in the chair, she folded her arms across her chest. "But I guess not everyone does." She jutted her chin toward Del and Jack.

Twyla released her furrowed brow to roll her eyes as she looked at Jack. "He's still getting to you, huh?"

Lena nodded. "I can't figure out why he dislikes me so much. I mean, I know he's protective of Del, like you said, and it's admirable, but what have I done to warrant so much hostility?"

"I think he's just taking his sweet time adjusting to you being in Del's life. Jack has seen Del not only go through a rough divorce, but also get his heart stepped on while dating." Twyla wiped the counter down as she spoke, to get ready for opening. "He's probably waiting for the other shoe to drop, you know?"

Frustration bubbled in Lena's gut, and she gritted her teeth. "What do I have to do to show Jack I'm not some fling?"

Twyla put her hand up in an I-don't-know gesture, then turned to stock glassware.

As Lena sat fuming over Jack's distaste of her, a hand came down on her shoulder. "Ready to go?" Del asked.

She turned, and as soon as she saw him, all her frustration melted away. It didn't matter what Jack thought. All that mattered was this man in front of her. He liked her, and she liked him. To hell with anyone who judged them.

***

Lena sat in the break room next to Del, counting the employee votes after closing on Saturday night. Beth had left when her duties were finished, leaving Lena and Del to themselves.

"Well, it was a pretty close call, but option B won." Lena tapped the stack of votes.

"I liked that one," Del said, brushing his fingers across her upper back.

"You liked them all."

"I did, didn't I?" He kissed her temple. "Well, I guess we're going paint shopping in the morning."

"Yep. How many people volunteered to help?"

"Everyone." Del tilted his head from side to side. "Well, almost everyone."

Disappointment settled in Lena's chest. "Jack isn't coming?"

Del tapped the tip of his nose, but didn't speak.

To avoid showing Del her discontent, Lena hung her head. "He's not on board?"

"How many votes did you have in total?"

"Um, eleven, but I didn't vote."

"I did, though." Del smirked, arching an eyebrow.

Lena's chest lightened. "So, he voted? That's encouraging."

"See? He's coming around." Del patted the table and stood up. "Now, let's get you home."

"Yeah," she said quietly as she gingerly touched the charm on her necklace.

"What's wrong?"

She sighed, crinkling her nose. "I don't like my house."

"What's wrong with your house?"

"Nothing is wrong with it, aside from the fact my mom doesn't live there anymore." Tears pricked Lena's eyes, so she raised her chin to look at the ceiling. "I grew up in it, but I hate how empty it is without her."

As she lowered her head, she found Del's sympathetic face smiling back at her. He slid back into his chair next to her and draped his arm across her shoulders. Del didn't have to speak, didn't have to move. All he had to do was hold her for Lena to feel safe and cared for.

"Can I... can I stay at your house?"

He jerked his head back. "I'm offended you thought you had to ask."

Lena laughed, wiping at her eyes.

"You're always welcome at my house, Lena." Del stood, offering her his hand.

Together, they packed the designs away, and did their last checks before locking up. They walked hand in hand to Del's truck, where he routinely opened her door and helped her into the cab. Once he settled into the driver's seat, he laid his upturned hand on the console, twiddling his fingers.

Lena gently placed her hand in his, smiling from ear to ear, and turned toward the window. The radio hummed quietly in the background with some country song Lena didn't know, but she didn't care. She'd listen to a million country songs in a row if it meant she had more time with Del. When he started singing though, she whipped her head over to look at him.

He sang softly through a tender smile as he stole glances in her direction. It wasn't the most melodic of singing voices, but he carried the tune well. It also would've been better if Lena knew the song.

When she furrowed her brow, he stopped singing. "You don't know who Tim McGraw is?"

Lena shook her head. "I told you I wasn't a country fan."

"Everyone should know this song." He slipped his hand from hers to turn up the volume and the gentle strum of guitars flitted through the air.

Lena listened to the words. Something about how the man would do anything to see his woman smile. A sweet sentiment, but the musical style still wasn't her favorite. She didn't want to be rude, though, so she sat quietly and let Del serenade her.

With another stolen glance in her direction, Del sighed heavily. "Okay. I can see there's no recruiting you." He clicked the buttons on the stereo, changing it from FM radio to CD.

Lena watched in confusion until a familiar voice came filtering through the speakers. Her eyes widened when she heard the lyrics to "Thinking Out Loud" by Ed Sheeran, but her mouth fell open when Del started singing along. He knew every word, every note, as if he'd been listening to the song for years. Del entwined his fingers with hers once more, squeezing tight.

When the song ended, Lena looked at him with an astonished grin. "I thought you didn't know his songs."

Del shrugged, feigning nonchalance. "I'd do anything to see you smile."

Chapter 20

The following morning, right at 6 a.m., when Home Depot opened, Lena and Del headed straight to the paint counter.

"These are the colors we need." Lena handed the employee her color swatches, listing out the amount and sheen of each.

The employee took his notes and double checked before glancing at Del. "Is this all?"

"Hey, don't look at me. She's the boss; I'm just here to do the heavy lifting," Del said, holding up his hands.

Lena lifted her chin.

"Okay, this should take me about fifteen minutes or so. Feel free to walk around while you wait," the employee said before turning to the paint machines.

Del held his hand out, motioning for Lena to lead the way. With her chin still raised, she tossed her hair back as she brushed past Del. Luckily, he laughed as she had hoped, and followed her with the shopping cart. They turned down the next aisle to gather supplies.

Lena grabbed an array of brushes from the shelf, but Del put them back and grabbed cheaper ones. Lena scoffed. "Good brushes are a must."

"These are as good as those, but five dollars less." He arched his eyebrow.

"We can spend a little more on better supplies since they're having that paint sale. We're already saving five dollars a gallon, and twenty on the 5-gallon buckets."

"And we'll save even more by buying the cheaper brushes."

With a roll of her eyes, she began gathering rollers and trays, to which Del also protested. When she came to the painter's tape, Del pointed at the plain masking, but Lena shook her head. "This is where I put my foot down. Masking tape doesn't cut it. If we want clean lines, we buy the good stuff."

Del huffed as he narrowed his eyes, but Lena stood her ground, her chin up. "Fine," he said, then took a step back.

Smiling, Lena slid rolls of blue painter's tape onto her arm like bracelets until it was covered from elbow to wrist. As she reached for the drop cloths, Del put his hand on her forearm, pushing it down.

"I've got plenty of those at home."

"Okay," she said, approvingly. Of all the things Del had argued over, drop cloths were one she could concede to. "I think this is all we need. Should we check on the paint?"

At the paint counter, they found the Home Depot employee buried in customers and only halfway finished with their order. They decided to walk around as he'd suggested, but left the cart next to the paint area.

Del linked his hand with hers. "Where are you taking me?"

"I don't know yet." She hummed as she strolled along, peeking down aisles of nuts and bolts, power tools, and plumbing supplies. "What should we shop for?"

Del grunted, but said nothing.

"We could look at curtains or blinds, unless you want to leave the windows uncovered. They're tinted, right?"

Del nodded.

"Or plants. A few small indoor plants can really liven up a space without taking up a lot of room."

"None of those words sounded like 'new rotary saw.'" Del's words were clipped.

"Are you okay?"

"I'm fine," he said, though the words sounded anything but.

Lena stepped in front of him, turning to place her hand on his chest. "Del, talk to me. What's going on?"

He groaned, letting his head fall back. "I don't like shopping."

"Could have fooled me," Lena said flatly.

He dropped his chin and gave her a pointed look. "Smartass."

Lena cupped his cheek. "I don't want you running away from this. I need you here with me, like you promised."

His warm palm covered hers against his face as his eyes searched the depths of her irises. Pain lingered in his gaze, but also a plea for understanding. "I'm here," he whispered before clearing his throat. "But it's hard."

"Why? What's hard?" She stroked his jaw with her thumb. "You were fine a few minutes ago. What changed? Talk to me, please."

He sighed. "Shopping for the supplies. It made me realize what an ass I can be."

"You're not an ass."

"I was back there." He jerked his thumb behind him. "You're trying to make sure this gets done the right way, and all I did was object to your choices." With a huff, he ran his hand over his hair. "And for what? A few measly dollars? I'm acting like a dick all over again."

"Del," Lena whispered, taking his hand in hers. "Wanting to save some money isn't being a dick. It's being responsible. And besides, you're right. Those cheaper brushes and rollers will work just fine."

His eyes looked everywhere except at her. "I thought I'd learned my lesson," he said quietly. "Thought I could do this *with* you."

She took his face in her hands, holding his head still so he had to look at her. "I'm here *with* you. That promise for us to do this together wasn't one-sided."

He turned his head to kiss her palm, his lips lingering on her skin. "I'm sorry." A shaky breath escaped him. "Every time you broach the subject of decorating, Amy's voice sounds in the back of my mind, and I think about how I fucked everything up. Now, it seems like I'm doing it again."

"Del..." Lena let go of his face to lay her cheek against his chest. "You said it yourself, I'm nothing like Amy."

"You're not," he said with strong conviction.

She turned her chin up to look at him. "Then you have nothing to worry about." Tipping onto her toes, she connected their mouths. "Now, let's get our paint. Maybe we can have some alone time before everyone shows up at Citadel."

***

"Okay, Del. I'm all done," Marky said, dropping his paintbrush into the drip pan. He took a second to admire the wall he'd finished before going to the bathroom to wash up.

"Thanks, Marky," Del called after him. He walked to Lena, wrapped an arm around her waist, and placed a kiss on her cheek. "I think we'd better call it a day. We can finish later."

"What? No. We're almost done!" Lena motioned to the last bit left to paint, then glanced out the window. "The sun isn't even setting yet. We've got plenty of daylight left."

Del groaned as he ran a hand over his hair, but stopped when he started picking at the paint stuck to the strands.

Marky returned from the bathroom, his hands and arms clear of navy-blue paint. "I'm gonna take off. You lovebirds staying?"

"I guess so," Del said, giving Lena a mocking glare.

She scoffed and went back to painting.

"Thank you for all your help today, Marky." The men shook hands, exchanged goodbyes, and then Marky was gone. Del let out a deep breath. "Well, if we're going to be here a while, I need a drink." He stepped behind the bar and grabbed a pint glass.

"You've been drinking *all* day," Lena said, a teasing tone in her voice.

"I have not. We've been here since 8 a.m., and I've only had four beers. It's called pacing."

Lena narrowed her eyes, studying him. His feet were firmly planted on the floor, and he didn't sway at all. The focus in his eyes didn't waver. There wasn't even a flush on his cheeks, so Lena nodded.

"See? I'm in control, so what's one more?" Del took his empty glass and tilted it toward Lena. "Want one?"

She shook her head.

"You haven't had one all day. We're on the last wall. Why don't you take a break and relax with me?"

"Because we're not finished," she replied sternly, continuing to apply paint.

"Suit yourself." Del filled his glass and took a long draw. "Mmm. There's nothing better than an ice-cold beer at the end of the day."

Lena turned her head over her shoulder, and wiggled her hips. "Nothing?"

A mischievous smirk crossed Del's face. "Well, I can think of a few things." He eyeballed her from head to toe, humming through his closed lips.

"Not on the clock." Lena winked and turned back to the wall.

His footsteps sounded on the floor as he joined Lena once again. Picking up his paint roller, he ran it up and down the wall, painting the same spot five times before Lena finally looked over at him. He stared at her and not the wall.

She gave him a pointed look and jutted her chin to his roller.

He shook his head, lifting his pint glass to take a drink.

Rolling her eyes, Lena went back to painting, until an idea sprang to her mind. She continued rolling on paint for a minute before pretending to stretch her back. She bent down to set her roller in the drip tray, but picked up her brush. Before Del could ask what she was doing, she spun around and dragged the sage green paint down his forearm.

He yanked his arm away, careful not to spill his drink. "What the?"

Lena feigned surprise, pressing her fingers to her lips. "Oops. Guess I was too busy watching you and not what I was doing."

Del's expression turned from confusion to conniving as a sly smirk crossed his lips. "I don't think you want to start this game with me, Lena."

"Whatever do you mean?"

Del snorted, bending down to set his beer on the floor. When he stood back up, his eyes flashed with determination. It was an incredibly sexy look, and unfortunately for Lena, distracting as well. He inched toward her before she knew what was happening.

She jumped back. "What are you doing?"

"Getting revenge," he said, picking up his paintbrush.

"No, Del. Don't."

"You started it." He licked his lips, taking a step closer.

Lena backed away right into a table, making her turn her head to avoid falling, and Del took his chance. He moved quickly, grabbing her wrist and spinning her around so her back was flush to his firm chest. With both her arms tucked under one of his strong ones, Lena couldn't do anything but squirm.

Del's deep laugh rumbled through her ribs as he waved his paintbrush in front of her face. "Resistance is futile, and will only make things worse."

Lena squealed as Del tapped the paintbrush to the tip of her nose. She whipped her head over and the brush slid across her cheek. Arching her back, Lena leaned her head against Del, but he dragged the brush down her throat, swirling it on her chest.

"Stop!" she whined.

Del tightened his hold on her. "Had enough?"

"I surrender!"

He kissed her unpainted cheek and released her from his grasp. She jumped away, bringing her fingertips to her nose, her cheek, and then tilting her chin down to attempt a look at her front. The trail of paint stopped above her cleavage.

When she raised her head to glare, she found Del staring at where his artwork ended, his irises burning. He licked his lips.

"Uh-uh. You don't get any shows after that stunt."

Del's trance was broken as he laughed. He held out his hand. "Truce?"

Lena narrowed her eyes, taking his hand. "Only if you finish the wall by yourself."

"Deal."

By the time he finished, the setting sun brought the coolness of nightfall, and Lena was glad the day had ended. "I hope the paint smell is gone by tomorrow." She glanced around at the box fans lining the room.

"It's not too bad. You just think it is because of this." Del poked the tip of her nose where he had dabbed paint. When she chomped at his finger, he yanked it away, laughing. "Down, girl. I doubt the smell will be gone completely, since we can't leave the windows open all night, but it won't be so bad." Del tipped up his glass to finish off the last few drops of beer, then smacked his lips. "Mmm. That's my favorite of ours."

"Which one?"

"Love Hops."

Lena's heart fluttered. The beer she had chosen as her fake favorite turned out to be Del's actual favorite. What were the odds?

"Which one is your favorite?" Del asked.

Lena's mouth opened, the "L" sound on the tip of her tongue, but she stopped. She didn't want to lie to Del, even if it was a harmless one, so she shrugged. "I don't know."

"Oh, I forgot you're not a beer person. Well, which one is the least worst?" He rinsed his glass.

"Um, well..." Lena chewed on her lower lip, unsure of how to answer. She didn't want to admit to Del she hadn't tried any of the beers. Her credibility would take a hit, but lying to him made a pit form in her stomach.

He turned to face her, an incredulous look on his face. "Have you had any of our beers?"

Lena crinkled her nose, biting down on her lip.

"You haven't!" Del's eyebrows shot to the sky. "You've worked here almost two months and you've never had our beer?"

She shook her head gingerly.

"Then how do you answer the customer when they ask about it?"

Lena put a finger up. "I know everything about them. All the stats." She counted on her fingers as she listed them. "I know their IBU's, their ABVs, their malts, hops, grains. I know the flavor hints and finishing tastes. I can answer any question thrown at me."

Del eyes gleamed with mischief. "Then which is your favorite?"

Lena swallowed roughly. "I picked one at random."

"Which was?"

"Love Hops."

A smile spread wide across Del's face, and he took a slow, deep breath. He held her gaze longer than a standard moment, but blinked himself out of his trance. "Well, that does it." He started taking tasting glasses from the shelf and filling them.

"What are you doing?"

"You are going to taste each and every one of our beers."

"Right now?"

Del nodded. "Right now."

Chapter 21

As Lena stared at the array of beers in front of her, a pit formed in her stomach. They looked bigger than normal. She'd poured plenty of tasters over the last month and a half, all in these exact same glasses, but these seemed gargantuan in comparison.

She tried to swallow down the icky taste at the back of her throat, but her mouth had run dry. She hadn't drank a beer since college. The memories of puking up cheap, warm beer made her gag.

"They're good. I promise," Del said.

She looked up from the tasting glasses to his bright, blue irises, immediately ashamed of her reaction. "I'm sorry. I haven't had a beer in a long time, and it wasn't a good experience."

Del steepled his fingers at his chest. "Let me guess. A generic lager type advertised as a beer for everyone?"

She nodded. "Something like that."

"Well, I'm going to go out on a limb here and say our beers are better." He picked up the first one, holding it out to her. "They'll have more flavor, be smoother, and finish better."

Lena took the glass from him without taking her eyes off his. When he jutted his chin toward the counter, she looked down at the taster. She knew from watching him at the tap, he had poured Jagged Little Pils, a lighter beer brewed with Pilsner malt and Perle hops, but she could've guessed what it was from looking at it. It had a bright, golden color which differed from the other beers.

With a deep swallow, Lena lifted the glass to her lips as Del watched intently. He nodded softly, as if to encourage her to continue. She inhaled, the familiar aroma filling her nostrils, and before she could think too much about it, she took a sip.

The carbonation danced on her tongue, the bitter flavor of the hops cascading across it. After she swallowed the tiny drink, there was a lingering malty taste at the back of her throat.

That was when she expected to gag, but she didn't.

The beer went down smoothly as Del had promised. The flavors were bold, but delicious, and Lena savored them as she finished the small taster. She smacked her lips. "Not bad."

A one-sided smirk crossed Del's face. "See? Told you." He picked up the next one. "Let's continue, shall we?"

Lena sampled the next few beers without fear. There was a mild hesitation with each one, but every time she took a sip, she felt more comfortable with the idea of drinking beer. They didn't make her gag. They didn't give her the sour stomach she remembered from all those years ago. These drinks were exactly like Del had said; flavorful and smooth.

When they were at the middle of the tasting tray, Del slid a glass of water to Lena. "You okay?"

She nodded, picking up the water and sipping it. "I'm good, actually. Who knew I would enjoy beer?"

"I did." Del picked up the middle glass and held it out to her.

"Love Hops?"

He nodded.

She crinkled her nose. "Would it be okay if we saved this one for last?"

"Why?"

"I don't know. It seems like the thing to do."

"All right." Del set it back down, picking up the next beer. "Mister Spock's Bock."

The Bock was not Lena's favorite, nor was the next one, a vanilla porter. "Too smoky," she said, reaching for her water.

"Porter's can take some getting used to." He handed the stout taster to her. "Stouts can be similar, but not as smoky."

Lena hesitated, the murky flavor of the porter still smoldering on her tongue. "Bottoms up," she said and tipped the glass to her lips. To her surprise, the stout was much better. It was smooth with hints of chocolate and coffee teasing her taste buds.

"Mmm," she hummed. "That one was good."

"Glad to hear it." Del picked up several empty tasters and proceeded to rinse them. "Only one left. Your favorite," he said, glancing at her.

"Hold that thought." She got up from her chair. "I have to pee."

As she walked toward the bathroom, Lena felt the room spin. She stopped to rest against the wall. *How am I this drunk?* She peeked inside the break room, glancing at the wall clock. *Oh, I haven't eaten in like, six hours and just drank fourteen tasters of beer. That'll do it.*

Pressing her fingers to her temple, Lena shook her head, steadied herself, and managed to get to the bathroom. It may have taken her longer than normal, but she finally made her way back to the bar to find Del patiently waiting.

Concern spread across his face as she stumbled to her seat. "Everything all right?"

"I'm fine." Lena shifted on the stool, trying to get comfortable. "Just a little lightheaded."

"We should stop," he said, taking the last taster glass from the tray.

"Del, I have one more. If we were going to stop, we should've stopped four beers ago."

He didn't chuckle like she expected him to. Instead, he stared at her with a furrowed brow and pursed lips.

Lena felt the urge to explain. "I haven't eaten in a while. There's nothing to soak up all this alcohol."

"We'll pick up a pizza on the way home." He didn't relinquish the tasting glass from his fist.

Lena flicked her gaze from him to the beer. "One more isn't the end of the world."

"Okay." He slid the taster to her, eyeing her suspiciously. "Enjoy."

Lena couldn't help but raise her chin as she lifted the glass to her lips. She inhaled the sweet citrus aroma. With one more glance at Del, she took a sip. It was crisp and refreshing. A hop-forward beer, bitter on the tongue, but smooth as it slid down her throat. The bubbles danced all the way to her stomach, where they fizzed and popped, making Lena feel lighter. A flutter ran through her.

"Well?" Del asked with his eyebrows raised.

Lena licked her lips, savoring the lingering flavor. She twirled the glass on the counter. "I could drink that all day."

"Good thing it's your favorite." Del winked, took the glass, and washed it. "Let me clean up, and I'll take you home."

Home. The word had a brighter meaning because it meant Del's house. Lena breathed easier knowing she'd soon be devoured by his warm embrace instead of hugging herself alone in her bed.

The breaths shortened as she ogled Del's backside. Heat crept into her cheeks. She dragged her tongue across her bottom lip just thinking about what would happen once Del took her home.

***

Lena's world still spun when they arrived home, but Del held her hand up the porch steps. They stayed connected until they crossed the threshold, where Lena whirled around to face him. She clasped her hands around his neck and their bodies swayed as his hands rested firmly on her hips.

"Bed?" she asked in her most sultry tone.

Del searched her face, his features warring between longing and concern. "Are you sure? It's been a long day, and we both could use some rest."

"I'm not tired." She leaned forward, pressing her lips to his. "At least not yet."

Del shuddered at her words, but composed himself before shutting and locking the door.

Once the door was shut, Lena pounced. She practically jumped into his arms and kissed him solidly. Their bodies were flush against each other, but there was still too much room between them. She longed for friction.

Lena's lips parted and she ran her tongue along Del's lower lip. He obliged her request by opening his mouth, and their tongues met in a tangle of desire, the kiss deepening with each second. Del's muscles tensed beneath her fingers, and his breath became shallow. As his hand ran up her side, stopping below her breast, she moaned.

With a grunt, Del squeezed her tight, but pulled away. "We can't do this," he said, his voice gruff, strained by self-control.

"What? Why not?"

He hung his head, taking deep breaths. "You're drunk." He lifted his gaze to meet hers, nothing but sincerity in his eyes.

"I'm not drunk." Lena tore herself from his embrace, staggering backward a step.

Del caught her by the elbow before she tumbled, giving her a knowing look with arched eyebrows.

"Okay, so what if I am?" She yanked her arm from his hand. "This isn't our first time. We've fooled around before."

"Yes, we have, but you weren't drunk."

She folded her arms across her chest. "Well, I wasn't exactly sober either. We drank a bottle of wine, remember?"

"Of course I do, but you weren't stumbling around or slurring your words."

"I'm not slurring." Even as the statement left her lips, the words felt sloppy.

Del sighed. "Look, I want nothing more than to tear those clothes off you and worship your body the way you deserve to be worshipped, but I'm not comfortable with it right now." A large groan left his throat as he threw his head back to look at the ceiling. "This isn't a decision I'm making lightly." His head lowered and Lena saw the struggle happening behind his eyes. "I don't want you to regret it later."

"Del," Lena whispered, placing her hand on his arm. "I won't regret it. I want this with you."

He covered her hand with his and squeezed. "And I want it with you, but you also told me last time you needed to take things slow. I don't want our first time to be a drunken impulse."

Lena laughed, hanging her head. She knew Del was right. Everything he said made sense, and she appreciated his respect for her, but she still longed for him. "Will you just hold me, then?"

When she lifted her head, she found a soft expression on his face as he took her hand. "I'd love to."

He guided her through the house to his room, where he handed her an oversized t-shirt. As Lena slipped out of her clothes, she heard Del moan. Not wanting to torment the man, she put on his t-shirt before removing her bra. Lena crawled into bed next to Del, who had stripped down to his boxers. She hummed contentedly as she snuggled into him, the urge between her thighs dissipating slowly. The warmth of his embrace comforted her in all the right ways.

She had no qualms about falling asleep next to a half-naked man, because this man, in particular, was trustworthy and honest. Something she hadn't known before in any other man.

Chapter 22

A godawful sliver of sunlight struck Lena in the eye, waking her from a blissful slumber. She squinted as she blinked and tilted her head away from the stream of sleep-destroying light. As she moved, Del stirred beneath her.

Lena froze. Taking a minute to get her bearings, she recalled the night before. The beer tasters on a mostly empty stomach. The striking urge to get naked with Del. His rejection of her advances. The fulfilling warmth radiating inside her as she lay blanketed in the safety of his arms.

And he was still there.

Lying on his back, with one arm flopped above his head, and the other still holding Lena against him, Del snored softly. His hair was only half made into a bun, and the loose strands framed his perfect face. The blankets were pushed down to his hips, exposing his chiseled chest and abs.

With him sound asleep, Lena was able to study the tattoo covering his ribs. She'd seen it a few times at the lake, but being mostly under his arm, all she could see was an array of differing shades of green. Now, the green blobs took shape, and Lena saw them for what they were.

Hops.

The majority of his ribs were decorated with a beautiful motif of hops cascading down his side. All sizes and colors, the hop buds entwined together with vines spiraling every which way.

Her eyes followed the trail of vines, and soon, Lena lost herself in the stunning visual.

That is, until Del stirred, sucking in a deep breath that made his chest expand.

Lena's attention was drawn back to the musculature of his body, and she fought the urge to drag her tongue across every defined ridge. She settled for using her fingers. The second her hand touched his firm pec, a jolt shot through her. She ran her fingertips down his chest, tracing the defined muscles of his stomach until she reached the edge of the blanket. Biting down on her lower lip, Lena glanced at Del's face.

He still slept soundly.

He must not be ticklish, she thought as her fingers inched under the blanket toward the hem of his boxers. She drew her gaze back down, only to see the blanket twitch. A mischievous grin grew across her face. Giving Del this kind of wake up would be a fantastic way to thank him for his patience the night before. Lena's hand slid all the way into his boxers.

He grunted in his sleep as she gripped him, but he didn't wake.

Lena took a breath and began pumping her hand up and down his hard length. When his breath labored, she scooted her body up to press her lips to his cheek. "Good morning," she whispered.

Del made some throaty noises as he smacked his lips, but when he opened his eyes, he did a double take of what was happening below his waist. "Lena, what□"

"Shhh. I want to do this for you."

He furrowed his brow briefly before letting his head sink into the pillow. "Can I touch you?" he asked through his strained jaw.

"Yes."

Del didn't waste a second with her approval. His hand raced to her breast, kneading and massaging. When her nipples hardened under her shirt, Del's fingers sprang into action. They tweaked and rolled the sensitive peaks, making Lena moan. Del responded with a deep groan, and his hips began moving with her hand.

Once he picked up her rhythm, it didn't take long for him to finish. He emptied himself into her hand, heaving breaths through his nose as he did. His body slowly relaxed, muscles easing as his orgasm subsided, and he stepped off to the bathroom to clean up.

Lena rolled to her side to grab tissues from the nightstand. As she wiped her hand clean, the self-satisfied smile never left her lips. She reveled in the fact she could turn Del on so easily, and the idea of him finding her sexy enough to be affected by something as simple as her hand made her swell with pride.

The only problem was how to handle the swelling happening elsewhere.

Del had already been taken care of. Would he want to give her the same satisfaction? He'd done it before, but that also had been his idea. This was all her doing, and while she didn't expect anything in return, some relief would be nice.

"Good morning indeed." Del's voice shattered Lena's thoughts as he crawled back into bed next to her. His arms swallowed her, and he gathered her to his chest. "What prompted the wake-up call?"

She brushed her fingers up his forearm. "I wanted to say thank you for being so respectful last night."

"Well, while I certainly enjoyed waking up to that, you didn't have to do anything." He kissed her head.

"I know, but I wanted to."

Del took a deep breath, pressing his chest further against her back. He put his lips to her ear. "What if I want to do something for you?" His voice was low, husky, and it made Lena shudder.

She tilted her head back. "I'm all ears."

"It's not your ears I'm interested in." He nipped at her lips before crashing his mouth to hers in a fierce kiss.

Lena rolled over to face him, but he kept her on her back, never breaking the kiss. His hand ran up and down her side, pushing her shirt up with each stroke. When her middle was completely exposed, Del left her mouth to trail kisses down her abdomen. He paused a moment in her belly button before coming back up to her ribs. Very slowly, he nudged her t-shirt over her breasts, taking one of her nipples into his mouth while his fingers rolled the other gently.

Lena moaned, arching her back so her breast was pressed against Del's mouth. She ran her hands along his back and shoulders as he laved her nipple.

His tongue swirled the hardened peak, flicking it before switching to the other, but he made no other movements.

He sure is taking his sweet time. Lena's impatience wanted to burst forth, but the pleasure she experienced from Del's attention to her breasts was enough to quell her frustration. She temporarily gave herself reprieve by rubbing her thighs together, but it wasn't enough.

Del must have noticed, because his free hand found its way south to massage her clit through her panties. Her head fell backward and if her underwear wasn't soaked before, it was now. Del moaned against her breast, obviously able to feel her arousal on his fingers.

He kissed his way back to her mouth. His tongue danced with hers for a minute until he moved his lips to her ear. "Lena," he whispered, his hot breath cascading down her neck.

"Mmm."

"Your nipples were delicious."

Panties drenched. "Mhm."

"I want to know how you taste here." Del pressed his fingers harder against her swollen clit.

Lena's breath caught in her throat. Fingers were one thing; tongues were another. It wasn't that she didn't enjoy oral sex, she just hadn't had a man's mouth between her legs in a long time. Ozzie hated it. He did it once for her and gagged practically the whole time. Would Del do the same? Would it even be enjoyable with his beard?

"Lena?" Del asked, kissing the skin below her ear.

She shook her head to clear it, and nodded. "Yes." She felt Del smile against her skin as he slid himself down her body.

He made a stop at her breasts to lick and suck on her nipples some more before moving south and taking the rim of her underwear between his teeth. His fingers still massaged her wet panties as he moved.

Lena tilted her chin down to look at him. His eyes held a world of desire with a hint of adoration. He bent his head to kiss her inner thigh before removing her underwear. With a flick of his wrist, he flung them across the room. Running his hands up her legs, he pushed them apart and settled his fingers on her warm, wet center.

"Mmm," he hummed as his fingers slid into her. "I love how ready you are for me."

All Lena could do was heave labored breaths in anticipation. She gasped as Del's mouth connected with her clit. The feeling was incredible. His tongue moved in perfect circles as his fingers pulsed inside her. Desire flared within her, and Lena began moving her hips.

Del moaned as his hands grabbed her waist, but his tongue didn't stop. He lavished her core, lapping and licking his way to her climax. He hummed and moaned in satisfaction, and he didn't gag once. When he slid another finger into her, she moaned his name into the air.

He picked up his pace.

The tension and pressure were deliciously unbearable. Lena wanted her release so badly, but didn't at the same time. When Del closed his lips around her clit and sucked, she didn't have a choice. She came hard in his mouth, his name leaving her lips in strained screams.

Del slowed his movements, but didn't stop until the waves of her orgasm were over. He kissed her intimate parts once more before rising to cradle her in his arms. He nuzzled into the crook of her neck, letting out a warm breath against her skin. "You okay?"

"Mhm," Lena hummed as she adjusted herself in his embrace.

"Good." With a contented sigh, he kissed her collarbone. "You taste divine, by the way."

Lena wanted to laugh. She wanted to turn over and kiss him, but she couldn't move. She was exhausted in the best way possible.

Chapter 23

"So, what's on the docket today?" Del asked as his lips grazed the skin of Lena's shoulderblade. He was lying behind her, his chest pressed to her back. Which was a growing favorite position on Lena's list of cuddling with Del.

It was Thursday and Lena's day off. She'd spent every night that week at Del's since their fun wake up Monday morning. It was seemingly becoming a common occurrence, and one Lena didn't mind at all. She didn't even miss her own home. "We're going furniture shopping, remember?"

Del groaned, rolling onto his back and flopping his arm over his face.

Lena flipped over to snuggle into his side and splayed her hand across his chest. Her eyes stayed focused on her fingers as they twisted into the hairs covering his sternum instead of peeking at his face.

Paint shopping was hard enough. "I guess I can go alone and send you pictures." She hated the meekness of her voice.

"What?" Del lifted his arm and tilted his head to look her in the eye.

She kept her gaze on her fingers still twisting his chest hairs. "After shopping for paint last weekend, I figured you—"

"Lena." Her name came out as a stern whisper, and he sat up to lean on his elbow. He tucked his knuckle under her chin, lifting her head to face him. "Yes, paint shopping seemed to open up a whole slew of issues I didn't realize I still had, but I made you a promise." Sincerity poured from his irises as they softened, and Lena lost herself in them.

A breath bled through her lips, one begging to be let out because the warmth spreading through her chest threatened to rupture her rib cage at any moment.

She hummed contentedly through closed lips and dipped her head to snuggle against him.

He kissed the top of her head. "I just have to ask for your patience."

"I can give you that." The moment was perfection. They were both warm and comfortable. Both relaxed. Lena never wanted to leave this position, but she knew if she stayed any longer, she'd fall asleep. They had already used up most of the morning lying in bed.

With a deep breath, she sat up to prop her head in her palm. "Showers and breakfast?"

Del arched an eyebrow. "Showers?" He emphasized the ending "s" sound.

"Yeah." Lena's forehead crinkled. "You do want to shower, don't you?"

"Of course I do." A sly smirk crossed his face before he leaned over to put his lips to her ear. "But I don't want to shower alone," he whispered gruffly.

A scrumptious shiver crawled up Lena's spine as she softly nodded. Sliding from the bed, she took Del's hand to lead him into the bathroom. After starting the shower, Lena removed her t-shirt, completely exposing herself, and she heard Del groan. She turned to find him staring at her ass, his Adam's apple bobbing several times. With a wry look, she spun to face him.

His posture was as straight as a board, his posture taut as she stepped to him. Her hands found his hips, and he sucked in a breath when she dipped her fingers into the waistband of his boxers. She pressed onto her tiptoes to kiss him, and he seemed to melt. Pushing his underwear to the floor, Del's cock sprang forth at complete attention. Lena nodded in approval as she opened the shower door and stepped into the steam, tugging Del with her.

Even in the over-sized shower, warmth enveloped them. Maybe it was the hot water, or maybe it was the heated desire growing within Lena. Either way, she couldn't complain. The fact Del created these feelings inside her was a milestone of great proportions, and she didn't want to squander the moment.

She reached up to slide a hand around his neck, pulling his mouth to hers. The kiss was searing even in the heat of the water, and Lena wanted more. More passion. More contact. More Del. She inched forward to close the gap between them.

Del's hand found her waist and yanked her flush against him. His erection pressed into her stomach, making her gasp into his mouth. As they adjusted to their standing position, their hands began roaming, sliding across each other's bodies like the water. Their fingers trickled down every muscular ridge. The velvety curves were drizzled in soft caresses. Not a single inch of their skin went untouched, and it set Lena on fire.

When Del leaned her against the tile wall, she welcomed the shock of the cool surface. It wasn't long before it heated under her skin, and she was right back where she started. Hot, drenched with desire, but seeping with anxiety of how to handle it.

Sex was the obvious answer. What else do two people do in the shower?

Was she ready, though?

Maybe it didn't matter. Spontaneity could be her ally. As long as she didn't think too much about it, she could ride out the moment in ignorant bliss while riding Del in all-consuming sexual gratification.

She was already thinking too hard about it. Spontaneity would have to wait.

"Lena," Del growled against her mouth.

The gruffness of his voice made her knees weak, and somehow wetter despite the water streaming down her body. "Del," she whispered back.

He held her up with one arm. "Come for me." Then, his other hand ran down her stomach to settle between her thighs, his fingers sliding inside her.

The pressure made her breath hitch, but three seconds later, she was grinding against his hand. His name rolled off her tongue in soft moans. With Del's mouth latched to her neck, Lena let him pleasure her in the heat of the shower. It was a magical experience, one she was beginning to get used to, but she wanted him to reap the benefits as well.

Their angle against the wall proved problematic, though. She couldn't reach his cock without compromising her stability, try as she may.

"Stop," Del growled. "Don't worry about me. Enjoy yourself. I sure am."

The deep rumble of his orders nudged Lena toward the edge. Her head dipped back to rest against the wall. With her eyes closed, she fell deeper into the moment, her crest edging closer with every second. She savored each precise movement of Del's fingers, relished every kiss he placed on her. When he nipped at her collarbone, she shuddered, gripping his shoulders and digging her nails into his skin. As her orgasm ebbed, Del slowed his pace, but didn't withdraw his fingers until she'd met her full satisfaction.

He slowly released her from his embrace, though he kept his hands on her. Without a word, he kissed her gently and reached for the soap.

Lena put her hand on his forearm, pushing it down, and shook her head at his furrowed eyebrows. "It's your turn."

"I told you not to worry about me."

"And I didn't..." A sly smirk crossed her lips. "While I was enjoying myself." She trailed her finger along his arm, tracing the curve of his deltoid to his bicep where the word "Stratton" was tattooed in script. "But now I want to enjoy you too."

"Well, I won't argue with you, I guess." He licked his lips as he reached for her.

Instead of falling into his arms, Lena placed her palm on his chest, and took a step back. She nudged him to do the same. When there was sufficient space between them, Lena knelt on the floor. Del's face changed from confusion to surprise as he watched, but his eagerness gave Lena the confidence to continue.

She glanced up at him through her eyelashes, the spray hitting the wall behind her head as his chest expanded with a huge breath. Her heart pounded in her chest as Del's erection stared her in the face. She wasn't surprised by it. She'd seen his cock several times in the past two weeks, but never this close.

Giving head also wasn't something new to her. She'd gone down on guys before, but she always used it as a way to get out of having sex, never because she wanted to pleasure the guy.

This was different. She wanted to make Del feel good. She wanted him to enjoy it, and her nerves were pinched at the notion that he might not. What if she wasn't good at it?

There's only one way to find out. Lena took Del in her hand, sliding her palm up and down his thick shaft. He moaned at her touch. Kissing his tip, she slowly took him in her mouth a little bit at a time. With each movement of her head, she took more of him in until his tip hit the back of her throat.

"Lena," he growled, running his hand over her wet hair to cup the back of her head.

His cock was too big for her to fit completely in her mouth, so she wrapped her palm around his hard length. She increased her speed, keeping the rhythm with her hand. When Del's hips started moving with her, she slowed her pace, but upped the pressure and swirled his tip with her tongue.

Del's legs shook, but he didn't waver. He dug his fingers into her scalp, but it was a gentle squeeze. He wasn't trying to keep her from pulling away, he was simply holding onto her in the only way he could at the moment.

Lena lingered in this position, at this tempo, for a few minutes, enjoying the sounds Del made. It wasn't until the initial drop of saltiness hit her tongue that she changed her actions. Knowing he was close, Lena sped up her movements, keeping her handhold on him firm.

His hips moved with her head. The moans and growls coming from him were insanely sexy and Lena wondered if the hot water would last long enough for her to have another orgasm. She didn't get long to ponder because Del hit his limit. As he came in her mouth, Lena welcomed it by gripping his ass. It hadn't ever bothered her, having a man climax in her mouth, but with Del, she could honestly say she enjoyed it.

After swallowing, Lena stood and ran her face under the shower spray. When she turned around, Del leaned against the wall, his head dipped back and his breathing ragged. Running her hands up his arms, she reached behind him to take the soap from the dish and lathered her hands.

As she splayed her soapy palm across his chest, Del reached up to cover her hand with his and lifted his head. A half-smile sat on his lips. His eyelids were low, his irises languid. He either couldn't speak, or had nothing to say, because he simply looked at her.

Lena rubbed the soap down his arm, entwining their fingers. "Time to get clean. We've got things to do today."

Del's fingers dug into her back. "What's the rush?"

Chapter 24

Lena ran her fingertips along the smooth oak tabletop of a dining set. Her eyes traced the round, beveled edge as she scrutinized the style. "This one's nice," she said to Del, who had been following her around the furniture store for an hour.

She didn't get a response, so she picked up the pricing sheet. "It's well within our price range." Flipping the sheet, her mouth ticked up to find it came in a variety of colored stains. "And we can get it in chestnut."

When Del didn't respond to any of her statements, she spun around to find him leaning against a sofa, engrossed in his phone. "Del." Lena huffed, her hands on her hips.

"Hm," he responded without looking up from his phone.

Lena stomped across the fake dining room and ripped the phone from his hand.

"Hey!"

"What is so important that you're ignoring me for?" She looked at his phone, and frustration instantly bubbled in her gut. Pinching her lips, Lena glared at Del. "Angry Birds?" she bit out.

Del shoved his hands into his pockets, shrinking back. "Sorry."

"What the hell are you doing? We're supposed to be picking out furniture for *your* brewery, and you've been drifting farther away every second."

With a sigh, Del tilted his head back to look at the ceiling. "Because we've been in here for an hour, Lena. Can't we just pick a set and be done?"

"No, we can't 'just pick a set.'" She folded her arms, tucking his phone against her ribs. "Don't rush this. It's an important decision."

Del lowered his head, a look of annoyance on his face. "Then stop talking so fast and let me think things through."

She gaped at him. "We need to make a decision sooner rather than later. I'm trying to get through as much as possible as quickly as possible."

"Now who's rushing things."

Her jaw tightened as did her clutch on his phone. "This is furniture we have to look at every day. Furniture our customers will have to use. It's not a light decision, so we need to explore all our options."

"We've explored every single table and chair set in this place." He swept his arm out, gesturing to the large warehouse store. "Why haven't you narrowed down our choices yet?"

Lena pinched her lips, her nostrils flaring. "Because you obviously can't be bothered to give me your opinion on anything." She shoved his phone into his chest before spinning on her heel and storming off.

"Lena..." Del called after her, but he was too late.

She stomped through the showroom and into a living room display with a large sectional. Flopping onto the cushy sofa, Lena tilted her head back and shut her eyes. Tears pricked her eyelids. The frustration coursing through her was palpable.

Why was he being so difficult? Did he not say he'd do this with her? Actually, he promised he would. So, why was he shutting down now?

A shaky breath escaped Lena. She wasn't being fair.

She had also promised to be patient, but hadn't held up her end of the bargain. They had, in fact, rushed through the showroom in the hour they'd been there, and Lena hadn't stopped talking. Over-excitement ran in her veins when it came to design.

The couch cushion next to her dipped with someone's weight, but the aroma of juniper wafting through the air told her who it was.

"Lena," Del said quietly. "I'm sorry."

She blinked her eyes open to avoid spilling any tears which remained, then turned her head to face him. "Me too."

He dipped his chin to look at her with apologetic eyes. "I never meant for things to escalate like that. I thought I had a handle on myself, but when you started in about what tables would go with which chairs and the color scheme and all the changes, I got overwhelmed again."

Lena's heart squeezed in her chest. "You were doing so well when we first got here, I thought you'd be okay. I'm sorry."

"No, don't be. It's not your fault." He laid his hand on hers. "I said I'd do this with you, and I meant it. I'm sorry I'm struggling."

"Don't apologize for being vulnerable." She flipped her hand over to entwine their fingers. "Besides, I told you I'd give you my patience, and I haven't exactly done that."

"I know you're excited. It's okay."

"Excitement doesn't justify me being a bitch."

Del smirked before hanging his head for a moment. "Not a bitch, just frustrated with this lousy schmuck."

"Yeah, but you're my schmuck." She leaned over to kiss his cheek. "Should we try again?"

He nodded, standing from the couch. "Sure, but could we slow it down some?" He extended his hand, which Lena took.

"Of course." She led him toward the front of the store where they had begun. "Let's start by eliminating some of the options."

***

The following Sunday morning, Lena tingled with excitement when she pulled into the Citadel Brewing parking lot to find a furniture delivery truck parked outside. The cargo door was still shut, so the unloading of the tables and chairs hadn't started. That fact flooded her with relief because it meant she could be there to do a quality check. She couldn't count the number of times she had waited on high-end, designer pieces to be delivered only to discover a gouge in the finish or a rip in the upholstery.

As she hopped out of her car, her phone dinged. Ignoring it, she grabbed the box with Del's surprise in it from her backseat and went inside Citadel. Del was speaking with one of the delivery men when his eyes found her in the doorway. They lit up and he waved for her to join him.

Lena stepped up in time to hear the last bit of information from the delivery guy. "We'll basically be replacing the old with the new. We'll bring one in, then take one out. You can sign for it all when we're finished."

"Sounds good. Let me know if we can help in any way." Del shook the man's hand before turning to Lena, greeting her with a kiss. "I just texted to tell you the truck was here. I was hoping you'd make it." His gaze fell to the box in her hands. "What's this?"

"Oh, it's for later." She sat the box on the bar counter. "Let's worry about the furniture first." Taking his hand, she gave him a squeeze. "Are you up for this?"

"Sounds like it'll be a slow process, so I should be fine. Besides, I can have a drink if I want." He jutted his chin at the taps, and Lena rolled her eyes.

As the moving men brought tables and chairs inside, Lena and Del unwrapped each one and assessed it for damages. The process was long and tedious, but completely necessary. After all the pieces were unloaded and inspected, which took a little over three hours, Lena was exhausted, but pleased there were no issues.

Del signed for the furniture and thanked the moving men. With a heavy sigh, he turned to Lena. "I suppose you want to arrange them all now, too?"

Lena nodded, bouncing on her toes, but reined herself in. "As long as you're okay."

"No time like the present. I'd rather do it now than in the morning before opening."

Lena had been prepared to take her time placing dining sets around the tasting room. After their furniture shopping fiasco, she didn't want to tempt fate.

Del surprised her, though.

His normal, easy-going attitude hung around, and she didn't get the slightest impression of tension from him. He moved faster than she'd expected, helping with every piece of furniture.

It also helped that Lena was calm herself. If Del paused, even for the briefest of moments, she paused. She didn't nudge him at all. Letting him take the lead on this was the best decision. After all, he had basically let her take the lead when picking out the furniture.

The tables and chairs looked as perfect as she had imagined them in the newly remodeled Citadel. The light wood tones contrasted nicely against the dark navy blue, but complemented the mossy green accent wall. Though the chairs were plastic, the scooped-back style made them comfortable. Their curvature was also a fantastic break to the harsh lines of the square tables.

After arranging the furniture, Lena ran the back of her hand across her forehead. "This is a lot of work. I can't believe I'm doing this for free on my day off." She gave Del a sideways glance, and when he furrowed his eyebrows, she smiled to show she was teasing.

Chuckling, Del pulled her to his side. "Well, thank you." He kissed her temple before lowering his mouth to her ear. "I'm sure I could think of some way to pay you for your time," he whispered, gruffly.

Lena elbowed him lightly in his ribs.

Still chuckling, Del leaned back against the bar and sighed. "So, I guess our next task is getting the word out about the release party."

"Yep. When do you want to have it?"

"Well," Del said as he scratched his beard. "The beer will be ready later this week, so we could have it as early as Saturday."

"I don't think that's enough time to advertise for it. We'd really have to work our asses off to get the word out." Lena pursed her lips, looking to the ceiling in thought. "Will the beer be okay until the following weekend? Two weeks gives us plenty of time."

"It'll be fine." Del nodded as he studied the room. "Looks pretty good in here." He tilted his head so their eyes met. "You did an amazing job."

"You helped."

"I was more difficult than anything." He arched his eyebrows, giving her a pointed look. "You had to pull all this together *and* deal with my shit."

Lena blushed. "Okay, you're right. I did an amazing job."

Del kissed the top of her head before reaching behind her to pat the top of the box she had brought in. "So, what's in here?"

"A little something I picked up last night." Lena beamed. She slid the box onto a chair and flipped it open. Pulling out several framed artworks, she laid them on the counter one by one before holding her arms out in presentation. "Ta-da!"

Del's eyes scanned the bar. Each time they landed on a new piece, they lit up, and the corners of his mouth ticked up. "Lena, these are awesome." He picked one up to eye it against the sunlight. "Where did you get these?"

"I found a specialty store close to downtown with a ton of pre-made stuff. Lucky for me, they're big beer fans, so a lot of it was beer or brewery related."

He whipped his head up, a frown on his face. "Wait, you said you picked these up late last night. From downtown? By yourself?"

"It wasn't terribly late." Lena crinkled her nose.

"I would've gone with you."

"Then the surprise would have been ruined." She laid her hand on his fore-arm, squeezing gently. "And I couldn't risk you seeing this before I had it ready."

"Seeing what?"

She took her bottom lip between her teeth before removing the last piece of artwork from the box. It was an 11" x 14" frame, protected by butcher paper. She held it out to Del. "Go ahead. Open it."

He arched a suspicious eyebrow as he took it from her. "Why is it covered? Is it one of those sexy pictures of you?"

"No, Del." Lena rolled her eyes, dropping her face into her palm.

"Shame."

"Just open it."

The rumble of Del's deep laugh and the tearing of paper made Lena take her face from her hand to watch. His expression went from curiosity, to awe, and finally settled on gratitude before he locked his blue eyes on hers. Adoration poured from his irises as he stared.

Lena squirmed on her feet. "Well, what do you think?"

He still didn't say anything for several seconds. He simply stared at her, like he was looking at the most precious thing on the planet and never wanted to blink for fear of it disappearing. Finally, he swallowed and said, "It's perfect."

A breath of relief blew from Lena's lips. "Glad you like it."

"I can't believe you did this." Del tore his gaze from hers to admire the artwork. It was a print of the Citadel logo, embossed on colored paper that matched the new interior of the brewery. Gold filigree adorned the outline, and below were the words, *I just feel it.* "What does that mean?"

"It was something you said to me after I first started here. You said you felt like I was the right choice for this job. I don't know, it seemed right to put there. Like a catchphrase for the brewery."

Del laid the frame on the bar and took Lena's hands in his. "Well, I think it's perfect. Thank you." He leaned in to kiss her. Gentle at first, the kiss turned passionate in a matter of seconds, and when they separated, they were both breathless. "You want to take a detour to the back office?"

The gravel in his low voice sent a shiver through Lena, but she shook her head. "Not here, Del."

"Shucks." He snapped his fingers in fake disappointment, a teasing tone in his voice. "Hang the art?"

"I think that's a good idea." She pulled him in for another light kiss. "Then we can take a *detour* to your house."

Chapter 25

The stress of the next two weeks was taxing. The entire Citadel staff were busy marketing for the beer release. Marky offered to take pictures and print flyers since he could use it as part of his photography portfolio. Twyla took charge of finding a musical act and a food truck, and Beth had social media posting duty. Del and Jack visited surrounding breweries and offered them a chance to be on the guest tap for the night, while Lena and the other employees acted as the street team.

The Monday before the big event, Lena took a handful of flyers, along with some brewery swag, to the business park across the street. Walking up to the first of five towers, she smoothed her pencil skirt before opening the over-sized glass door. Her heels clacked on the marble floor as she crossed the foyer to the reception desk.

There had been many office spaces in her portfolio at Designology. Offices, for her, were both a blessing and a curse. Usually seen as easier projects, they bored Lena because the color palettes were often monochromatic and muted. She was always drowning in a sea of gray or beige, very rarely allowed to bring in bright accent colors, and the uninteresting furnishings sat as blobs of fabric grouped together.

When commissioned for an office design, Lena gave it her all, but knew it would be nothing more than another dime on her paycheck.

This office was another story.

The floor was a dark gray marble, streaked with gold. It grounded the room as the light-colored walls lifted the ceiling, and the jade accent panel behind the receptionist desk drew the focus. The chandelier hanging in the center of the foyer mimicked a double helix, crystals dripping from its every curve. Even the sitting area was stocked with sleek, modern furniture.

Everything about the space took Lena's breath away. If this was what people were looking for, maybe she'd given up on design too soon. Redoing Citadel had sparked that fire in her again, but she didn't look at that as a design job. It was something she did to help *at* her job.

Still, excitement flitted through her at the idea of designing a space so different than she'd done before.

A woman cleared her throat. "Can I help you?"

Lena blinked herself out of her trance to find the receptionist staring at her from behind the desk. "Hi, my name is Lena." She extended her arm to shake the woman's hand, and glanced at her name tag. "Nice to meet you, Holly. Can you tell me how many businesses operate in this building?"

Holly gingerly shook Lena's hand, furrowing her brows. "Um, only one. National Epic Finance."

A familiar lump formed in Lena's throat. Anything finance related caused the memory of Ozzie to slither into her mind. Lena swallowed, but kept her professional smile. "Perfect." The word even tasted sour on her tongue. "I work for the brewery across the street, and I'm here to invite your company to an event we're having this weekend." Lena handed a flyer over the desk. As Holly took it, Lena noticed an emerald ring on her forefinger. "Oh, how lovely. Green is my favorite color."

Holly smiled sadly, holding up her hand to admire her ring. "Thank you. It was my grandma's. She left it to me when she passed."

"I'm sorry to hear that. She sounds like a lovely person."

"She was." Holly took a breath before looking Lena in the eye once more. "Now, what did you need?"

The ding of the elevator sounded in the hallway. "Is there a mail room I can leave these in, or a common room, where I can pin one?"

"Um, maybe." Holly chewed on her lip, bright pink lipstick smudging onto her tooth. She licked it away. "The finance partners get pretty uptight about what gets posted around here. What exactly is the event?"

Lena pressed her lips together, keeping a smile, albeit tight, on her face. "We've given the brewery a makeover, so we're inviting people to come see our new look. Plus, there will be new beers on tap for everyone to enjoy."

"I'd tap that," a man's voice said, making Lena whip her head up. An attractive guy in his mid-thirties wearing a black Dolce & Gabbana suit walked up, stopping to rest his hip against the desk. "The beer, I mean." His smirk exuded confidence as he offered his hand. "Hi, I'm Justin."

Lena forced a polite smile as she turned to face him, placing her hand in his. "Lena."

"Nice to meet you, Lena." His large palm held on to hers longer than necessary, giving a light squeeze before letting go. "Can I be of assistance here?" He looked between Lena and Holly.

"That depends," Lena said, shuffling the flyers in her hand. "Do you like beer, Justin?"

"Are you selling beer?" He pursed his lips, arching an eyebrow.

Closing her shrug over her corset top, she feigned a giggle. "No. I work for the brewery across the street, and we're having a release party this Saturday." She handed him a flyer.

Justin took the paper, glancing at it briefly before his gaze slithered down her body. "You don't dress like you work at a brewery."

She stifled an uncomfortable shiver. "I'm a consummate professional. Something I suspect you can appreciate in such a fine suit."

"This old thing?" Justin dipped his chin, pinching the lapel of his jacket and twisting the fabric. "I've got a dozen like it." His voice dripped with arrogance.

"Well, if your taste in drinks is as good as your fashion, you should absolutely come to our event."

Justin's mouth ticked up in smug satisfaction as he scanned the flyer for details. "Last time I was in there, I wasn't impressed." He popped his dark eyes up to meet hers. "No offense."

"None taken." *I honestly wasn't the first time I walked in there, either.* "But we've actually redesigned. You should come check it out."

"I'd rather take you to dinner, Lena." The thirst in his tone as her name slid from his lips shook her. She'd heard that tone many a time in Los Angeles, and its effectiveness in drawing her in never failed.

She fought hard against herself, knowing what she had with Del was better than anything this jerk could offer. "I'm flattered, but I'm seeing someone."

"Shame." Justin stood upright, putting his hands in his pockets. "A beautiful, confident woman with an appreciation for professional men is hard to find."

"Well, who knows? Maybe you can find another one like me at the release party on Saturday."

"I doubt it."

Lena tilted her head to the side, crinkling her nose. "And why is that?"

"Because I'm guessing you're one of a kind." Justin's eyes flashed, and Lena dipped her chin to hide her blush.

This man may have been a little on the sleazy side, but his flirting was working. He wasn't overtly lewd, his compliments were on point, and he happened to be young and handsome to boot. Justin's charm threatened to break Lena's resolve. She'd sworn off men in suits, but this one made her second guess herself.

Justin cleared his throat. "So, this redesign... is it a Coyote Ugly thing, where women dance on the bar?"

Lena rolled her eyes. "No. It's a design I did myself."

Justin's eyes widened. "Oh, so you're not just a pretty face. You've got talent too?"

"Yes. I worked in design for years doing renovations for restaurants, hotels, and offices." She held her chin high as she examined the foyer, letting out a deep breath. "This space had me reliving my glory days when I walked in."

Justin rubbed his clean-shaven jaw. "You know, if you want to do some more design, my apartment could use an update."

Lena arched a skeptical eyebrow. "Oh, really?"

"Sure. I'd love to see your talents at work on my place." He leaned in close to whisper. "Especially in my bedroom."

Lena's mouth turned up in an amused smirk as she dipped her chin. This was all too familiar. A conversation laced with flirtatious innuendo, followed by a proposition for a good time, had been Lena's social life for years. Which meant she knew exactly what the next morning would look like.

She'd wake up alone, or be asked to leave shortly thereafter. The hollow ache in her chest would consume her while she tried to convince herself she didn't care, then she'd gear up for another night. She'd go out and do it all over again just so she could feel whole for a few hours.

That wasn't what she wanted anymore. Now, she had Del.

With her head still lowered, Lena let out a breathy giggle.

"What's so funny?" Justin asked quietly, but his tone was laced with irritation.

Lena lifted her chin to look at him through her lashes. "You're predictable."

"What?"

She sighed. "Justin, I've met a lot of men like you, and at one point in my life, I would have let you take me home. We would have had a fun night, parted ways, and never spoke again. It's not what I want anymore."

Justin ran his tongue along his teeth. "Your loss, honey." He spun on his heel with a huff, and stormed out of the building.

Lena watched him leave, not feeling an ounce of regret.

"Wow," Holly said, startling Lena. "I've never seen a woman turn Justin down."

"Well, there's a first time for everything." Lena tilted her head. "But I suppose he won't be coming to our release party."

Holly giggled. "Probably not, but I'll be there. And I'll bring some girlfriends."

"Sounds good." Lena shook Holly's hand and left with her chin held high.

Chapter 26

Saturday finally arrived and all the Citadel's employees' hard work paid off. The release was scheduled for four o'clock, but people began showing up at noon. From that point on, business steadily grew, and by the time the beer was set to tap, the line extended out the door. It took three employees to run the front counter, and even Jack had to come help run tables.

Jameson and Johnnie stopped in to congratulate Del. Jameson had a shift at The Landing Pad, so he had a quick beer, and went outside with Twyla for a not-so-quick goodbye, before leaving. Johnnie stayed for a while, drinking more than his share of pints. When Del cut him off, Johnnie called an Uber.

While he waited, he chatted with Lena in between customers. "So, you and my dad, huh?"

"Mhm." Lena tried not to smile at the way his words strung together.

"You like him?"

"Of course." She gave him an incredulous look as she handed a customer their credit card.

Johnnie narrowed his eyes with a smirk as he swayed in his seat. "He likes you. A lot."

"I know, Johnnie," she said flatly before greeting the next customer with a smile. "Hi, what'll it be?"

"He's a good man, Lena." Slapping his hands on the bar, he scooted the stool away. "In more ways than one." He arched an eyebrow, giving her a knowing look, then ambled out the door.

Lena shook her head. *What's he being so cryptic about?*

Despite the craziness of the release, Lena had a skip in her step the entire day. Every time she overheard someone compliment the décor, her smile widened. Each "wow" or "looks good" was empowering. She had done this. She made this place better, and she had to take credit.

"Need a break?" Del's low whisper in her ear startled her.

She gasped, whipping around to face him. "Del, you scared me. No, no break yet. This is crazy."

"And it's all thanks to you." He quickly kissed her before stepping away. She watched as he climbed onto a bar stool with a wireless microphone in his hand. The sound of him clearing his throat echoed through the speakers, and a hush fell over the room. "Hey, sorry about that. I wanted to introduce myself to those of you who don't know me. I'm Del Stratton, the owner of Citadel Brewing, and I'm excited to share our latest releases with you. We have three new beers in addition to our normal line-up. We also have several guest taps from other local breweries, so give them a try tonight too."

He gestured to the bar. "Our wonderful staff has been working double time tonight, so please show them some appreciation." The room exploded with applause and a few hoots and hollers. "They'll take good care of you." He locked eyes with Lena and took a deep breath. "The last thing I want to say before we tap these new beers, is a special thanks to a special woman."

Lena's cheeks heated, and she tried to hide behind Twyla, but to no avail. Twyla grabbed her by the arms and dragged her to the bar, front and center.

"Miss Lena Bouras, the mastermind behind our beautiful remodel. Come here, please." Del waved her on.

Lena inched out from behind the counter, face no doubt brilliantly red. She sidled up next to Del, and fought the urge to bury her face into his chest.

"Without Lena, this place would still be..." He turned to her. "What was it you said? Shabby?" There was a collective laugh from the crowd. "She single-handedly redesigned this place to be what you see today. Lena, do you want to say anything?"

She wasn't one for grand speeches, so she took the easy way out. "I used both hands," she said into the mic, receiving a boisterous guffaw from the room.

"Modest and funny." Del shook his head before kissing her temple. "Well, folks, enough from me. Let's drink!" Cheers went up all around. Del took Lena's hand, kissing her knuckles before heading behind the bar to do the honor of pouring the first pint.

The rest of the night passed like some sort of surreal dream. People would stop Lena to compliment her work, and it felt amazing. Not only was Citadel booming with business, the main point of all this, but Lena received recognition for a job well done. Her cheeks hurt by the time closing came, and everyone took a minute to sit down.

"What a fucking crazy day," Twyla said exuberantly as she sat on the bar, swinging her legs in the air. "I've never seen such a crowd!"

"And I've never worked up this much sweat," Marky chimed in, waving his hand at his armpit. "Hopefully, it's not like that every night."

"Oh, shut up. It was awesome!" Twyla countered. She turned to Del. "Do you have any idea how much we did tonight?"

Del shook his head. "I won't until I run end-of-day, but I can tell you it's probably more than normal," he said with a hint of sarcasm.

Twyla rolled her eyes. "Well, duh." Her phone dinged and her eyes lit up as she read the message. "Jamie's here. See you guys on Monday." She hopped off the bar to give Lena a huge hug. "You did it. Total success." As she pulled away from the hug, Twyla playfully punched Lena in the arm. "You boss bitch."

Lena laughed. "Thanks."

She, Del, and Marky closed up, but Marky was the first to leave. Lena sat at the bar, patiently waiting on Del to finish running the closing procedures. As she waited, Lena traced the woodgrain in the countertop with her finger, her mind replaying the day.

Every time she thought about it, her sense of accomplishment blossomed. She'd forgotten what it was like to complete a project, to be proud of what she'd created. An overwhelming airy feeling filled her chest. Flutters ran through her back to back, chasing each other's tails and keeping Lena on such a satisfying high, she didn't think it could get any better.

Until she felt the biggest flutter of them all.

This one came not from her design accomplishment. Nor did it stem from any of the compliments she'd received. It was a flutter unlike anything she'd ever felt, and it was accompanied by an all-consuming desire begging to be satiated. It shot through her in an instant, leaving a tingle in its wake.

All because Del had taken the time to credit her with the design.

Suddenly, thoughts of Del flooded her mind. His sweet smile beneath his graying beard. The adoring look in his cool, blue irises when he spoke to her. The way his deep voice rumbled through her when she was locked in the safety of his warm embrace.

His touch.

Lena shivered. She'd be lying if she said she hadn't been thinking about touching him from the moment they met at the lake. She may have denied it then, but deep down, she'd known what she wanted. And she wanted Del.

Right now, more than ever.

"All finished." The sound of Del's smooth voice melted into her ears. "Ready?"

She shook her head, blinking at him as he stood leaning on the wall by the end of the bar. Lena couldn't believe how sexy he looked. Several pieces of his wavy, salt and peppered hair had fallen from his man-bun, and they dangled in front of his eyes. The top two buttons of his shirt were undone, and he'd rolled the sleeves up his forearms. The way his muscles flexed as he pushed off the wall made her breath heavy.

"Lena? You okay?"

She nodded quickly. "I'm fine. Just still can't believe how well today went."

Del's mouth ticked up on one side. "You want a drink before we go? To celebrate?"

"Sure. Sounds good." Although delaying their private time wasn't what she wanted, Lena decided some liquid courage wouldn't hurt.

Del took two pint glasses from the shelf, expertly filling them before sliding one to Lena. "Your favorite, my dear."

"Thanks."

He winked, turning to fill his own pint glass. "So, how does it feel to design again?"

"Surreal. Especially because of all the compliments this place got today."

"Those compliments were for you," he said over his shoulder. When his glass was full, he turned back to the bar, setting his drink down and leaning against the counter with his forearms. "All I did was make the beer. You're the one who made this place what it is. Take the credit, Lena." Picking up his glass, he tilted it toward hers. "Cheers."

"To what?" she asked, lifting her glass to clink it against his.

"To everything."

The smolder in his eyes stole Lena's breath, and she took a drink before she could blush. As she licked her lips, Del's Adam's apple bobbed, and he let out a soft moan.

The colors of the room swirled together like melted wax as they revered each other. All the noises of the world ceased except for the pounding of Lena's heart. If it hadn't been for the bar being a physical obstacle, Lena would have smashed into Del with such force, their bodies would've melded into one.

She tried to breathe, but the air was so thick, Lena couldn't inhale. The electricity coursing between them stifled her lungs from working.

The spell broke when Del cleared his throat. He lifted his glass before taking a drink. "Well, uh, let's finish up and get out of here. I'm ready to go home."

Lena finally took a steadying breath. *Home.* "Okay."

Del nodded, but said nothing, as he took another drink. The next few minutes were silent as they enjoyed their beers, catching eyes every so often and smiling as they did. Lena's stomach flipped when she slid her empty glass across the bar and her fingers grazed Del's.

She internally laughed at herself. *You're acting like a teenager. Get a grip, Lena.*

Once finished, Del followed Lena outside, locking the door behind them. His hand found the small of her back as they walked toward his truck, his fingers pressing into her. Lena sighed, nuzzling against him.

He kissed the top of her head. "I like driving you to work because you have to come home with me."

"I don't have to. I could tell you to take me home."

"You said you don't like to be at your house." He shrugged, making her head bob. "But I can stay there all the same."

She snorted. "Maybe I want a night to myself."

"Do you now?" Del whispered as he spun her around, pushing her against the door of the truck. He framed her in with his strong arms and leaned in close, his mouth only millimeters from hers. "I don't know if I believe you."

Lena's chest heaved with anticipation. If she shifted slightly, their lips would connect, but she savored the moment. The magnetism between them was intense. It made desire coil low in her abdomen, her heart fluttering a mile a minute.

"Do you want to be alone tonight?" Del asked, his breath hot against her skin.

"Del..." His name rolled off her tongue in a soft whisper.

He moved his head, his lips brushing her ear. "I asked you a question," he said low with gravel in his tone.

"I don't ever want to be without you."

Del didn't move for several seconds, and Lena waited not so patiently for him to process her words. Finally, he straightened his posture so he was once again facing her. As she looked up at him through her lashes, he studied her eyes. The look on his face was an adorable mixture of curiosity, confusion, and contentment, and all Lena wanted to do was kiss him.

So she did.

Chapter 27

They rode to Del's house in silence laced with tense anticipation. As he drove, Del's hand traveled the length of Lena's thigh from her knee to below the crease of where it met her hip. Every time it came devastatingly close to touching her more intimately, her heart picked up speed.

She shifted in her seat, groaning as he slid his fingers back toward her knee.

Del chuckled. "Antsy, are we?"

With a mocking glare in his direction, Lena decided to play his game. She lifted her arm to rest across the seats and began massaging his scalp with her fingernails. He moaned, dipping his head back and pieces of his hair came undone. Twirling a lock around her finger, she gently tugged before dragging her nails down his neck.

He shivered. "Don't distract the driver."

"Then drive faster."

The growl from Del almost matched the roar of the engine as the truck sped up. The normally twenty-minute drive only took a record ten with Del's hand never leaving Lena. He parked in his driveway, cut the engine, and turned over the console to face her. She held his fiery gaze and watched his eyes flash with desire.

"Lena..." Her name was a strained whisper on his lips.

"Yes?"

His eyes flicked to her mouth, his Adam's apple bobbing with his deep swallow. "Let's go inside." He slid the keys from the ignition and got out of the truck.

Lena furrowed her brow. *That wasn't what I expected him to say.* She shook it off and followed him to the front door. Once inside, Del kept his back to her as he shucked his shoes and tossed his keys into the dish on the entry table. When he didn't say anything, Lena stepped to him, placing her hand on his bicep.

The second her fingers grazed his shirt, he spun around. He took one big step, pushing her against the door and closing the gap between them. Cupping the back of her head with one hand, his other hand snaked around her waist to grip her tightly. Lena's arms flew around his neck as her chest pressed into his, but their mouths stopped short of connecting.

There was no space between them, aside from the small gap where their lips should be touching. Lena's jaw quivered as she looked up at Del. His irises locked onto hers with fiery passion, and Lena's mouth ran dry. His grip tightened, bringing them ever closer as their breaths mingled, dancing on their lips.

"Del," she whispered.

His mouth crashed onto hers in a deep, searing kiss. As her tongue slipped along his lips, he let out a contented groan. It rumbled through Lena, weakening her knees. Her body went slack. Del held her tight, but took advantage of her head dipping back to pepper kisses across her cheek and down her throat before nuzzling into the crook of her neck.

She rolled her hips, sliding her thigh between his to rub along his ever-growing erection. Lena's desire for Del filled her in a way she had never known, and though it frightened her somewhat, the sensation thrilled her more than anything.

Del nipped at her earlobe. "What should we do?"

Lena's heart pounded against her sternum as her lungs expanded into her ribs. She knew what she wanted. "Make love to me, Del."

He went stock still, but Lena felt his shaking breath cascading down her neck. Leaning back to look her in the eye, he blinked several times. A crease formed between his brows. "Are you sure?"

She nodded. "I'm ready."

Del pressed his lips to hers before scooping her into his arms and carrying her to his bedroom. He flew so fast, it was as if he'd grown an extra set of legs. Inside the dark room, he laid Lena onto the bed, crawling up to hover over her. Illuminated by only the light from the full moon, his eyes sparkled as he searched her face, as if looking for one last confirmation.

Lena lifted to kiss him. She arched her back so her chest brushed his, her nipples hardening at the contact.

With a groan, Del ran his hands around her back, supporting her weight as he scooted their bodies toward the headboard. Gently placing Lena's head on the pillows, he sat onto his knees and began unbuttoning his shirt. His eyes stayed fixed on hers, his stare immensely intense.

As she watched him undress, her lower lip found its way between her teeth. The buttons came undone excruciatingly slowly. Her breath hitched when he slid the shirt off his chiseled torso and down his muscular arms to reveal the silhouette of a Greek god sitting before her, the moonlight dancing across his body.

Each ridge was highlighted. Every flexing muscle pronounced as the soft light kissed their nuances. Even his tattoos seemed to glow.

Desperate for contact, Lena grabbed his belt buckle, yanking him down to connect their mouths once more. The kiss was hot, like molten lava, and she craved the burn it left on her lips. Her hands held onto him tightly. She needed him as close as possible and didn't want him leaving her space ever again. Losing a hand in his hair, she removed the elastic tie from his head, his silvery locks hanging like a curtain around their faces.

When she hooked her legs around his, he sat up. Lena couldn't protest because he brought her with him to remove her Citadel Brewing t-shirt, tossing it on the floor. She expected him to remove her bra, but instead, he laid her back down and crushed her with his weight. Lena reveled in the closeness.

The heat of his bare skin against hers was borderline tortuous. Not for being too hot, but because she never wanted it to end. It had become an addictive sensation. Like everything she felt with Del, his touch was more than a craving, it was necessity.

He broke away from the kiss, his lips trailing down her body to her chest. "I know what you asked of me downstairs," he said against her skin, peeling back her bra to take her pebbled nipple in his mouth. Lena moaned through ragged breaths as his hand massaged her other breast. Del flicked her nipple with his tongue, giving it a small kiss before lifting his head. "But I told you, I'm not here to rush anything."

Del's mouth returned to her breast, but his fingers ran down to caress the seam of her shorts, Lena moved her hips. Moaning against her breast, he flipped the button of her shorts open and slid them down her legs. Lena kicked them off without hesitation.

"Mmm," Del hummed as his fingers moved over her panties. "Wet already. I like that."

Lena only breathed in response. Del's fingers on her most intimate parts, even through the barrier of her underwear, felt incredible. That combined with the way his tongue laved her nipple, left Lena in a pleasure coma, only capable of barely audible words and noises she assumed cavemen made.

Del pushed her panties aside and slipped his fingers inside her, making Lena gasp. Del had touched her like this many times in the past month, always adamant she came first, but this felt different. It felt more intimate somehow. Was it Del? Had he changed his moves to be more sensual? Or was Lena anticipating the main event to come later? Either way, she got lost in a swoon of lust and pleasure, not wanting it to end.

But when Del hooked his fingers inside her and swirled her clit with his thumb, Lena tumbled over the edge. Her body shuddered as Del's name rolled off her tongue in cries of passion. As her orgasm ebbed, Del slowed his movements. It wasn't until she was completely relaxed that he removed his hand and scooted up to cradle her in his arms.

She couldn't do anything but breathe. Her eyes wouldn't even open, so she simply laid with Del and soaked up his warmth.

"Don't tell me you've had enough," he teased.

Lena flopped her head from side to side. "No. Just need a moment to compose."

Del planted a kiss on her cheek. "Take all the time you need. We've got all night."

The realization rejuvenated her, and she popped up onto her side. "All night?" She arched an eyebrow as she dragged her gaze down Del's body. "Has a nice ring to it." Leaning in for a kiss, she slid her hand to Del's pants, palming him through his jeans.

He promptly snatched her wrist, stopping her movement. "Don't. Please."

"Why not?"

"Because if you touch me like that, I won't be able to... you know, later."

"Del," Lena said softly as she reached up to tuck some of his hair behind his ear. "I want to touch you. I like touching you, and if you're serious about us having *all* night, you're going to need some release too."

He watched his hand as he brushed his fingers down her side, but didn't reply.

"Let me do this for you, and then you can spend however long you need making me come until you're ready again."

He shuddered as the word "come" left her lips, and she nudged him onto his back, throwing her leg over his hips to straddle him. As she stared down at him, his eyes raked her over, his hands resting on her waist. "Now," she said, leaning down to put her lips to his ear. "What should I do with your cock?"

Del's breath hitched, and his hands slid to grip her ass, but he still said nothing.

"Come on, Del," Lena breathed. "I want to hear you say it."

"Your mouth." It was so low and gruff, Lena almost didn't hear him.

She moved her head to hover her face over his, grinding her hips down against the strain in his pants. "What was that?"

"Use your perfect mouth on my cock." He slid his thumb over her lips, so she kissed it.

Lena didn't say anything as she moved down his torso. She took her time, peppering kisses across his collarbone, down his firm chest and defined abdomen, until she reached the waistband of his jeans.

When Del moved his hands to undo the button, she swatted them away. "Uh uh." She waved her finger in the air. "I'm doing this *for* you. Enjoy yourself." With that, she undid his pants as Del folded his arms behind his head.

With a bit of assistance from Del's hips, his pants came off, and Lena admired the bulge beckoning her from his underwear. She'd seen his dick before, even tasted it a few times, but she couldn't wait to find out how it felt inside of her.

Later, Lena. She shook her head before sliding her body up to hover her face over his erection. As she released him from his boxer briefs, Del's hard cock sprung from the opening, standing at full attention. Lena took him in her hand at first. As soon as her fingers wrapped around his velvety skin, his eyes closed and his head dipped back. She watched his muscles strain as he tried not to lose himself in pleasure.

The moment her lips kissed his tip, Del flinched almost involuntarily. Her stomach fluttered before Lena took him fully into her mouth. She moved slowly, keeping the pace between her mouth and hand, simply enjoying the sounds Del made. It was her favorite part of all this.

Sure, the orgasms were fantastic, and she'd be lying if she said she didn't enjoy his hard cock in her mouth, but she really liked how good she made him feel. The idea she could give him this kind of pleasure empowered her. It made adrenaline pump even faster through her veins.

When Del's cock jumped, and the salty taste of precum hit her tongue, Lena picked up her pace. She hollowed out her cheeks, swirling his tip with her tongue with every pass, and tightened her hand around his base.

He hardened even more, one of his hands twisting into her hair. He breathed her name over and over until he pulsed in her mouth, releasing his orgasm which she happily swallowed. Swirling his tip one last time, she kissed his length as she made her way up his body to snuggle into his side.

His chest heaved, but otherwise he laid still. His eyes stayed closed.

Content to let him savor the moment, Lena nuzzled against him and reveled in his bliss. When he cleared his throat, she lifted her head to see his face. His eyes were still closed.

"Can I say..." He opened his eyes, irises languid with relaxation. "It's incredibly sexy when you swallow my cum."

Heat rushed to Lena's cheeks as she bit her lower lip. "Ditto."

Del arched an eyebrow. "Is that so?"

She nodded.

"Well, then..." Del sat up to kneel before Lena, the sleepiness gone from his eyes, replaced with palpable lust.

She twisted her legs together, squirming. Her skin burned as he placed his hands on her knees to spread her legs before sliding his large palms up her thighs.

He tucked his fingers into the waistband of her panties. "These need to go," he said gruffly, and pulled them down her legs. Tossing them over his shoulder to the floor, Del leaned down so his face was inches from her core. His thumb found her clit and made small circles.

Lena threw her head back with a moan.

"I love that sound, Lena. Keep it up." The depth of his voice sent a shock wave through her, and Del hummed. "Spread wider for me." He nudged her legs apart, lifting one over his shoulder. All the while massaging her clit.

Every time he spoke, Lena felt his hot breath caress her center. If she had still been wearing panties, they'd be soaked.

Del slid a finger inside her. "I love how wet you get for me." Another finger found her opening. "I can't wait to get my dick inside you, but first" —one more finger, all three pulsing together, and all Lena could do was moan— "I want to eat."

Del's mouth crashed onto her, his tongue replacing his thumb with delectable swirls, leaving her gasping for air. His fingers moved inside her like satin. The fluid motion paired in tempo with his mouth made a symphony of noises erupt from her. His other hand gripped her ass, keeping her close.

When she bucked her hips to grind against his face, he hummed. Not only a delicious sound, it also vibrated through Lena, pushing her toward the edge of her orgasm. "Del," she breathed. "I'm going to come."

He didn't stop. Instead, he closed his lips around her clit. When he sucked on her bundle of nerves, she came hard in his mouth. Her back arched off the bed as his name spewed from her mouth in screams of pleasure. The shuddering lasted longer than ever, but Del kept a firm hold on her until it ebbed.

When she finished, he released her and crawled up the mattress to lay behind her. Swaddled in his arms, Lena was content, but exhausted. Briefly, she allowed her eyes to close and her body to relax to the point of dozing off. In a fit of panic, she realized what she was doing and jolted awake.

"Shhh." Del ran his hand over her head. "If you're tired, go to sleep."

"I'm not tired. Just incredibly relaxed. I guess I have your mouth to thank."

"The pleasure was all mine."

She shook her head. "No, I'm pretty sure *I* got all the pleasure, but I'm glad you enjoyed it too."

"I always enjoy the way you taste," Del whispered against her ear. "The way you feel." His arms folded around her tightly, pulling her back to his chest, and Lena felt him harden against her ass.

"Ready for more?" She reached her hand back between their bodies to palm his erection.

He groaned, tipping his head forward to rest his forehead against her hair. "Up to you."

Lena spun in his arms to face him, splaying her hands across his chest. "Make love to me, Del."

His mouth devoured hers almost on command as he nudged her onto her back. Lena threw her legs around his waist, hooking her ankles, and Del settled between her thighs to slide out of his underwear. Locking his eyes with hers, Del's irises flashed in the moonlight, adoration pouring out of them and into Lena.

"Say it again," he whispered.

Lena fluttered her lashes, pouting her lips, and slid her hand around Del's remarkably hard cock. "Make love to me."

The second she released him, he shifted his hips so his tip was at her entrance, but stopped abruptly. "I, uh, need something..."

"What?" Lena asked, frustration lacing her words.

"Something I haven't needed in a long time. I hope they're not expired." He leaned over Lena to reach into his nightstand, taking out a pack of condoms.

"You don't need them, Del. I've got an IUD."

"Really?" His enthusiastic tone shined through before he cleared his throat, becoming more serious. "I haven't been with anyone since my last doctor visit a little over a year ago. Just so you know."

"I got tested after I found out I'd been cheated on. I'm clean."

Del heaved a relieved breath and settled to hover over her once more. He moved forward, sliding inside her a bit, and groaned. "You're so wet, you might kill me."

"Wait until you're all the way in."

Del let out a strained growl, pitching forward to latch his lips to her neck, and Lena closed her eyes. He moved inside her slowly, carefully, giving her time to adjust to his impressive size, but moaning with every inch. Lena held her breath until he filled her. When she released her breath and opened her eyes, she found Del staring at her intently.

"Everything okay?" he asked between pants. He was working hard to restrain himself.

"Everything's perfect."

His mouth ticked up on one side. "Good." He moved his hips. "You tell me what you like. Faster, slower, harder, softer. Whatever you want, I'll do it."

Lena's hands ran up his arms, her fingertips brushing his biceps. "Let's go slow a minute. You're a big guy."

"Mmmm. How big?"

"The biggest."

A smug smirk overtook Del's face as he kept his pace. It didn't take long, though, for the desire to build in Lena. She wanted more.

"Faster."

With a curt nod, Del's hips moved into action. Their speed increased, but the rhythm stayed steady. Each on-point thrust hit Lena in the right spot every time. Sliding her hands to his shoulders, she dug her nails in. He tilted his head to kiss her arm, his lips burning on her skin.

"Harder, Del."

He didn't change his movement as he asked, "You're sure?"

She nodded. "I want you to fuck me." Lena stifled a smile as Del seemed to choke on her words.

He recouped quickly, though. "Yes, ma'am."

His hips picked up speed as he thrust into her. The movement was hard, deliberate, and it made Lena cry out his name. The sound of skin against skin filled the air, mingling with their pants and moans. Lena's arms fell from Del, settling above her head.

"You're so beautiful," Del said as he bent down to take her nipple in his mouth.

Lena arched her back to give him better access, but the new position also made his cock rub her clit differently. The pleasure that had been steadily building, suddenly shot through her without warning. His name left her mouth in an enraptured scream as she tightened around his erection and her body shuddered with release.

Del grunted a string of swear words before chasing his own release. His forehead rested on her chest, his chin between her breasts, and his beard scratching her skin. The huge breaths that had been heaving from him ebbed. He lifted his head to meet her gaze and planted a gentle kiss on her lips.

Rolling to his side, he gathered her to his chest. "How are you?"

"I'm so good. You?"

"Lena, I'm not going to lie." He cleared his throat. "I've never had so much fun in my entire life."

She giggled. "Glad I was here for it."

"No, not just tonight." Del moved so he could see down into her eyes. "I mean all my time with you. Every minute we've been together has been better than the last, and it makes me want all the minutes in the world."

A blush came over her face. "Del..."

"I mean it. This thing with you is so good, it makes nights like tonight the cherry on top."

"Oh." She pursed her lips, looking away.

"I didn't mean it like that. I meant even if we never have sex again, I'll still take every second of time you'll give me."

Lena's chest vibrated, like a million butterflies were vying for space inside it. An exhilarating feeling bubbled in her gut she'd never felt, words on the tip of her tongue she'd never thought she'd say. Until tonight. "I love you, Del."

His sincere, adoring expression didn't waver. "I love you too, Lena."

The kiss they shared before succumbing to sleep was one of pure affection. It was completely different than any one before. A tender yet claiming kiss, it sealed the declaration that they belonged to each other.

Chapter 28

"Why are you so nervous?" Del asked, giving Lena's hand a reassuring squeeze.

"I'm not."

Del snorted. "Lena, your hair is twisted so tight around your finger, it's turning purple."

Lena glanced at her hand. Del was right. She quickly untangled the lock from her finger and dropped her hand to her lap. "This feels like a family thing. I'm not family."

"Neither is Twyla, but she'll be there."

"It's her apartment." Lena rolled her eyes.

"And Jameson's."

"Exactly. They're at least living together, which makes her more family than me."

Del gave her a sideways glance. "You've been staying at my house every night for two weeks. Aren't we basically living together?"

She tilted her head from side to side. "I think of it as more of an extended sleepover."

Del chuckled.

"I feel like I'm out of place in your life with your boys."

"Lena," Del said, his voice suddenly stern. "You are not *ever* out of place in my life. My boys like you. If they didn't, Jameson wouldn't have told me to bring you tonight."

She sighed. "I guess you're right. But having dinner with all of them seems intimate, like something I shouldn't be in on yet. I mean, aside from working with Jack, I've really only hung out with them once that day at the lake."

Del squeezed her hand even tighter. "Well, the only way you're going to get in on things, is by attending them." He pulled the truck into a parking spot labeled "visitor," and cut the engine. Turning his body to face her, his eyes softened in the late afternoon sunlight. "Ready?"

Lena nodded, and Del gently kissed her before they exited the truck, walking hand in hand to the front door.

It wasn't an apartment as Del had originally told her. This was a townhome wedged between two identical buildings. The façade was modeled after an old Swiss cottage, which gave it a welcoming, cozy feeling, and Lena's tension ebbed.

Del paused for a moment on the stoop to admire Lena before opening the door without knocking. "We're here," he announced as they stepped inside.

"Hey!" Twyla shouted from the kitchen to the right of the door. She was busy arranging tiny finger foods on a tray. "Come on in, and make yourself comfy. I'm almost done in here." She craned her neck to see through the doorway. "Hey, girl."

Lena waved as she removed her sandals. She followed Del into the living room, where Jameson and Johnnie were arguing over what music to play. They briefly halted their quarrel to give a curt nod. Jack sat in the corner, playing on his phone with his fingers pressed to his temple.

Del gave Lena a pointed look with arched eyebrows, and motioned for her to sit on the couch. She shook her head. Instead, walking into the fight and placing her hand on Jameson's tattooed forearm.

"You have a lovely townhome," she said quietly. "I've always been a fan of quaint spaces. Can I see the backyard?"

Jameson furrowed his brow for a moment, but softened. "Yeah, sure." He slapped the stereo remote into Johnnie's hand, then turned toward the patio door at the back of the room.

Lena shot Del a sideways look, and he nodded in approval.

As she and Jameson stepped out into the small yard, a hip-hop beat bumped through the speakers, and Jameson groaned. Lena slid the patio door closed to muffle the sound. "Not a fan, huh?"

"No. We're a punk rock house, through and through."

"Well, let Johnnie win for now, and he'll be easier to sway later."

Jameson looked at Lena, arching an eyebrow and looking exactly like his father. "I'll give you twenty bucks if you can get him to change the music when we go back in."

"I can't make any promises it'll be punk rock." She turned, holding her hand out.

"I don't care, as long as it's not that shit." He firmly shook her hand.

The hip-hop music grew louder as the patio door opened and Jack leaned out. "Twyla said she needs your height. I offered, but she said you know what bowl she needs." The last part came out as more of a question.

"She can't reach the tall cabinets, and she's very particular about our dishes." Jameson laughed.

The three of them stepped back inside with Jameson heading to the kitchen, Jack sitting down next to Del, and Lena setting her intentions on changing the music. She walked to where Johnnie was bobbing his head to the beat as he stared at his phone. He did a double take as she sidled up next to him.

"Can I ask you a favor?"

"Uh, sure..." Johnnie eyed her suspiciously.

Lena glanced at Del, and licked her lips. "I'm trying to get your dad to expand his music tastes past country, but I don't think this is helping. Can I commandeer the stereo?"

Johnnie furrowed his brows, his blue eyes flicking between Lena and Del. "On one condition."

"Which is?"

"Jameson isn't allowed to play any more punk rock tonight."

Lena rolled her eyes. "Okay."

Johnnie gave Lena a nod, handed her the remote, and took a seat at the dining table. Lena took out her phone, luckily finding a usable cable already plugged into the port on the stereo. She scrolled through her music and chose the perfect song. When the words to "Thinking Out Loud" began, Lena turned to smirk at Del.

He pursed his lips, giving her a sarcastic look. As the lyrics poured over her, it wasn't Ed Sheeran serenading her, it was Del's sweet voice singing in her memory. The flutter in her chest was almost overwhelming, but the moment was broken when Jameson crossed the room. He slid a twenty-dollar bill into her hand and walked back to the kitchen.

With a satisfied smile, Lena stuffed the money in her pocket.

Shortly thereafter, Twyla sounded the dinner bell, and everyone filed into the seats to eat. Dishes were passed around and portions were doled out, until Johnnie tried to grab a stuffed pepper.

Twyla smacked his hand. "Those are Lena's." She shot him a pointed look, sneering back when he stuck his tongue out. With a huff, she turned to Lena. "You get first dibs on those. There's no meat in them."

"Thank you," Lena said.

After everyone settled, they all dug in. The food tasted delightful, the conversation flowed as easily as the drinks, and Lena felt more comfortable with each passing minute. She was particularly pleased she didn't have to rely on Del to include her. The boys spoke to her as if she were an old friend, and it warmed her heart.

When dinner was over, Del leaned back in his chair. "Well, Twyla, everything was delicious. Thank you for cooking. Johnnie and Jack will be happy to clear the table."

Johnnie groaned, looking physically pained, while Jack chuckled quietly.

"Thanks, Del, but before you start, Jamie and I have something to tell you all." Twyla's eyes gleamed with excitement. She threw her left hand up, a dazzling diamond on her ring finger, and squealed, "We're getting married!"

The table exploded with exuberant congratulations with everyone rising to exchange hugs.

As the buzz quieted and everyone took their seats, Del put his arm around Lena. "Jameson," he said in a fatherly tone. "I'm happy for you, son. You and

Twyla are perfect together, and I can't think of two people who deserve each other more."

"Thanks, Dad." Jameson took Twyla's hand, lifting it to his lips.

After Jack and Johnnie had cleared the table, everyone went to the backyard for some after-dinner yard games. They set up horseshoes, ladder ball, and giant Jenga. Though Del's sons chided each other and argued over points, the competition between everyone stayed lighthearted. Even Jack seemed to relax the longer they played.

Lena's heart swelled over being a part of this huge family moment, and she couldn't wait for the wedding.

Chapter 29

"Remind me why I ever schedule you to open?" Del grumbled as he pulled Lena against him.

She squirmed in his grip, kicking the blankets off the end of the bed. "Because I told you not to treat me any different than the other employees because we're dating. I don't want preferential treatment."

"It wouldn't be preferential if I scheduled you to close because you were a good closer."

Lena rolled her eyes and sat up. "I've got to get in the shower." She turned to press a finger to his chest. "And you've got a dentist appointment, remember?"

"Yes, I know," Del groaned, but glanced at the clock. "Do you have enough time for an extended shower?"

She leaned down and planted a kiss on his lips. "Not unless you want to hear about it from Jack."

Del groaned again, this time with a little more frustration. "Okay, fine. You shower, and I'll make breakfast."

Lena beamed as she watched Del rise from the bed, wearing nothing but his boxer briefs. Not only was this man a fine specimen with his rippling muscles, hard stomach, and perfect ass, but he was hers. Fully, wholly, completely hers.

After putting his jeans on, he turned to find her staring. "What?"

"Nothing. I just like that you're mine."

Del leaned over, putting his hands on the mattress to hover close to Lena's face. "I've been officially yours for a month now. It hasn't gotten old?"

"Not in the least."

"Mmmm," Del hummed as he pressed his lips to hers, but the kiss didn't last long. "Get your ass in the shower before I make you late," he called out as he strode out the door.

Giggling, Lena bounced her way to Del's bathroom. She flipped the shower on, turning the knob all the way to scalding, and began brushing her teeth. It was satisfying how comfortable she felt in his home. Ever since the "L" word had come out a month ago, Lena had spent every night at Del's house, only going to her own home to cycle out clothes, or get her mail.

She opened the shower door to test the water. It seared the back of her hand, telling her it was time to get in. As she stepped under the spray, it enveloped her in steamy warmth. Oddly enough, reminding her of being in Del's arms.

Del...

It didn't seem real. Even after ten weeks of dating and a month of being in love, Lena still couldn't believe things were as good as they were. Every time she thought about being with Del, a flutter ran through her. Unless she thought about being *with* him, then the reaction was much different.

In fact, all the feelings she had about Del were different.

For one thing, he'd awakened the long-dead concept of love within her. After fruitlessly chasing meaningful relationships throughout her twenties, Lena gave up on the idea. One-night stands were not only fun, they were an easy way to protect her heart, and after Ozzie's betrayal, she never believed she'd love anyone.

A knock on the shower door ripped Lena from her thoughts. "You'd better hurry up, or your breakfast will have to be to-go," Del's deep voice echoed through the running water.

Lena laughed. "Okay, I'm done." She turned off the shower and opened the door to grab her towel. She found Del waiting with it in his hand. "Thank you."

"Pleasure's all mine." His gaze raked over her naked body, before reaching in to playfully smack her ass. "Now, hurry up."

***

Del helped Lena into the cab of the truck before heading to the driver's seat. He put the keys in the ignition and looked over at her. "Ready?"

"Mhm."

He started the truck and backed out of the driveway. After turning onto the main road, he reached over to take Lena's hand, holding it tightly on the console. "So, I have something I want to talk to you about."

"Okay. What?"

"What would you say about doing more design work?"

Lena's breath stopped short. "What do you mean?"

"I had lunch with a buddy of mine the other day. He owns one of the other local breweries and we were discussing how well Citadel has been doing in the last month. I told him it was because of you and your design."

"Del…" Lena internally groaned. "It's not just due to the redesign. We've also brought back trivia and live music. The food trucks have drawn a crowd. It's not only me."

"Those things have helped, yes. But not a day goes by where I don't hear someone compliment our décor, or one of those art pieces you found. People are talking about the look of Citadel and it's all thanks to you." He turned his head between her and the road, a proud expression on his face.

"Okay, so what does that have to do with your friend, or me doing more design work?"

"Well, my friend—his name's Jason, by the way—and I were discussing the improvements. I brought up some numbers, which impressed him. He said he'd been thinking of redoing some of his brewery and asked if you'd be interested in helping."

Lena squirmed in her seat as she chewed on her lower lip. "I'm not a designer anymore. I work at Citadel, and I'm happy there."

"I know you are." Del squeezed her hand. "But, Lena, I've never seen you as alive as when you were working on the redesign for Citadel. You're not even that animated when we're in bed."

Lena almost choked on her laugh.

"Seriously, though, the way your face lit up when you showed me the designs. The lift in your voice when you spoke about them. Your excitement while shopping and painting and moving furniture, it was all so cool to see." He glanced at her briefly, and Lena glimpsed the adoration in his eyes. "You may not work as a designer anymore, but it's what you are, and it's what you love to do. Don't deny it."

With a deep breath, Lena dropped her gaze to her lap. "You're right."

"I'm sensing a 'but' coming."

"But..." she drew out the word in one long syllable. "Doing the redesign for Citadel was fun because it wasn't my *job*. It was a project, and one I took very seriously, but those days of doing design for work are behind me."

"What if they weren't, though?"

"What are you talking about?"

"Think about it. You do this redesign for Jason. Things go well, and there are two projects you can put in a portfolio. We can pitch your services to other breweries, which could include a couple brewpubs in the area. Brewpubs have kitchens, which would be a good segue into restaurants, and you know who has restaurants?"

"Who?" she asked dryly.

"Hotels." His eyes gleamed as he glanced at her. "And you know what else hotels have?"

"Ballrooms, conference rooms, banquet halls?"

"Bingo. And who uses those rooms?"

"Jesus, Del. Quit talking to me like a child." Lena snatched her hand from his to run it through her hair. "I know who uses them. Businesses. They're used for all kinds of things, so if I work my way into those, I can also pick up office building clients. Is that what you're getting at?"

He swallowed, nodding, but didn't say anything more.

Lena sighed. "I know how it works, okay. I was in the design industry for over ten years. I've trudged my way through all those steps, and it's a lot of work."

"But it's work you enjoy, right?"

"Yes, but I'm also enjoying my time with you, and if I start designing again, I'll be at the mercy of clients. Not to mention my new boss won't be as nearly as cool as my current one." She gave him a teasing smirk.

"Unless the new boss is you."

The liveliness dropped from her face. "Me?"

"Mhm. You start your own design firm, Lena. That way, you're in control of your hours, your projects, your life. You can do what you truly love."

"While being with the man I love?"

The expression that slid over Del's face was sheer perfection. It was as if he'd taken all the emotions associated with love and rolled them into one divine look. It took Lena's breath away.

Del pulled the truck up to the curb outside Citadel, where Jack leaned against the wall with his arms folded. He put the truck in park and turned to face Lena. Taking her hands in his, he lifted them to his lips. "Would you at least think about it?"

"Del..."

"Lena..." His tone matched her whine.

"Okay, I'll think about it."

He kissed her fingers. "Thank you. Now, get to work before my son has a meltdown."

Lena laughed as she kissed Del goodbye before getting out of the truck. Once she was on the sidewalk, Del rolled down the window to say hello to his son. Then, he was off to his dentist appointment.

"Good morning, Jack."

"Good morning, Lena," he said with more warmth than usual when he greeted her.

It wasn't much, but it was a change, and Lena took it as a good sign. "Who else is opening this morning?"

He shook his head as he turned to unlock the door. "Marky will be here at opening. Until then, it's you and me." He stepped inside, leaving Lena on the sidewalk in confusion.

Why is it just us? Three people always open; a manager and two shifts. She swallowed the lump forming in her throat before entering the brewery. "Why is Marky coming in later?" she asked as she locked the door behind her.

"Because I told him to."

Lena shook her head to clear it. "Jack, I'm not following you here. What's going on?"

Jack took a deep breath, letting it out slowly. "I needed to talk to you. Alone."

Lena's throat quickly closed around the now double-sized lump, making it impossible to swallow or speak. She stood in place as she watched Jack walk around the room. He stopped every few feet to look at the different artwork she and Del had hung.

"I need to thank you." Jack's words were almost inaudible. Or maybe they sounded so strange, Lena wasn't sure she heard him right.

"Thank me? For what?"

"For all of this." He held his arms out as if embracing Citadel. "You really turned this place around." Lowering his arms, he spun to face her. "Your remodel, your event ideas, all of it. It's all made a huge difference in this place. So, thank you."

Lena blushed from the pride filling her chest.

Jack stuffed his hands in his pockets as he stepped toward her. "And also, I need to apologize."

Now Lena was certain she didn't hear him correctly. "What?"

He looked to the floor, shuffling his feet. "When you first came into my dad's life, he was so excited. Like a kid on Christmas. And, while everyone else could accept his happiness, I was skeptical." He lifted his head to look at Lena through his eyelashes. "I'm always skeptical of the women my dad dates."

"I know. He told me."

Jack let out a breath of relief. "Good. Then I don't have to explain how I've watched my father be broken time and time again."

Lena shook her head.

"I got so tired of seeing him hurt, I stopped being glad when he found someone new, and started off disliking them. I never gave any of them a chance. So, when you came along, I treated you the same, but you were different."

"How so?"

Jack took a hand from his pocket to run it through his hair. "Most of the women my dad dated over the years were... high maintenance. They wanted my dad to treat them a certain way. Expected him to make concessions for them, but never gave him the same courtesy." Something resembling a smile pulled at Jack's lips. "You know, you're the first woman he's dated who's gone to the lake with us?"

Lena blinked, shaking her head as she tried to comprehend Jack's question. "What? You can't be serious."

"In fact, you're the first one he's ever asked."

"Why?"

"Because he saw something in you he liked so much, he wanted to share his favorite thing with you."

"The lake is his favorite thing?"

Jack nodded. "It's his happy place. When he and my mom split, he would take us there a lot. The house we lived in was a painful place to be, and the brewery wasn't exactly a kid-friendly venue, so the lake was the perfect substitute. It kinda became our sanctuary." His gaze fell to the floor, but his lips stayed upturned. "I never saw my father sad while we were at the lake."

Warmth bloomed in Lena's chest. She hadn't given a second thought to being at the lake with Del. It was something so simple, she'd assumed it was just another activity to pass the day. Now, Jack was telling her it was some kind of test she'd passed. Apparently, with flying colors.

"So, you see, you've become something very special to my dad. And us."

Lena blinked, furrowing her brow. "*Us?* As in you and your brothers?"

"After seeing the way you diffused Johnnie and Jameson's argument over the music, and the way you coaxed Johnnie into letting you change it, I knew they'd accepted you." He motioned around the tasting room. "And everyone here seems to like you."

Lena bit her lip, hesitating to ask the question burning on her tongue. "What about you?"

Jack took a deep breath, expanding his chest. "I'm glad you're in our lives."

Happy tears pricked Lena's eyes as her heart swelled so much, she thought it would burst. She and Jack smiled at each other, but it was different than the usual courtesy smiles they gave. This was understanding. They had cleared the air between them. Things in Lena's life were finally falling into place. She was happy, something she hadn't felt in a long time.

Chapter 30

Later in the week, on her day off, Lena headed into Citadel to take Del to lunch for once. As much as he tried to take days off when she had them, he was still the owner and had certain responsibilities requiring him to be at work more often. Lena didn't mind. It balanced everything, allowing their relationship to bloom more organically.

As she strode through the door, she found Del at the counter with his back to her while talking to Marky. She admired him from head to toe; her handsome man in his black denim pants and flannel shirt. It may have been seventy degrees outside, but it was September after all, and autumn would be upon them in no time.

Marky jutted his chin in her direction, and Del spun around, his eyes lighting up at the sight of her, and he greeted her with a kiss. "So, how'd it go?"

Lena rocked back and forth on her feet. "It went really well."

"That's it?" Del's excitement faded. "It went well?"

She stopped moving, locking her eyes on Del's. "I told Jason I'd have designs for him this weekend."

"Excellent." He leaned down and kissed her cheek. "I'm proud of you."

"Me too."

Marky cleared his throat. "As sweet as this moment is, I have customers to check on." He hiked his thumb back before scooting off to bus tables.

Lena glanced around the tasting room, where several groups of people were gathered, all seemingly enjoying themselves. The deep breath she took almost lifted her off the ground. "I think this is the start of something good." Her gaze traveled the room before meeting Del's again.

"I think it's already good," he said, his voice low. He took her hand, lifting it to his lips in a gentle kiss. "Let me finish up real quick in the office, and I'll be out for lunch. Tacos?"

Lena nodded, and Del let go of her to head down the hall. As light as she felt, Lena was also grounded. Her life was finally beginning to come together in a way that not only made her feel secure, but more importantly, happy.

The chime on the door made Lena spin around to see a man and woman enter the brewery. Her arm was laced through his, though it didn't seem to be a romantic embrace. It was more chivalrous and professional.

They were both impeccably dressed. Him in a nicely pressed suit with his hair slicked back, and her in a fabulous pink Houndstooth pencil skirt with a matching jacket. Her cream blouse was flowy, but tucked into the skirt to accentuate her curves. She tilted her head back in a laugh, her long, blonde hair cascading down her back and over her shoulders like a golden waterfall.

As Lena watched the woman, something in her brain ticked. Lena felt as if she'd seen this woman before, but had no idea who she could be. Frantically, she searched the recesses of her mind, scrounging for any clue as to who this woman was and why Lena thought she knew her.

Maybe she'd been in the brewery before? She was stunning enough for her image to cement itself into anyone's memory.

The clacking of her sleek, black Jimmy Choo pumps broke Lena's fixation. The woman stopped a few feet from where Lena stood at the bar. "Hi, table for two?"

Lena opened and shut her mouth, most likely looking like a fish. "I, uh..."

"Don't you work here?" the woman asked, a bit on the snotty side.

Marky rushed around the counter. "She does, but she's off the clock. What can I do for you, honey?"

With a sneer, the woman turned to Marky at the register, tugging the man along with her. They chatted about the beers until the man's phone rang. He held a finger up to the woman before walking outside to take the call. She smiled, not-so-genuinely, and waited for Marky to pour their pints, though Lena noticed one pint glass was water.

"Ready to go?" Del's voice sounded from behind Lena, but when she turned to greet him, his eyes were fixed on the blonde woman, and there was tension in his jaw.

"Del? What's wrong?" Lena tilted her head, staring at him, but he wouldn't budge. Even though she wasn't touching him, she could feel the agitation radiating off him.

"Amy," he bit out.

With a gasp, Lena spun around. *Then I definitely don't know her.*

The blonde woman very casually turned, batting her long, fake lashes. "Why, Del, so nice to see you."

Del's chest heaved into Lena's back. "What are you doing here, Amy?"

"I need a reason to come visit my favorite brewery?"

Del didn't say anything, but continued to breathe deeply.

"Oh, you mean here in Aurora?" Pursing her lips, Amy turned fully to face Lena and Del. She glanced out the door at the man she'd come in with. "Relax, Del. I won't be here long." Her tone changed from feigned politeness, to a cold indifference. "My client outside is opening a new hotel in Denver and is a huge beer guy. Apparently, your little brewery has been getting great PR lately, so he wanted to come check it out before we fly back to L.A."

Silence filled the air once more as the three of them stood, locked in conversation limbo. The only reprieve was when Marky slid the pint glasses to Amy.

She picked them up, not bothering to thank Marky, and sipped the water as she looked around the room. "I do love what you've done with the place, though. I mean, it's a bit of a downgrade from my original design, but such an improvement from the slop you redecorated with."

Lena's hair moved with Del's huff. "That's all thanks to Lena here." His hand found hers, squeezing it.

Amy's eyes landed on Lena, and suddenly, it wasn't the wistful look she'd been eyeing the brewery with. This was intense, scrutinizing. She ran her tongue along her teeth, narrowing her eyes. "You did this?"

Lena nodded.

Amy arched an eyebrow. "Impressive."

"We have her to thank for getting Citadel back on its feet." Del squeezed her hand again, but this time, Lena moved their entwined hands to her stomach, folding Del's arm around her.

Amy's eyes flicked between the two of them and a malevolent smirk crossed her lips. "Oh, Del." She shook her head, tsking. "Don't tell me you're dating the help. You could do better."

Lena felt Del flinch, like he wanted to take a step, but was restraining himself. "Amy, you can come in here and belittle me and my brewery all you want, but I'll be damned if I'll sit here and listen to you insult the woman I love."

"Love?" Amy's eyebrows shot to the sky. "Does that mean he's made you give up on your dreams too?"

Lena squeezed Del's hand as she felt him bristle behind her. "No," she said sternly. "In fact, he's helping me start my own design firm." She was surprised by how easily the words left her lips. Though she hadn't officially decided anything, after her meeting with Jason, the idea of having her own firm had been growing on her.

A vicious sneer overtook Amy's face, twisting into malicious amusement. "Well, don't be surprised when he rips the rug out from under you."

"Pay your tab and get out, Amy," Del bit out through an obvious sounding clenched jaw.

"Already done," she snapped, and spun on her heel to march through the door. The air in the room noticeably changed, becoming lighter and lighter the farther away Amy got.

Del's hand relaxed against Lena. "I'm sorry about her."

She spun around to face him, reaching up to cup his cheek and stroking his beard with her thumb. "It's not your fault she's here, or is such an awesome person." The sarcasm hanging in her words was palpable.

Maybe that was why Amy had seemed so familiar. Lena had met women like her left and right in Los Angeles. Amy was just one of the dime a dozen bitches who felt the need to belittle others in order to keep their heads afloat. Lena could lump her in with the rest, and never pay her a second thought.

Del dropped his chin to look her in the eye, earnestness flooding his irises. "Do you see what I meant when I said you're nothing like her?"

"I do, and I take it as the utmost compliment." Lena tipped up on her toes to kiss Del. "Still want to go to lunch?"

"Of course, I do."

Her hand lowered to fiddle with the top button on his shirt. "I wasn't sure if your mood got ruined."

Del reached up to entwine his fingers with hers, and Lena stepped to press herself flush against him. "Doesn't matter how bad my mood gets, you always make it better." He brushed his knuckle down her cheek before connecting their mouths in a kiss filled with affection, the tension from a few minutes ago ebbing with each passing second.

Chapter 31

"Yes, thank you. I'll have an answer for you on Friday. Okay, bye." Lena hung up the phone and stared at the now blank screen, her head spinning.

Deftly, her fingers swiped the screen, and she dialed Nicole. The chain of her necklace furiously wound and unwound around her finger as she willed Nicole to answer the phone.

"Lena, hey! Long time, no talk. I thought maybe Del had kidnapped you, or something."

"I got my job back."

Nicole was silent for a moment. "What?"

"I just got off the phone with the HR at Designology, and they want me to come back."

"Oh, yeah. I totally meant to tell you, Hatfield doesn't work here anymore. She got moved to the new corporate office." Nicole huffed a breath.

Lena pinched the bridge of her nose. "Not exactly what I'm worried about, Nicki."

"Oh, right. Okay, what do you mean you got your job back?"

"I guess you were right about my absence having an impact on business." Lena ran her hand through her hair. "Not only did they lose clients, but new ones refused to come aboard since I wasn't there."

"You certainly had a reputation." Nicole popped her gum. "I hope you told them to shove it."

"It took everything I had not to laugh in her face and hang up."

"Why didn't you?"

"Because she went on to tell me what they were offering." Lena took a deep breath, pulling her lower lip between her teeth. "They want to bring me back as a senior consultant at double my pay."

"HA!" Nicole cackled. "They had that chance and chose to fire you instead. Did you tell her off? I would have let her have it. They wouldn't be able to hire me back after all the dirty words I'd call—"

"Nicole!" Lena waited for her to pause her tirade. "They want to make me a partner." Nicole went silent. So silent Lena thought the line was dead. "Nicki?"

"I'm here. Are you effing serious? Partner?"

Lena nodded, quickly realizing Nicole couldn't see her. "Mhm. I'll come back at a senior position for a pay period, and then they'll announce my partnership. I would be a *partner*, Nicole."

"But why would you want to be a partner out here in L.A. for a firm that fired you six months ago, when you told me Del was helping you start your own firm there?"

"Because I'd be coming into the position for an established company." She began pacing her living room. "I wouldn't have to do all the groundwork because it would already be done. Right now, I'm a no-name designer trying to build her clientele. I wouldn't have to do that at Designology."

"Okay, yes, it would be easier, but..." Nicole paused, and Lena could picture the way she crinkled her forehead as she looked to the ceiling in thought. "I'm not trying to say you don't deserve it, or you aren't qualified, but why? Why are they offering you such a big promotion?"

"The HR said the new owner, Hatfield's sister, Amelia, did some digging as to who the designer was that all these clients were attached to, and when she found my portfolio, she was impressed. I suppose they're trying to sweeten the deal to get me to come back."

Nicole popped her gum a few times. "What does Del say about it?"

Lena's stomach sank into her feet. "I haven't talked to him yet. You were the first person I called when I got off the phone with them."

"I think you need to talk to him. Didn't you tell me his ex left him for Cali to be a designer?"

"Yeah." Lena dug her toe into the carpet. "But this is different."

"How?"

"Del and I aren't married. We don't have kids. It's not like I'm leaving a family or anything." *Does that make it any better?* Shit, we've only been together a couple months."

"Don't cuss." Nicole took a breath. "But you love him, right?"

Tears pricked Lena's eyes. "Yes," she said, her voice shaking.

"So, love isn't enough to make you stay?"

Lena huffed, stomping her foot. "This is my dream job, Nicole. It's what I've wanted for years, and now I have a chance at it."

"Okay, okay. When do you need to give them an answer?"

"Friday."

Nicole sucked in a breath through her teeth. "That doesn't give you much time."

"No, considering today is Wednesday." Lena rolled her eyes before dropping her face into her palm. "What do I do, Nicole?"

"When are you seeing him next?"

"Tonight. We're going out for dinner, and tomorrow we're spending the day at the lake. Just the two of us. So, do I ruin tonight *and* tomorrow, or do I wait until□"

"Lena, the only way you're going to ruin anything is if you've made up your mind to come back here. Is that what you want?"

A crease formed between Lena's eyebrows as she stopped pacing. "I... I don't know."

"Well, if you don't, who does?" Nicole sighed heavily. "Tell you what. Go to dinner tonight, enjoy the evening with your perfect man, and if by the end of the night, you're not convinced you should stay, then you'll know your answer."

Lena took a deep breath. "Good idea, thanks."

"You're welcome, Leen. Good luck."

Lena hung up the phone, feeling a bit lighter than when she'd begun the conversation. Nicole was right. Lena shouldn't be making any decisions without discussing things with Del. Next to her own, his opinion was the most important. She hoped it would mesh with hers.

***

"Lena?"

"Hm?" Lena whipped her head up.

Concern laced Del's eyes as they flicked to the fork her hand was absentmindedly twirling around in her spaghetti. "Is your food not good?"

"No. I mean, yes." She huffed a breath, sitting up and wiping her mouth with her napkin. "It's very good, Del."

He furrowed his brow. "Then what's bothering you? You've been quiet all night."

"I'm tired."

"Tired, huh? It wasn't too busy at Citadel today." He attempted a laugh, but it sounded stilted.

"Well, sometimes those are the days that wear you out the most." Lena tried to keep her tone lighthearted. "You know, when you don't have too much to occupy your mind, *and* you're listening to Twyla rattle on for hours about the concert she saw last night. It can be exhausting."

Del actually laughed, but a curious concern lingered in his eyes. "Okay, I'll give you that."

Lena was thankful he accepted her answer. It wasn't a complete lie. Work had been slow, and Twyla had droned on about her night out, but Lena wasn't exhausted. More so, the inevitable future conversation, the one which would most definitely ruin the night, plagued her.

She and Del finished their dinner at Enzo's Bistro with light chatter. Lena tried to keep the topic on their lake day tomorrow, steering their conversation in that direction whenever Del strayed toward something else. Mainly, Lena wanted to avoid anything having to do with design.

Relief flooded her when Del paid the check without asking whether she wanted dessert. The drive to his house was quiet, but far from their normally comfortable silence. Without any noise to occupy the space between them, Lena feared Del would hear her heart thumping in her chest. It was already hard enough to keep her fingers from finding her hair.

"How about some music?" he asked, turning the radio up.

Lena nodded softly, relieved to have some background noise as she turned her head to look out the window. The setting sun was almost on the horizon. She eyed the sky streaked with a myriad of reds, oranges, and pinks as clouds dotted the atmosphere. Lost in the beauty of a Colorado sunset, Lena almost didn't realize they'd arrived at Del's house.

Once inside, Del took Lena's jacket as she removed her shoes. "Straight to bed?" he asked, hanging her jacket in the closet.

"What?" Lena glanced at the kitchen clock. "Del, it's only seven-thirty."

"I know, but you were so tired at dinner, I thought maybe you'd want to go to sleep right away."

A soft smile crossed her lips. "I'm not *that* tired."

"Well, maybe if we go to bed, I can make you tired." He bobbed his eyebrows.

The smile dropped as Lena rolled her eyes.

With a self-satisfied smirk, Del asked, "How about a glass of wine and a movie?"

"Perfect."

After the wine was poured, Lena and Del settled onto the couch. At first, they sat next to each other with Lena leaning into him slightly, but not enough to hinder her from reaching her wineglass on the coffee table. As the movie progressed, and after the wine was spent, Lena melted more and more into Del's side until the length of her body pressed against his. Her cheek rested on his chest, her head rising and falling with his breath.

The movie, *Y Tu Mamá También*, may not have been the best choice for Lena's frame of mind. Certain moments in the movie had Del's hands roaming. He wasn't copping feels, but his fingers lightly brushed Lena's arm, sending little jolts of electricity through her with every stroke.

It was enough to make Lena need to touch him. She ran her hand up his abdomen to the collar of his shirt, where she undid the top two buttons. Her fingers slid under the fabric, the warmth of his skin against her palm tingling her fingertips. The deep hum he let out didn't help anything either.

She tilted her chin up as he tilted his down, and their mouths connected. His tongue ran along her lips, parting them and sliding inside. The kiss, while deep and passionate, was also sensual. More so than usual.

Del cupped her cheek as he shifted onto his side. Lena was pinned between his weight and the couch, but she savored every second of it. In fact, she craved it. Her favorite place to be was pressed against Del, and right now, he had her deliciously trapped.

She rolled her hips to meet his erection.

He moaned. "Should we take this to the bedroom?"

"Why wait?"

Before he could answer, Lena pushed him onto his back and climbed over to straddle him. Splaying her hands across his chest, she dragged her gaze up his body, coming to rest on his eyes. They flashed with need as his hands gripped her hips. She bent down to press her lips to his once more.

Piece by piece, their clothes came off, but their kiss was never broken for more than a few seconds. Lena feared losing the connection would break her completely. She needed this closeness. She needed Del.

He slid his hand between her thighs, groaning as his fingers slipped along her wetness. "Lena," he breathed.

Still not breaking the kiss, but needing friction, she moved her hips. Soon, they perfected their rhythm. Del's fingers moved with her body in a way that had her diving over that euphoric ridge in no time. Her body shuddered, but she still gasped when Del replaced his fingers with his cock.

With a stiff groan, he paused before moving inside her. Much to her disappointment, his mouth pulled away from hers and trailed kisses across her cheek and down to her shoulder. He cocooned her in his arms, keeping their chests together as their hips moved in perfect harmony. His embrace tightened, as if he was afraid she'd float away.

It was slow, sensual love making, much different from their usual fun. This was a deep need to feel each other. Del moved in and out of Lena with precision, hitting her in the right spot to build the pleasure, but not rushing it. Excruciating, yet enjoyable.

Lena wanted more, though.

She nipped at Del's collarbone, loosening his constraint, and sat up. His hands slid to her hips briefly before running up her sides to her breasts. He rolled her hardened nipples between his fingers, and Lena's head fell back as a fervent moan escaped her lips. Even in this position, the intimacy was fierce.

One of Del's hands left her breast, his fingers brushing the skin of her stomach before moving farther south. They found her center and his thumb made circles on her clit. Desire bubbled low inside her as she rolled her hips to get more contact.

Del groaned, the hand still on her breast pausing.

He's held out long enough, I think. Lena tilted forward, bringing her mouth to his ear. "Fuck me, Del."

He grunted, shivering at her words. "You sure? I can keep going." If it weren't for the strain in his voice, Lena might have believed him.

"I'm ready." She bit his earlobe. "Fuck me."

No words left Del as he lifted himself up, taking Lena with him. She yelped in surprise. When he was on his knees, he shifted his hips to remove himself from her before connecting their mouths in a strong, forceful kiss. Different than the passion they shared earlier, this was an all-consuming, lust-filled kiss that had Lena scrambling for contact.

She slid her hand between their bodies, but Del grabbed her elbow. "Uh, uh," he whispered against her mouth. "You told me to fuck you, which is what I'm going to do."

Without warning, Del grabbed her hips, spinning her around so she was bracing herself on the arm of the couch. He sidled up behind her, his hard cock resting at her entrance. His fingers traced the length of her spine before twisting into her hair. His other hand moved between them, finding her clit.

Lena moaned, trying to dip her head down, but Del pulled on her hair. The hand circling her clit nudged her legs apart. "Open up for me."

As Lena obliged his orders, Del replaced his hand with his cock, and she gasped again. No matter how many times he'd been inside her, and never mind the fact he was in her only a minute prior, it never ceased to amaze her how well-endowed he was.

He slid his hand over her ass to her hip. "Now, what was I supposed to do?"

She groaned, pushing her hips back against his.

"Say it, Lena," he growled, the hand lost in her hair tightening.

"Fuck me, Del."

And he did. Del thrust into her hard and fast, the sound of skin on skin filling the air. Lena's screams of pleasure soon joined, and they mingled with Del's groans. The faster he pumped, the harder he seemed to get. Lena lost herself in the pure bliss of friction, the edge of her orgasm inching closer with every second.

Del ran his hand from her hip up her spine and down again, grabbing her ass. "I love this position," he said between breaths. "But I'm missing something." He untangled his hand from her hair, and gripped her waist, hoisting her up so her back was flush against his chest. Sitting on his heels, he ran his hands around to cup her breasts. "Two things, actually."

His fingers expertly rolled her nipples as his hips still moved. He latched his mouth to her neck, kissing every spot he could reach.

All Lena could do was whimper. The noises coming out of her were small, meek moans because every movement brought her closer to her crest.

Del kept this position for a few minutes, seemingly composing himself from the zealous pounding he was just doing. Then, he lifted back to his knees and nudged Lena forward onto all fours again. She protested when he slid out of her.

He clicked his tongue. "Don't worry." Flipping her onto her back, he lifted one of her legs over his shoulder so she was fully opened to him. His fingers found her entrance and pumped into her. "I'm not done. I want to watch you when you come."

Lena ground against his hand, seeking the friction that had been taken from her moments ago. Her moans grew louder. Her breath grew shorter. She was on the precipice of another fantastic orgasm.

Del had other plans. Right as the wave was about to hit her, he slid his cock inside. Her orgasm broke with the hardness of him, and she screamed his name into the air. As she tightened around him, he pumped faster into her. He held out as long as he could before his own release caught up to him, and he pulsed against her walls.

Both out of breath and thoroughly exhausted, they stayed connected for a while before Del pulled out. He grabbed some tissues off the side table and cleaned them both up. When he was finished, he snuggled up to Lena so she was between him and the couch, her head resting on his chest.

"Isn't this the position that started everything?" she joked.

He kissed the top of her head. "Yeah, but if you're wanting another round, I'm going to need some Gatorade or something."

She laughed. "No. I'm good. Better than good. I'm perfect."

"You certainly are," Del whispered, grabbing the throw blanket from the back of the couch. "Now, get some sleep. I love you."

"Love you too," Lena said, though she wasn't sure if the words were audible.

Lost in a euphoric stupor after probably the best sex she and Del ever had, Lena melted into him. It may have been the best, but it was also the most intimate. It began so sensually as if they were two beings who could never be separated. The way it ended, though, was one for the history books.

This is what it's supposed to be like, she thought as the soft tendrils of sleep curled around her. *How could I even think about leaving him?*

Her eyelids fell heavy. Her breath evened. Her whole body went slack.

But what if I end up resenting him like Amy did?

Chapter 32

The next morning, they arrived at the lake at 9 a.m. Del said it was always best to get there early so they could secure a good spot on the beach. Lena wasn't sure why since the reservoir sat fairly bare. A few boats floated across its surface while the swim beach lay empty, and the last straggling fishermen packed up their gear before heading home.

Being September, it wasn't cold, but it wasn't exactly warm. Lena gripped her swimsuit cover-up tighter around her as she watched Del unhooking the jet ski from the trailer. "Are you sure going out on the lake is a good idea today?"

"It'll warm up, don't worry."

She shivered in the slight breeze. "It better."

He smirked before guiding the jet ski into the water. He hopped onto it and started the engine. "I'm going to dock this, and then I'll come back to move the truck. Hang tight."

I'll hang tight inside the truck. Lena climbed in the passenger seat to wait. She watched the trees and tall grasses around the reservoir sway in the wind as clouds built steadily on the western horizon.

A knot formed in Lena's stomach. She felt as unstable as the swaying grasses with her inability to make a decision about her job offer. The growing clouds mimicked the anxious storm brewing inside her. Sooner or later, it would all come to a head, and she didn't know what the outcome would be. Either way, someone would end up losing. The biting question was, would it be her, or Del?

The driver's side door opened, startling Lena, and Del climbed inside. "All right, let's get this day started, shall we?" He reached over to take her hand and drove the truck to the parking lot.

A few hours later, the weather did indeed improve. Lena sat on the beach, sweat beading on her skin as she watched Del glide across the water, making sharp turns and jumping waves. When he beached the jet ski and made his way toward her, she knew what he was coming for.

"No," she said flatly without looking up from her book.

"Oh, come on. It's warmed up, the water is fairly calm, and I'm lonely."

Lena glanced up from the pages to see Del's face twisted into a sad puppy-dog look. She laughed. "I told you no more rides."

Del pursed his lips, narrowing his eyes. "I seem to recall you stipulating that was only if the boys were here." He turned his head from side to side, surveying the area. "I don't see anyone except you and me."

Lena huffed, dropping her book to her lap.

He held out his hand. "Please?"

She couldn't deny the poor man some company. If anything, it would cool her off. With a nod, Lena tucked her book away, put on her life jacket, and followed Del to the water. Even though she'd been on the jet ski before, her heart still hammered away in her chest.

Del was accommodating, though. He didn't take off at full throttle, or make any sharp turns. He didn't even bring the jet ski up to full speed while Lena was riding. The ride was actually enjoyable, and it definitely cooled her down.

Maybe too much.

Del turned his chin over his shoulder. "Are you done? I can feel your teeth chattering."

"Mhm. Done."

They returned to the beach, where Lena promptly bundled up in a towel. Del dropped to his knees next to her. "Do you mind if I go out for a little longer?"

She shook her head, unable to respond without her jaw quivering.

"Thanks." He leaned in for a kiss before returning to the shoreline.

After several minutes of watching Del perform panic-inducing maneuvers, Lena finally stopped shivering. Instead of relaxing, though, she felt tense. There was too much intensity on the water, so she grabbed her book and sprawled out in the sun. Now that her skin was dry, she could enjoy the warmth of the soon-to-be fall afternoon.

Try as she may, she couldn't concentrate. The words on the page escaped her memory the moment she read them. At first, she thought it was due to her anxiety over Del's daredevil antics, but she soon realized it was because there was something else plaguing her mind.

Today was the day. She had to talk to Del about the phone call she received the day before. But when would be the right time? Not here at the lake, his place of harmony. She couldn't destroy that. Back at his house wouldn't work either. What if she decided to break his heart? She had no way to get home other than him taking her, and that would be the most awkward drive in the world.

Lena yelped as cold drops of water hit her back. With a fiery glare, she flipped over to find Del standing over her, his chin lifted and a teasing eyebrow arched.

"Sorry, you looked hot."

Her eyes narrowed, intensifying the glare.

Del stifled a chuckle, holding his hands up in defense. "My mistake. You *are* hot, but water won't help." He winked and settled onto his towel next to her, folding his arms behind his head.

Lena let the glare fall, her eyes bouncing from Del's last name tattoo to his hops. Of the four tattoos he had, she knew the meaning of three of them. There was only one left to be explained. "What's the tattoo on your back for?"

"Hm?" Del hummed, not opening his eyes.

"I know what all your other tattoos symbolize, but I don't understand the snakes that run across your upper back."

"Oh. Those." Del huffed a breath, then rolled to his side, propping his head in his palm. "Well, I got that one a while after the divorce. When I finally started to feel like I was healing from everything, I needed to do something to close off that pain. Snakes shed their skin when they grow. They transform almost, and that's what I felt like I had done. I wasn't the person I was when I was with Amy, nor was I the person she'd hurt. I was... new."

Lena stared at Del in admiration, and a smile crept across her lips. "How incredibly brave."

"Pffft." He waved her off. "Not brave. Just, tired of being broken."

She reached over to take his hand, the pages of her book flopping back and forth.

He glanced down at it. "How's the book?"

"It's fine," Lena said flatly as she closed the book and set it aside.

"So, it's a dud, huh?"

"What? No. I haven't really gotten into it yet."

"What's stopping you?"

Lena sighed, letting the book flop on the towel. "I don't know."

A crease formed between his eyebrows. "Lena, what's up? You've been super quiet, distant almost, ever since dinner last night. I believed you when you said you were tired, but now I'm not so sure."

"Del..." She grimaced, squeezing her eyes shut.

He reached over to take her hand. "Hey, it's okay. Talk to me."

"I..." Opening her eyes, she took a deep breath. "I got an interesting phone call yesterday."

Del's hand tensed, his fingers digging into her. "Okay..." He drew out the syllables. "What kind of phone call? Medical?"

She shot him a sideways glance. "No."

"Good." He ran his hand down his face, letting out a slow exhale. "Well, whatever you have to say can't be that bad, then. Go on."

"It's not exactly good, though."

"Lena, whatever it is, we can figure it out."

Can we, though? She fidgeted with the corner of the towel. "I don't want to talk about this here. Can we go home?"

Del licked his lips as he nodded. "Sure. Let's load up."

Relief washed over Lena. After waiting patiently for Del to load the jet ski, she steeled herself before climbing into the truck. As they drove away from the loading ramp, they left the reservoir behind them. All of Del's happy memories would remain intact.

The notion she wouldn't ruin the lake for Del comforted Lena, but only for a moment. Driving down the road, silence hung in the air, thick like molasses. Lena couldn't bring herself to start talking, though.

So Del did. "Okay, I'm not waiting until we get home. What's bothering you?"

With a groan, Lena propped her elbow on the door and rested her cheek in her palm. "I got a call from my old design firm in L.A. They want me to come back."

"Oh." Del shrank back, the void between them widening. "What did you tell them?"

"I didn't tell them anything, yet."

"Which means you didn't tell them no." It wasn't a question; it was a statement, and one laced with hurt.

"They want an answer tomorrow, and I wanted to talk to you first."

"What is there to talk about, Lena?" Del's tone was angry, but he wasn't yelling. "Obviously, you've made your decision if you didn't turn down the job. What are they offering that's so good?"

Lena's eyelids fell heavy as her body sunk into the seat. "They want to make me partner." It came out almost inaudible. "So? I thought we were going to start your *own* company? You know, one where you'd be the proprietor, not just partner?"

"I know, Del, but..." She sat up straight, turning slightly to face him. "This way, I'm coming into an established company. All the groundwork will be done. I won't have to fight for clients, scrounging my way into the industry."

"In other words, the easy way out?"

Lena sighed. "Nothing about this is easy."

With a groan, Del ran his hand down his face, pulling on his beard. He kept his eyes on the road, but his knuckles were turning white from his strong grip on the wheel. "I don't understand what's so great about Los Angeles."

"It's not L.A., Del, it's the job. Ever since I started in the design world, my dream has been to be partner at a big firm. It's what I worked toward for over ten years."

"Until they fired you," he bit out.

"Yes, until that. But they said they've lost clients and have had trouble getting clients to sign without me there. I'm an important part of the business. They need me."

"I need you too." He reached over to take her hand, squeezing it hard.

Lena's chest constricted as tears pricked her eyes, so she squeezed them shut and took a shallow breath. "That's why I couldn't make a decision." The words shook out of her mouth.

Del paused, completely silent. "I think you should go," he whispered.

Lena blinked her eyes open, swiping at her eyelids. "What?"

"You should go to Los Angeles."

"Why?" She sniffled. "A minute ago, you—"

"A minute ago, I was angry and hurt. I still am, but not enough to make you stay somewhere you don't want to be."

His words punched her in the gut. "I want to be with you, Del. I do."

"But you're a strong woman who was taught to rely on herself. Your mother showed you what it meant to be independent, not to let anyone get in the way of what you want."

Lena shut her eyes again, nodding softly. Her mouth tightened as she thought about how proud her mother would be if she could see Lena getting what she'd wanted all these years. Her hard work paid off. It was finally being recognized; she was finally being seen.

Del cleared his throat. "I made the mistake of trying to force Amy to stay here, and look how that worked out. I can't bear the idea of you hating me the way she does."

"I could never hate you," Lena said quietly as he lifted her hand to kiss her knuckles. "But I have to do this. I'd be doing myself and my mother a disservice by letting all my hard work go to waste."

"I know." He swallowed deeply. "I'll, uh, take you home." The tone in his voice told her he wouldn't be driving to his house.

Lena's jaw quivered. More tears threatened to well in her eyes, so she took a deep breath. This is what she wanted, what she'd always wanted; her dream come true.

Why then, did she feel so empty?

As Del parked in her driveway, Lena looked up at the house. This had been her childhood home, the one she left when she moved to California. The one she'd come back to sporadically while her mother had undergone chemo treatments before being placed in hospice care. She called it "home" for a few months after losing her job, but it hadn't ever felt like one. Now it looked as uninviting as a cheap motel.

They sat in silence for several moments. Neither said a word, nor did they look at each other. It was unnerving, but Lena couldn't bring herself to say the one thing she wanted to say. The words might have broken her if she uttered them. Instead, she slipped her hand from Del's and opened the door of the truck.

To her surprise, Del followed. He met her on the porch as she unlocked the front door. It slid open, squeaking from decreased use over the weeks, and she turned to face Del.

His face was sullen. The usual brightness in his blue eyes was muted, making them more gray, as if his light had gone out.

Lena wanted to touch him. She wanted to cradle him in her arms and tell him it was going to be all right, but she refrained. His heart was broken enough; she didn't need to add to his heartache by giving him false hope. "Thank you for everything, Del."

Shoving his hands into his pockets, he let out a sigh. "I wish it had been enough."

Lena stifled the sob trying to force its way from her throat. She hung her head as a tear slid down her cheek. Del's words cut her deep, though she knew he didn't say them out of malice. It was a genuine statement, one she agreed with.

He watched the rolling tear, and took a step forward. His hand found her face, cupping her cheek and wiping the tear away with his thumb. Though his features were laced with hurt, the longing remained, buried deep behind the pain she'd caused him.

As he bent down to kiss her, her heart fluttered. He'd kissed her many times on the porch, but this was both the best and worst of them all. It was a gentle kiss, full of love and devotion. The kind that made Lena's knees wobble.

But when Del moved away, it left a sourness on her lips because she knew he was no longer hers.

His hand lingered on her cheek, brushing the skin lightly, and Lena fought the urge to nuzzle into his warm palm. He was still so close, his breath tickling her lips and his juniper scent tantalizing her senses. When he straightened to stand, his hand fell from her face, and she immediately missed his warmth. Without a word, he turned, walking to the truck and getting in. Lena watched him pull onto the street and drive away until he was out of sight.

She made it as far as her sitting room before she collapsed onto an armchair and unleashed the tears which had filled her to the brim. Best to get them all out now. She'd need time to compose herself before making the phone call that hopefully would be worth the heartache.

Chapter 33

Nicole kicked Lena's foot hanging off the edge of the couch. "Come on, stop moping."

"I'm not moping, I'm dwelling."

"Same difference." Nicole huffed, putting her hands on her hips. "At least you've stopped checking your phone every five minutes."

Lena blew a forceful breath through her lips, puffing her cheeks out. For the first few days after leaving Colorado, her phone had blown up with texts from people wanting to know what happened. Twyla mostly, but others from Citadel were worried about her. Lena hadn't been able to give them more than a "sorry" or "can't talk now" reply.

Even Johnnie and Jameson had asked after her, and it wasn't surprising that Jack didn't.

Lena wasn't sure if she was relieved or disappointed by not receiving a message from Del. She knew it was silly to think he'd reach out. After the way she hurt him, it was feasible he'd never speak to her again, but a painful sliver of hope took root in her heart, and she couldn't remove it.

Nicole nudged Lena with her knee. "Look, you told Elle and Brook we'd go out tonight. Not my fault you lied to them."

"I didn't lie," Lena protested. "I just didn't tell them all the details."

Nicole took a seat on the couch near Lena's head, stroking her hair. "I don't know why you didn't tell them about your summer with Del. They would've understood why you didn't want to go clubbing."

"It's too soon." Lena's eyes welled with tears. She'd shed many of them over the past week whenever she thought about how she'd left Del. It was the right decision, at least *she* thought so. He likely disagreed. Lena sighed.

"Well, maybe getting out will help keep your mind occupied. Come on, they'll be waiting."

With a groan, Lena slid from the couch, rising to follow Nicole to the bathroom where she helped Lean get ready. Nicole did Lena's makeup, pinned up her hair, and even chose an outfit for her. As much as she felt like a child, Lena appreciated her friend's help. She wasn't sure she'd be able to do it herself.

At the club, Lena and Nicole met Elle and Brook in the VIP line. The duo squealed as they pulled Lena in for a group hug.

"OMG, Lena!" Elle screamed in her ear. "I'm so glad you're back!"

"Thanks, me too," Lena said, telling herself the tightness in her chest was from Elle's embrace. She took a breath when she was released from the hug and smoothed her black cocktail dress. "I'm also glad Brook moved up to senior editor. Even if it is for a tabloid magazine."

Brook scoffed, smacking Lena's arm. "Hey, that tabloid magazine is getting us in the VIP room tonight, so don't talk shit."

"Don't swear," Nicole chimed in.

Brook rolled her eyes as she turned to the bouncer, waving her hand between Lena and Nicole. "The judgy ones are with me."

The security guard's mouth twitched as if he fought a laugh, and lifted the velvet rope to allow the four women to enter. Inside the club, Lena was hit with a blast of air-conditioning as the familiar thumping of dance music fell on her ears. Another security guard escorted the women down a corridor to a roped off section. They claimed a private table enclosed with curtains, then ordered drinks from the server.

Lena wanted to protest doing shots, but her friends didn't know the old Lena had been replaced, and denying the drinks would arouse questions she wasn't ready to answer. Against her better judgment, she downed the shots in stride. After taking three each, the group ordered cocktails, and Lena felt relieved to have something she could nurse.

Elle yanked on Lena's arm and yelled, "Let's dance!"

With a forced smile, Lena obliged. She needed to appear as her former self; fun-loving, clubbing, bar-hopping Lena. She could fake it for a night, but she hoped the girls wouldn't attempt to pry out one-night-stand Lena. That person was long gone.

Out on the dance floor, the alcohol kicked in. Her legs wobbled, and the room spun around her, but most importantly, she'd had enough drinks to allow the music to muffle her aching heart. As her body moved to the beat, her muscles eased and all the pain from the summer slid from her like a waterfall.

Surrounded by her friends, engulfed in a familiar song, Lena was transported back seven months to a time before Del. Before being fired. Before her mother's death.

She danced for multiple songs, losing track of how many, until she felt two hands on her hips. She stopped mid-step and whirled around to find Ozzie smiling at her.

Suddenly, the prior year of her life flashed before her eyes, and her heart leaped into her throat. "Ozzie?" She had other questions, but the music was too loud to speak any further.

He jutted his chin toward a table, but she shook her head. Rolling his eyes, he nudged her off the floor. She pushed back, refusing to go with him, so he took her by the forearm, practically dragging her until they were far enough away from the dance floor to hear each other.

Lena ripped her arm from his hand. "Don't touch me, Ozzie. What do you want?"

"Fuck, Lena. It's nice to see you too," he said harshly.

She gritted her teeth. "I didn't say it was nice to see you."

"Look, all I want to do is talk, okay? I've got some stuff to say."

"And I don't care." She pushed by him, but he caught her bicep, yanking her close.

"You're going to listen, Lena." His dark brown eyes bored into her, a menacing fire in them. The stench of gin rolled off his lips.

"Why don't you go talk to Shannon?"

He grimaced. "I'm not with Shannon."

"Oh?" Lena asked with a snotty tone. "What happened? Did she figure out what a prick you are, or did you cheat on her too?"

His grip tightened on her arm. "She's not who I want." Drunken lust poured out of his irises as he eyed Lena up and down. "You are."

Lena choked down the urge to vomit. She didn't want to ruin her dress. "Ozzie, I don't want your fake affection. If you wanted me, then you shouldn't have taken Shannon back to *my* apartment to fuck her!"

"Are you going to hold that over my head forever?"

"Um, yeah!"

Ozzie growled, running his hand through his cropped brown hair. "I came to talk to you like an adult, but I see you're still the same snotty bitch you always were." A malevolent smirk crossed his lips. "That's why I had to have side pussy; to deal with your attitude."

Lena wound up and slapped Ozzie so hard, his head snapped to the side. When he righted himself, Lena grinned at the fingernail marks across his cheek, but the twisted sneer on his face made her blood run cold. Ozzie lunged, ready to choke the life from her, but a security guard caught him by the upper arm, twisting his arm behind his back.

"Is this guy bothering you, miss?" the security guard asked as Ozzie yelped.

Lena swallowed her panic and nodded.

"Got it. Come on, buddy. Let's call you a cab." The security guard led Ozzie away, and Lena stumbled back to her table.

Tears streaked her cheeks, no doubt smearing her eyeliner, but she didn't care. She was a fool to come to the club tonight. This life, her old party life, wasn't hers anymore, and wasn't one she wanted.

Lena paid for her drinks, and texted Nicole she was going home. This would be her last night of clubbing.

Ever.

Chapter 34

"**E**arth to Lena..."

"Huh?" Lena whipped her head up to find Nicole sitting on the edge of the desk, looking down at her with confusion on her face.

"Where were you?" Nicole crossed her arms. "Don't tell me you were daydreaming."

"No, not daydreaming. Just thinking about the announcement."

Nicole relaxed her arms, her eyes gleaming. "Not long now."

"Nope." Lena glanced at the clock on her desk. It was 9:35 a.m. "Ten minutes and they'll call everyone into the conference room." She sat back in her cushy swivel chair, wiping her palms on her creased black slacks.

"What's with the nerves? You know you've got the spot."

"I don't think it's nerves, just excitement. This announcement solidifies things. And it means I can actually start looking for apartments instead of crashing in your guest room. I'm sure Jayce is ready to get rid of me."

Nicole rolled her eyes. "Oh, girl, you know you're welcome in my house anytime. In fact, I went six months without my BFF, so these last three weeks of non-stop girl-time have been great." She stood from the desk, motioning for Lena to do the same. When Lena stood, Nicole rubbed her palms up and down Lena's arms. "Now, get yourself together. You've got a big moment coming."

Lena gave a crisp nod and pulled Nicole in for a hug. "Thank you. I don't know what I'd do without you."

"Be a daydreaming homeless lady, probably."

Lena laughed as they separated. She said goodbye to Nicole, watching her disappear through the office door. With a deep breath, Lena spun in her chair, doing a full 360 and taking in her spacious office. Bigger than she'd expected, it still sat bare. She hadn't had time to decorate it yet considering she'd been in it less than two weeks.

After calling to accept the job, Lena spent a week packing and setting up to move into Nicole's apartment before starting at the office. She'd taken as much as she could fit into the small guest room, but the house in Colorado still held the majority of her belongings. Lena decided not to sell it right away. A voice in the recesses of her mind told her to wait in case something went awry.

But that was three weeks ago. Nothing had even come remotely close to ruining what was about to be the best move of Lena's career.

Best move of my life, she corrected herself.

Now, she had one more day to go before she would officially become partner at Designology. In less than twenty-four hours, Lena would be signing the paperwork she'd never thought she'd get the chance to even see. Today, the owner of the company, Amelia Hatfield, was coming in to address the entire office and announce Lena's partnership.

Lena spun in her chair again. This time, with so much enthusiasm, she nearly lost her high heels in the process. The office intercom cut her light-hearted laugh short.

"If we could have everyone's attention, please," the nasally voice of the front desk receptionist said. *"There is an all-hands meeting in conference room A in fifteen minutes. Please finish what you are working on and join us. Thank you."*

"Let's get this show on the road," Lena said before rising from her chair. She walked to the mirror mounted next to the door to check her hair and makeup.

It had been an odd thing to get back into the routine of wearing makeup every day. She'd gone practically all summer without it. Her heart sank as Del's voice echoed in her mind, *But for the record, you always look beautiful.*

She shook her head. No time for thoughts of Del. She'd been practicing not thinking about him for weeks, and this was not the moment to relapse. Lena smoothed her slacks, fluffed her flowy light-pink blouse, and gave her reflection a crisp nod.

The walk to the conference room felt different than ever before. The hall seemed more spacious, the lighting seemed brighter. Even the air tasted sweet. Maybe it was because she knew what waited for her. She'd been in the conference room countless times, watching as someone else lived out their dream. Now, it was her turn. Lena held her head tall as she opened the door and stepped inside.

Nicole jumped from her front row seat, waving her arm in the air. With a small laugh, Lena headed to the front of the room. Nicole squealed as they took their seats.

"Shhh. You're not supposed to know, remember?" Lena scolded quietly.

Nicole bounced in her chair. "I know, but this is exciting." She glanced around the room. "I don't see Amelia Hatfield anywhere."

Lena furrowed her eyebrows. "I know we Googled her after she bought the firm, but I don't remember what she looks like."

"You don't?" Nicole's eyes widened. "Well, I'm sure you'll remember when you see her, but she doesn't look anything like her sister. She's just as venomous, though."

"It's always so interesting to hear the words you use instead of cussing. I never would have said 'venomous.' I would have said bitchy."

Nicole smacked Lena's thigh, giving her a teasing smirk. "That's why my vocabulary is more extensive than yours."

The two friends fake sneered at each other before bursting into giggles. They were forced to corral their festivities when the office HR manager walked to the front of the room.

She tapped the microphone, the thump echoing through the speakers. "Hello. Can you all hear me?" She waited for confirmation before continuing. "Good. Thank you all for coming. We've got a few announcements we wanted to make in person rather than through emails."

There was a collective grumble from the room, making Lena shift in her seat. Nicole reached down and took her hand.

"First thing's first..." The HR manager went on to address recent office issues, updates on clients, and other such information. A half hour went by with Lena's necklace twisted tight around her fingers. "Now, the reason you all probably showed up on time." She cleared her throat. "The rumors are true. We have a special guest here today. The owner of Designology, Miss Amelia Hatfield." The HR manager floated her hand to the side door of the conference room, and everyone's heads turned.

The door opened, allowing a picturesque blonde woman to enter. When she flipped her hair to greet the crowded room, Lena's stomach dropped into her feet. "Amy?" she whispered.

Sure enough, Del's ex-wife, Amy, sauntered across the room to take the microphone from the HR. Lena could hardly keep her jaw from dropping. How was this possible? Amy was Amelia Hatfield? Amy owned the firm that bought Designology? Amy was responsible for rehiring Lena? She pressed her fingertips to her temple as her head spun.

"Thank you for the introduction," Amy said into the mic. "And thank you to everyone here. Designology would not be so successful if it was not for your hard work." With a fake smile on her lips, she paused to allow for a brief applause. "Speaking of successful, I have a success story to share before I do my big announcement."

Lena planted her feet firmly on the ground to keep herself from running away.

"You have a colleague among you who has proven to be a real asset to our company." Amy began pacing the front of the conference room. "Time and time again, she made our clients feel valued while giving them the best possible designs she could. She worked tirelessly for hours. Came in under budget consistently. I heard once, she even met a client at their child's tee-ball game in order to sign paperwork. *That's* dedication."

As Amy's pacing slowed, Lena's heart sped up.

"Which is why I've decided to reward her dedicated efforts." Amy stopped right in front of Lena, looking down at her with false appreciation in her ice-cold eyes. "Meet your new senior partner, Lena Bouras." A round of applause sounded from the room as Amy held her hand out.

Reluctantly, Lena took Amy's hand and stood from her chair. She smiled and waved at the co-workers she'd known for so long, and some who were new, but still clapping for her. When the riotous noise died down, Amy handed Lena the mic.

Lena paused to brace her nerves. "Thank you. I appreciate each and every one of you for such a gracious celebration." She glanced at Nicole, who was grinning from ear to ear. "I'm not one for speeches, but I can say this is a long-time dream come true for me. As partner, I promise I won't let you down. I'm still the same Lena I always was, hard-working, honest, and willing to go the extra mile for our clients. Thank you." She handed the mic back to Amy and waited for yet another round of applause to quiet.

Amy motioned for her to take a seat, then continued on with her speech. Lena didn't hear much of what she said because her head was a jumbled mess of thoughts. This entire situation was surreal. Lena had been handed her dream job by someone she loathed. Could she still take it? What would that say about her? More importantly, did she care?

When the meeting officially ended, Nicole jumped from her seat and pulled Lena in for a strong hug. "I'm so proud of you. Want to go have lunch and celebrate?"

Lena nodded, letting go of Nicole. "Yeah, but I need to touch base with Amelia first. I'll come to your desk when I'm done.

Nicole hugged Lena again, and bounced away, leaving Lena to wait for Amy to end her conversations with other employees. As Lena approached her, Amy's exasperated expression turned to false cheerfulness as she met Lena's gaze. "Ah, there's the woman of the hour. How's it feel?"

"Amy, what are you doing here?"

Amy scoffed, waving her hand in the air. "Don't act so surprised, Lena. I really thought you'd have figured it out, but I guess that's why you're a designer and not a detective."

Lena pinched the bridge of her nose. "What exactly is going on?"

"What do you mean? You're getting promoted, that's what's going on."

"Why?"

"Because you're going to do great things at Designology, Lena." Amy's eyes flashed with something Lena could only describe as greed. "You are going to make this company huge by bringing in new, exciting clients."

"So, is this about keeping me at Designology, or keeping me away from Del?"

The annoyed expression on Amy's face twisted into amusement. "Lena, do you really think I rehired you to get you away from my ex-husband?"

"You didn't answer the question."

"Okay, fine." She let out a groan, rolling her eyes "Yes. I rehired you to get you away from Del."

Lena's chest tightened so quick, her heart jumped into her throat. There was no breath left in her lungs as she stared at Amy with wide eyes.

"But it's not for the reason you're panicking over."

Lena finally sucked in a breath. "What?"

Amy pursed her lips, sighing. "Lena, you are an incredibly talented designer. Your portfolio here at Designology was stupendous, and after I saw it, I couldn't fathom how they fired you in the first place. I couldn't sit idly by knowing you were stuck in a hellhole of a city with Del who was going to suck the creativity out of you an ounce at a time." She took a deep breath, raising her chin. "He would've destroyed you, Lena. Like he tried to do to me."

"How did he try to destroy you?"

"By attempting to make me stay. He knew what my dreams were, but he insisted I give them up to stay with him. He was selfish, and pig-headed men like him don't change."

Lena let out an offended laugh. "Wanting his wife, the mother of his children, to be in their lives was being selfish?"

"That was his angle." Amy folded her arms, lifting a hand to study her manicure. "And aside from the lack of vision in their lives, the boys grew up fine without me."

Lena almost threw up in her mouth, disgusted by Amy brushing off the pain she caused both Del and the boys. She composed herself, licking her lips before speaking. "You abandoned them for a career."

Amy ran her tongue along her teeth, looking at Lena through lowered lashes. "Did you not do the same?"

"I…" Lena's chest constricted. She wanted to refute, but every last breath had been squeezed from her lungs. Her eyes dropped to the floor, scanning the carpet for some sign of Amy's words being lies. She came up empty.

Tears pricked Lena's eyes, so she shut them. In the darkness, she could only hear her heart thumping in her ears, its heavy beats pounding out every noise in the room. Deep breaths and swallows couldn't rid Lena of the overwhelming fact she was exactly like the one person Del hated the most.

Lena, you are nothing like my ex, Del's voice whispered in the recesses of her mind. Her chest loosened at the sound of his voice, even if it was imaginary.

"Soon, Lena, you'll figure it out like I did," Amy said. "You'll realize what you really want."

Lena opened her eyes, a tear rolling down her cheek. "I already have."

Amy smirked. "Good."

"I quit."

Amy's jaw dropped. "Wait, what?"

"I quit, Amy. I don't want this job, this position."

"You signed a contract," Amy said, her laser-focused stare burning a hole through Lena.

A sly smile crossed Lena's lips. "Technically, I haven't. I signed an agreement to come aboard as a senior consultant. The contract paperwork isn't scheduled until tomorrow." She lifted her chin, arching a triumphant eyebrow. "Goodbye, Amy."

Lena turned to leave the room, but Amy stepped forward to grab her arm, her eyes filled with fury. "You don't want to do this, Lena. I'll make sure you never do design in the entire state of California ever again."

"I don't want to work in California." Lena ripped her arm from Amy's hand. "Everything I need is in Colorado." With that, she strode from the room, her chin held high.

Chapter 35

Adrenaline pumped through Lena's veins as she walked briskly through the office. Reaching Nicole's desk, Lena braced herself on it, afraid her legs would give out any minute. Her chest heaved as she waited for Nicole to get off the phone.

When she did, she spun in her chair to face Lena, furrowing her brows. "Hey, what's up?"

"I'm hungry," Lena said with a huff as she straightened to stand. "Let's go to lunch."

Nicole held up a hand. "Okay. Hold on." She clicked around on her computer, grabbed her purse, and hooked her arm through Lena's as they left the office.

They slid into their normal booth at the deli across the street after ordering their usual meals. Nicole bobbed in her seat. "So, how's it feel? Are you on cloud nine?"

"I quit," Lena whispered so quietly, she wasn't even sure she heard herself.

"What?"

"I quit."

A puzzled look came over Nicole's face. "You quit, as in, you quit eating carbs?"

Lena shook her head, letting out a breathy, frustrated chuckle.

"Is this, like, some weird metaphor thing? You quit the senior consultant position to become partner?"

"No. I quit my job," Lena said, full of conviction this time. "I told Amy, I mean, Amelia Hatfield, to take the partner position and shove it."

Nicole's jaw dropped to the floor and her eyebrows hit the ceiling. "What? Why?"

Lena rubbed her palms up and down her thighs. "Amelia Hatfield is Del's ex-wife, Amy. She came into the brewery about a month ago with a client she was schmoozing. I guess my redesign impressed her, so she researched me and found out I used to work at Designology. My portfolio was even more impressive, so she rehired me, sweetening the deal with the partner thing."

"Okay," Nicole said, drawing out the syllables. "So, you think she wanted to hire you to get you away from Del?"

She swallowed deeply, shaking her head. "She wasn't jealous. She only saw me as a way to further her career. My talent and success with my clients meant she could expand business. It had nothing to do with Del."

Nicole folded her arms, a knowing look on her face. "But your decision to quit did?"

"Yes." Lena dropped her chin, looking at her hands wringing together in her lap. When Nicole didn't say anything, Lena lifted her head to find Nicole beaming at her. "What?"

"I'm just so... proud of you."

Lena arched an eyebrow. "Proud?"

"Yeah, Lena. I mean, a year ago, you were dating that scumbag Ozzie, content to work and party without any thought of the future other than becoming a senior design consultant." She pressed her lips together as if she was fighting tears. "And now, you're choosing happiness. Choosing love."

Lena sighed, resting her elbow on the table and dropping her forehead into her palm. "Yeah, and what would my mom say? She'd probably scold me for letting all my hard work go to waste on a man. I'm chasing a guy instead of furthering my career. I'm stupid."

"No, you're not." Nicole leaned forward and smacked Lena on the forearm. "Your mom wanted you to be happy, and when happiness was your career, she supported you. If she were here now and saw the new you with Del, and what a difference he's made, she'd be on board. You've just figured out what's important to you."

"But I gave up a secure, well-paying, and well-respected position for a man."

Nicole groaned, letting her head fall back. "Love, Lena. You gave up a pretentious, over-hyped position for love. The love of a man who not only adored you with all his being, from what you told me, but also wanted to help you start your own company. He was going to give you everything."

Lena's heart felt like it was going to leap from her throat. "And I threw it all away."

"Nah, I bet he'd take you back in a heartbeat. You just have to ask."

"You don't think it's been too long?"

"I mean, it's been a month, and you did do the one thing you swore you wouldn't, so I'd say you have some pretty heavy groveling to do. But it's nothing a blow job won't fix."

Lena laughed, the pit in her stomach lightening. She took a deep breath, lifting her chin and setting her jaw. "I'm going to have to do more than that."

Nicole grinned. "What are you thinking?"

"Well, I have to do something to show him I'm serious."

The grin fell from Nicole's face as she scrunched her eyebrows. "You don't think quitting your job after only two weeks and moving back to Colorado is enough?"

"No," Lena said confidently. "It needs to be big, but not like, some grand gesture. Del's too laid-back for that." She chewed on the inside of her cheek before her face slowly lit up as an idea sparked in her mind. "I have an appointment to make."

***

Lena cocked an eyebrow at Nicole who stood in the bedroom doorway, leaning against the frame. "Why are you looking at me like that?"

"I just can't believe you're leaving me again." She sighed.

Lena scoffed as she folded clothes into her suitcase. "You said you were proud of me."

"Oh, I know, and I am. I'm so proud of you for going after Del." Nicole slid her arms around her middle, hugging herself. "I just have dèjá vu watching you pack."

A laugh escaped Lena, but it did nothing to ease the heavy ache in her chest. She knew she had Nicole's full support, and returning to Del was what she needed to do, but the idea of leaving her best friend again weighed on her heart. She tucked a shirt into her suitcase. "Sorry."

"What? No. Don't you dare be sorry." Nicole walked to the bed, taking a seat at the end. "Lena, you are chasing down love, and that's a path I never thought I'd see you take." She placed her hand on Lena's. "Am I sad I'm losing my BFF? Yes, but it's for the best reason."

Lena looked wistfully at her friend, and a sad smile crawled across her lips before drawing in a breath. "At least this time I'm not running away."

"Exactly." Nicole squeezed Lena's hand. "Although, escaping to Colorado last time did land you one hunk of a man."

Lena's heart fluttered as she pictured Del, but it sank almost immediately. "What if he hates me?" The words were soft, meek, as if speaking them would make them true.

"He won't."

"But what if he does?" Tears pricked her eyes at the thought.

Nicole sighed and patted the bed for Lena to sit. When Lena joined her, Nicole threw her arm around Lena. "Do you remember what happened to me and Jayce right before he proposed?"

Sniffling, Lena nodded. "When you ghosted him for almost a week because you saw him with his sister, but didn't know it was his sister?"

"Yes, that." Nicole rolled her eyes. "I was a crazy person. I knew his sister, but when I caught them hugging and only saw her back, I immediately assumed he was cheating on me. After that, I convinced myself I didn't want anything to do with him."

"I remember, because even I told you what a nutjob you were being."

Nicole feigned offense, then smirked at Lena with a sideways glance. "And *you* persuaded me to talk to him." She turned, taking Lena's hands in hers. "Lena, if I hadn't listened to you, if I hadn't swallowed my fear, then I would've missed out on the most spectacular man. Jayce was... *is* everything I ever needed, and I can't imagine living without him."

Lena swiped at her nose. "But you didn't move to another state, doing the exact same thing his ex did that traumatized him."

"Oh, gosh no." Nicole placed her hand on her chest. "I didn't do anything like that."

Lena's jaw tightened. "Not helping."

"What I'm saying is, it didn't matter what a crazy person I became. Jayce loved me for me. He knew who I was, and he knew I wouldn't have acted in such a way if I wasn't supremely upset. Del knows you, doesn't he?"

Lena nodded.

"And he wouldn't have told you to go if he hadn't known how badly you wanted this job. He knew your love for him was holding you back because you loved him *that* much." Nicole wiped a tear from Lena's cheek. "He let you go, Lena. So, I'd bet one gazillion dollars, he'll take you back in a heartbeat."

Lena nodded, straightening her limp posture. "Either way, I have to try."

"There's the Lena I know." Nicole beamed as she shook Lena gingerly from side to side. "When does your plane leave again?"

"Sunday morning. Early. It was the first flight I could get, and it wasn't cheap."

***

Lena thanked the Uber driver as he lifted her suitcase from the trunk. As he drove away, she took out her phone to finalize the payment and leave him a glowing review. Mainly, she was happy he hadn't spoken at all during the drive.

Even if he had, she wouldn't have been able to respond because thoughts of Del had consumed her mind.

It had been two days since she quit her job and made the decision to move back to Colorado. Two days seemed like two years with a cloud of uncertainty looming over her. She'd hardly slept. Trying to hone in on exactly what she was going to do about Del proved to be harder than she'd thought.

With an exhausted breath, Lena stepped inside her Colorado house. As she surveyed her surroundings, a strange comfort engulfed her, an unusual feeling whenever she was at home. When she'd moved there seven months ago, it had been like crawling into a deep hole to lick her wounds. The pain of Ozzie's betrayal, the humiliation of being fired, and above all, the stinging loss of her mother had demolished Lena. She'd retreated to the house.

Now, returning there was different. A light at the end of a dark tunnel. She was headed in the right direction, and that direction was toward Del.

But how would she fix the rift she'd caused?

Her fingers wound her hair around them as Lena walked to the kitchen. She had a lot of thinking to do, and she couldn't do it without some tea. As the water heated, Lena circled her kitchen island, one hand in her hair, one picking at her pursed lips.

"First thing's first," she said quietly. "Where am I going to find Del?"

He'd be in one of three places; the lake, home, or Citadel. Lena crossed off the reservoir right away. Not only was it October and much too cool to be on the water, but the lake was Del's place of refuge. She couldn't risk destroying his happy place if he didn't receive her well.

His house seemed like a good option. At least there they could talk if he wanted to.

Lena's heart stopped. *What if he doesn't want to?*

He would have every right to slam the door in her face. Or worse, not answer the door at all. What would she do then? Sit on his porch day and night until he came out? Slink away in utter defeat?

No. Going to his house wouldn't work unless he knew she was coming.

Lena pulled her phone from her pocket, unlocking the screen. She clicked the contacts icon and stared at Del's name under the favorites list. She hadn't erased him. *Couldn't* was more like it.

Her finger hovered over the green call button as her heart pounded in her chest. Panic inched up her spine, threatening to constrict her throat.

Lena practically dropped her phone when the teapot whistled. A breath gushed from her lips, and she slid her phone back into her pocket.

Calling Del wasn't an option. She needed to talk to him in person. This was a face-to-face conversation, and if all her years in design had taught her anything, it was to relay important information physically whenever possible. And if spilling your guts about love and devotion to someone didn't qualify as important, Lena didn't know what would.

She poured the hot water into her mug, resigning herself to the fact that Citadel would be the place to talk to Del. It wouldn't be overly private, but she'd have a better chance of him listening to her. There was also less of an opportunity for him to make a scene if he became upset. Nodding as she dipped her teabag into the water, Lena made her decision.

Shit, it's Sunday. They're closed. "Well, that just gives me more time to figure out what I'll say."

All the things rushing through her mind dizzied her. Obviously, she would tell him how sorry she felt, and how much she loved him, but what else could she say? Those were the biggest points she needed to assert. Maybe she'd tell him those things, and then he'd take the reins? He could spend however much time he needed talking out his feelings, or yelling at her, or whatever he wanted until he felt satisfied.

But what if he just tells me to leave? Like he did to Amy.

Lena drooped against the counter. Her planning wasn't as fruitful as she'd hoped it would be. Tears stung as they welled in her eyes, and she lifted her gaze to the ceiling.

"Maybe I should just give up," she whispered through her quivering jaw. "Mom never wanted me chasing after a man, anyway." Her mother's voice echoed through her mind, *Do something today that your future self will thank you for.*

As the words repeated themselves, Lena focused hard on them. She'd always assumed her mother had been referencing school or work, never her personal life. When Lena had cried to her mother after failing a test in college, her mother used that quote to encourage Lena to join a study group. The time Lena had competed with a colleague over a client, her mother's quote told her to go above and beyond to solidify her competence. Every time that quote came around, Lena had used it as motivation to further her career.

Now, she saw it in a totally different light.

If she wanted her future self to ever be happy again, she needed to woman up, and get closure from Del. Whether that closure was good or bad didn't matter. She'd never be able to move forward if she left her questions unanswered.

Chapter 36

Lena's heart pounded in her chest as she sat in her car in the Citadel Brewing parking lot. Her hands were clammy, but she couldn't let go of the steering wheel. Every nerve in her body had been stretched to the point of snapping. Walking in there meant facing everyone she'd abandoned. It meant crawling back for forgiveness.

What if they didn't forgive her?

The thought had plagued her for the last four days. There were people in Aurora who might hate her. People she had called coworkers, and some she had even called friends, but none of their hatred haunted her more than Del's.

Could she move on knowing he hated her? Knowing he would never be in her life again? The idea shredded her heart, but she needed to know.

Three deep breaths later, Lena went into autopilot, letting her body guide her from the car to the front door. The familiar chime sounded as she stepped inside. It was followed by another familiar sound, Twyla's customer greeting, but it was cut short by a confused question.

"Lena?"

"Hi, Twyla." Lena put her hand up in a small wave, pressing her lips together as she eyed the Halloween decoration littering the bar. "All ready for Halloween I see."

"What are you doing here?" Twyla rounded the bar, completely ignoring Lena's comment, and pulled her in for a hug. "We thought you went back to California."

"I did, but I realized it was a mistake."

Twyla let go, a knowing smirk on her face. "So, you're back for good, then?" She squealed when Lena nodded. "We've missed you. All of us have."

"I've missed you guys too." Lena glanced around the tasting room. It looked exactly as it had when she left, aside from the skeletons and spiderwebs. Del hadn't felt the need to redo anything like he did when Amy had left him. *Del.* "Speaking of missing people, is Del here today?"

"He's not here, Lena," a deep, disgruntled voice said from the end of the bar, and Lena knew exactly who it was.

She grimaced as she turned to face him. "Hi, Jack."

He didn't say anything as he eyed her with stony discontent.

Lena cleared her throat, a dryness suddenly impeding her voice. "I don't suppose you know where he is, do you?"

"Even if I did, why would I tell you?" He squared his posture and folded his arms across his chest.

She licked her lips, stepping toward Jack slowly, but not meeting his icy glare. "Because he needs to know how sorry I am. Even if he can't forgive me." She raised her head, looking into Jack's brilliant blue eyes that matched his father's, and expecting to see malice. Instead, for once, she found sympathy. "I know I messed up big time, but I want to at least try to make it right. If I can't, then I'll leave Del alone forever. I swear." She ran her finger over her heart in an X. "But, if there's even the slightest chance I can fix this, Jack, I have to."

Jack pursed his lips, his chest heaving with deep breaths. He studied her face through his narrowed eyes, as if he was searching for an indication of a lie. When he came up empty, he sighed, dropping his arms to his sides. "Come on," he said, brushing past her and heading for the door.

Lena spun to follow him. "Where are we going?"

"For a drive."

She stopped dead in her tracks. A car ride alone with Jack? It wasn't her first choice in activities, but since it might lead to finding Del, she hurried along to catch up to him.

"Get in," he said as Lena heard the locks to his black SUV click.

She slid into the passenger seat and put on her seatbelt. Jack said nothing as he pulled out of the parking lot and onto the road, staring straight ahead. Lena wondered if she should speak first. What would she say that she hadn't said in the brewery? Jack knew her intentions. He heard her explain herself, what more could she say?

Several minutes of silence passed before Jack spoke. "Why did you come back?"

"Because I realized I made a mistake."

"It took you this long? You've been gone over a month."

"I think I knew it was a mistake from the beginning, Jack. I just needed something to prove it to me. A catalyst of sorts."

"And you got it?"

"Mhm." Lena wrung her hands together in her lap, unsure if she should divulge the information about Amy. *He needs to know.* "Your mother is the person who rehired me in Los Angeles."

Jack's head whipped over to look at her before quickly turning back to the road. "My mother? How?"

"It's a long story."

"So start talking."

Lena sighed, but let the story come spilling out. Jack listened intently, though his hands tightened on the steering wheel every so often. The anger radiating off him filled the car with an unbearable stuffiness. So much so, Lena had to roll her window down as she finished recounting what happened. "So, I quit my job to come back here. For your dad."

Jack stayed focused on the road. His chest rose and fell as he adjusted his position in his seat. "You know, she never said goodbye when she left?"

Lena knew the story, but had never heard it from Jack. She chose to stay silent so he could get this off his chest.

"They had their biggest fight ever, and the next morning, she was gone. No goodbyes. No hugs or kisses. Not even a note. She just left." The muscles in his jaw visibly tightened. "I spent years hating her for it. Jameson and Johnnie were so young, they sort of forgot, but I didn't."

"I can't imagine having to carry a burden that big at such a young age."

"Eventually, I came to terms with my feelings toward her. I gave up hating her, and just moved on." He ran his hand over his bearded chin. "Then you went and did the same thing."

Lena's heart broke in two. It hurt so badly, she placed her palm against her breastbone. Never in a million years would she have thought Jack would have been hurt by her leaving. She didn't only abandon Del, she abandoned his kids too. She shut her eyes, stopping the tears from forming. "Jack, I'm sorry," she said quietly.

"You don't have to tell me."

"Yes, I do." She opened her eyes, fixing them on his stoic expression. "I'm sorry I left without saying anything to you or your brothers. You deserved better, and I'm sorry. From the bottom of my heart, I am sorry."

Jack's mouth ticked up into a smile before he cleared his throat. "Thank you, Lena. It means a lot."

Lena beamed at him.

He glanced over at her, and his shoulders slouched as he sighed. "My dad said he told you to go."

"Yes, he did, but I still could've chosen to stay."

Jack shook his head. "No, you couldn't have."

Lena furrowed her eyebrows as she waited for him to continue.

"Lena, we all saw how you changed when you were redecorating Citadel. Everyone saw the brightness and excitement in you, like you were a different person." He took a deep breath. "I know it wasn't an easy decision for you to make, and so did my dad. That's why he told you to leave. He wanted you to have everything you wanted, and he knew you wouldn't take it if he didn't nudge you."

"So, he manipulated me?" Lena was relieved when Jack laughed at her joke. "It wasn't an easy decision, Jack, but coming back here was. I figured out I have everything I want right here. Starting with Del."

"Well, good. 'Cause he's home," Jack said, turning the steering wheel to park behind Del's truck in the driveway.

Lena gaped at the house. She had been so enthralled in the conversation with Jack, she hadn't realized where he was driving. Blinking back happy tears, she turned to Jack with a shaky smile. "Thank you."

"You're welcome." He pointed a finger at her, a teasing expression on his face. "Just don't make me regret it."

Lena laughed as she wiped a tear from her eye. "I won't." She started to exit the car, but stopped to throw her arms around Jack and hug him tightly. He flinched, but slowly eased and put his arms around her. When she felt all the tension ebb from his muscles, she let go.

"Go on," he said, his voice cracking. "He's waiting for you."

Lena pulled away with all the confusion in the world displayed on her face.

"I texted him you were back when I heard you in Citadel." He shrugged, a sheepish smirk on his lips. "I had to know whether he wanted to see you."

Warmth bloomed in Lena's chest. She gave Jack one more big hug before getting out of his car. Her steps felt lighter as she ascended Del's porch. He *wanted* to see her. After everything she'd put him through, he still wanted to have her in his life.

Her breath caught in her throat as he feet stopped moving.

What if that wasn't the case? What if this was an elaborate ploy between Del and Jack to humiliate Lena? What if Del opened the door only to slam it in her face?

It didn't seem likely considering Del's character. That kind of malice wasn't in his personality, but what if being hurt again hardened him? Could he be a different person?

Lena ran her sweaty palms up and down her thighs before ringing the doorbell. Her toes tapped the ground as she waited, tears threatening to well with every second the door went unanswered. She raised her finger to ring the bell again, but let it fall to her side. If he didn't answer on the first, he wouldn't on the second.

Her heart began to crack. It split right down the middle, spilling her fragile feelings onto the concrete, where they shattered into a million pieces. She felt heavy, as if she couldn't move her weight of her own volition. Dizziness set in, and she braced herself on the wall.

Before she could break down completely, the door whipped open. Del stood in the entry way, his chest heaving, his face lit up in eager excitement.

A tear ran down her cheek as longing spilled from her lips in the form of shaky breaths.

Del cleared his throat before straightening his posture and setting his jaw. "Of course you'd show up when I was in the bathroom."

The lilt of Lena's laugh was drenched in relief. "Sorry."

"For your timing, or something else?" He arched a skeptical eyebrow.

She tried not to giggle. Jack told her he alerted Del to her presence, and she could play along. Del deserved some sort of payback. "For everything. For breaking my promise. For entertaining the idea of my career being the most important thing to me." She dropped her chin. "For leaving."

Del cleared his throat. "I told you to go."

"I know, but I shouldn't have listened." She lifted her head to meet his watery gaze. "It was harder than I thought."

"It was the hardest thing I've ever done."

A smile appeared on her face, but her heart sank knowing he'd suffered because of her.

"Lena," Del said, stepping forward to tuck his knuckle under her chin, his eyes flicking between the two of hers. "When Jack texted me that you were back, and asked if I wanted to see you, my answer was instantaneous, a resounding 'YES.' But while I waited here for you, my mind began to wander."

Lena's heart stopped beating. Her insides shook, locked in a grapple between fear and hope.

Del's blue irises swirled with pain and confusion, but warmth pooled in their depths. "I can't do this if it's not permanent. My heart won't take it." He took a large breath. "How do I know with certainty that you're here to stay?"

Her jaw quivered as she whispered, "Because of this." She reached up to take his hand, placing his fingers on the underside of her wrist.

When he glanced down, his eyes widened. "What's this?"

"I got it last Friday." Lena watched Del's fingers as they traced the tattooed lines of a snake twisted into an infinity symbol, eating its own tail. "I've changed, Del. I've transformed."

Their gazes met, Del's face scrunched into adoring appreciation.

"And I'm sorry that it took breaking your heart and moving a thousand miles away to make me realize the old Lena doesn't exist anymore. But if you're willing to forgive me, even if it's only an inch at a time, I'll spend the rest of my life showing you how sorry I am."

He sniffled, swiping at his nose before his features relaxed. "The *rest* of your life, huh?" Pursing his lips, he rubbed his bearded chin with his hand. "That's a good start." He reached out to yank her to him, their mouths colliding in a kiss to end all kisses. It was a kiss to seal their commitment. There would be no more questions, no more second-guessing, only she and Del solely together.

He stepped back, looking down at her with love brimming in his blue eyes. "Would you care to show me how sorry you are right now?" His voice was low, husky, and it made Lena's knees wobble.

"I'll show you all night."

Epilogue

"Ready?" Del asked, his hand hovering over the doorknob.

Lena nodded as she bounced on her toes.

"Three, two, one!" Del turned the knob and threw open the door to Lena's new office.

The smell of fresh paint and carpet freshener wafted into Lena's nose as she stepped through the doorway. It was a small office, only one room with enough space for Lena's workstation, a couch and coffee table for meeting with clients, along with a coffee and tea bar. It wasn't much, but it was all Lena needed.

Del put an arm around her waist, pulling her to his side and kissing the top of her head. "You did it, Lena," he said with pride in his voice. "You've started your own design company."

"Yeah, it only took six months." She nudged him with her elbow. "And I couldn't have done it without you." Tilting her chin up to kiss him softly, she broke away to do a lap around her office.

Del watched with admiration in his eyes. "This can be your first design gig, decorating your own office." He laughed. "Though, I bet you already have ideas for it."

Lena gave him a knowing look, nodding as she walked to the large window and took in the view. The office was on the west side of the twelfth floor of the building, so she had a fantastic view of the mountains. She looked forward to many sunsets.

"Penny for your thoughts?" Del sidled up next to her, taking her left hand in his and fiddling with the diamond ring on her finger before she could.

Lena took a deep breath. "It's all very surreal." She turned to Del, splaying her hand on his chest. "A year ago, my life was in the toilet. I had lost my mother, and my job. Left the only life I'd known for over a decade to move here and start all over. I thought I'd never recover."

Del lifted his hand to cover hers.

"And now, here I am, starting my own design firm, married to the most wonderful man" —she tipped up onto her toes to kiss him— "and loving every minute of my life with him. Things I never thought I'd do, never thought I'd want, are what make me happier than I've ever been."

"I'm glad you're happy. Glad our life makes you happy." He arched an eyebrow. "But you know, you can stop working at Citadel so you can concentrate on design."

Lena dropped her head for a moment before locking her eyes back on Del's. His bright blue irises held her whole world. Everything she could ever want shone in them as he looked down at her. She had been blinded by her past. The things she thought were the most important things in the world, turned out to be superficial. A high-profile career, party life, and her failed relationships clouded her judgment, but Del was the light shining through the tempest.

"I like working at Citadel." She snuggled into his chest. "Let's go home."

"Mmmm," Del hummed. "I like the implication in your voice, but we've got Jameson and Twyla's rehearsal dinner, remember?"

Lena pursed her lips, feigning disappointment. "Why couldn't they go to the courthouse like we did?"

Del held up his hands in defense. "I offered you a big wedding. You said, and I quote, 'I don't care about anything except being your wife.'" He lowered his hands to pull her to him again. "And we don't have to leave, yet. We can stay longer and make some plans for this space."

She shook her head before nuzzling into him again. "I've already got it all planned. I've had it planned since we first saw it."

"Are you serious? You knew we were going to get this place right off the bat?"

"No, I didn't. I decorated every space in my head when we toured offices, so I have an idea already."

Del laughed. "Always working, aren't you?" He kissed her forehead.

"Yep. And I've got some work to bring home." She trailed her finger down his firm pec and defined abs to the buckle of his pants. "I'll need your help, though."

Del growled. "Whatever you need, Lena, I'll give to you." His mouth closed over hers as he swathed her in his strong embrace.

Lena melted into Del. Her stomach flipped a million times over, hopping with the effervescent tingle of love.

The End

Preview of Mud, Love, and Chemistry

Chapter 1

The fresh mountain air fills my lungs as I exit the car and step into the hot July sun. Sweat immediately beads on my forehead, so I slide on my headband. I double check my braid is secure, and round the back of the car, a light skip in my step.

It's my favorite day of the year; Mud Down race day.

"Fuck, it's already so hot, and it's only eight-thirty," complains Lisa, my high school BFF now turned college roommate, as she meets me at the trunk.

"We've done this race four years in a row, and it's always this hot. It's July in Colorado, remember?" I ask, rolling my eyes.

She huffs a breath. "You've done this race four years in a row. I didn't go last year."

A shaky breath bleeds through my lips before my throat closes up. I can't swallow over the lump that forms.

Lisa's eyes immediately widen when she realizes what she just said, and she wraps an arm around my shoulders. "Sorry, Brynn. I didn't mean to bring him up. I was just☐"

"It's okay," I say, but it's not entirely true. Refusing to let this sudden reminder of my heartache ruin my adrenaline high, I link my arm with hers and tug her through the dirt lot toward the huge purple and black tent. "Come on, let's go find Jenny and Sarah."

The frigid burst of air-conditioning blasts me in the face as we enter the tent. Lisa lets out a sigh of relief, while I for one can't wait to get out of here. I hate air conditioning. It always makes the air taste weird, like it's stale, or something. There's no comparison to the crisp, energizing feeling of fresh air flooding your lungs.

When our friends, also our college roommates, Jenny and Sarah, arrive ten minutes later, we all share a hug before checking in. We make sure to take the ceremonious selfie in front of the Mud Down sign, then head out to put our backpacks in a locker.

Stepping back into the warmth of the sun, my eyes readjust to the light after being in the dim tent. I relish the open air with a deep breath. As we walk toward the starting area, I take a minute to survey the grounds. The same vendors from the previous year already have their tents up, and racers congregate near the race entrance. I admire their enthusiasm.

Watching the eager racers, a pang of jealousy rips through my heart as I notice there are several couples. Boyfriends and girlfriends dressed in matching race gear, holding hands or sharing kisses while they wait. I thought I had that. I thought I had a partner to share this race with, but he wasn't who I believed him to be.

I huff a breath, and square my shoulders. There's no sense in letting my past heartbreak get the best of me. Sure, I may have spent the last year solo, and in a dating rut, but today is the best day of the year, and no memory is going to change that.

No matter how painful it is.

At the starting line, we all stretch while waiting for the emcee to begin his usual motivational speech. More people file in around us, and soon, we're surrounded by other racers.

The Mud Down is cool because anyone can participate. Sure, it's challenging, every 10-K race is, but this one's designed for everyone. There are people old and young, men and women, tall, short, lean, muscular, all waiting to partake in my favorite race.

"So, Jenny, Sarah, ready for your first Mud Down?" I ask as I slide into a side lunge.

"Would be if I didn't have to get up so early." Jenny mockingly glares at me. "Why'd you sign us up for such an early race time?"

I throw my hands up in defense. "Because it's just going to get hotter as the day goes on. Better to get it done early." If it were up to me, we'd have arrived at eight when the event opened, and we'd already be on the course. My friends, while excited for the Mud Down, don't share my tenacity for it.

"And get used to it," Lisa chimes in. "Brynn always signs up for the earliest race she can."

I bump Lisa's shoulder with mine. "More like the earliest one you'll let me." We stick our tongues out at each other before sharing laugh.

Sarah puts her hands on her hips. "Do you drive all the way to Grand Junction every year? Isn't there another race that's closer to school?"

"Not one with this good of a vibe," I say cheerfully.

"And at least we spent the night here instead of driving up the morning of." Lisa places her hand on my shoulder for balance as she pulls her leg behind her into a quad stretch. "Be glad you came this year, though. Now that we're twenty-one, we get a finisher beer at the end." Lisa holds up her arm in triumph, the words "Legal Drinking Age" printed on her wristband.

After a few spirited high-fives, the four of us huddle together, arms wrapped around each other's waists, and begin bouncing on our toes as we psych ourselves up. Our uplifting affirmations get interrupted by the screech of a microphone.

"Good morning, Mud Downers!" the emcee yells from a tent next to the starting line. "Y'all ready to get dirty?"

A collective cheer goes up from the crowd, and Lisa fist bumps me.

"Now, before y'all get out there, let's go over the legal stuff I have to tell you." The emcee proceeds to explain the liabilities of the Mud Down, the safety regulations, and the partner rule. "Look at the person to your right and to your left. Those are your teammates."

I look left at Lisa, then right at Jenny. We grin cartoonishly at each other.

"Those teammates are out there with you. All running the same course, doing the same obstacles, getting dirty, just like you. If someone needs a hand, lend one. You'll probably need one later."

The crowd laughs.

"Here at the Mud Down, we take care of each other." The emcee leaves the tent, cordless microphone in hand, and steps into the middle of the group. He asks everyone to take a knee. "But don't just take care of each other out here. Take care of each other at home, too. Take the Mud Down sentiment back to your lives, and spread the idea of teamwork around. The world needs it." He motions for us to stand up. "Last thing, I want you to turn to your neighbors, give them a fist bump and say 'you got this.'"

I turn left and fist bump Lisa again, but when I turn right, Jenny isn't there. Instead, I find myself staring straight into a guy's bare chest. A fairly muscular guy's bare chest.

I raise my gaze to meet the most beautiful pair of dark brown eyes I've ever seen. They're like sparkling muddy pools flashing in the morning sun. My breath catches in my throat as I take in the face surrounding the eyes. This guy is gorgeous. Shaggy light-brown hair held back by a sweatband, a strong jaw covered in just the right amount of stubble, and a dazzling smile that has my stomach flipping when his mouth ticks up.

"You got this." His low, smooth voice is full of confidence as he bumps his fist against mine.

The second his knuckles tap my own, the spell I'm under breaks, and I blink before returning the bump. "You, too," I say, much quieter than he did.

His half smile melts into a full one before he turns back to his friend, and I spin to face Lisa. I suck in a breath, but luckily, she doesn't seem to notice what just happened.

To be honest, I don't even know what just happened. I've been off relationships and guys in general for a year, and I'm certainly not looking for a casual hook-up. Even if I talked more to that guy, there's a minuscule chance we'll see each other again, so I move on. I focus on the race ahead of me.

That's the whole reason I'm here, anyway.

The emcee blows the whistle, officially starting the race. All the racers take off at different speeds, some at a full sprint, some walking, but my three friends and I fall in the middle. We jog. Liberally. We aren't in any hurry, but we have the energy and stamina to keep a brisk pace.

After a half mile, we reach the first obstacle; the muddy crawl. It entails us crawling through a mud pit underneath barbed wire, some of which hangs so low, we're forced to dunk our faces into the muddy water to get under it.

I take the lead. I slide into the murky water to crawl under the low-hanging barbed wire, then hold it up so my friends can slither through safely. That starts a chain reaction, and other racers begin copying me.

When the four of us make it safely to the other side, I use Jenny's shirt to wipe my face. She didn't get as dirty as I did since I did all the footwork to get them through.

Another few obstacles, and we get to one that really requires teamwork. The mud mounds are exactly what they sound like; several mounds of mud over six feet tall with water filled ditches in between. People give you a boost, then you reach down to pull them up. The slippery mud offers no footing, and it's a riot watching people slide face first into the next ditch.

The four of us jump in, and I begin giving the boosts. Lisa first, then Jenny, then Sarah, and lastly, me. This order goes on for all of the mounds, five total. When I lift Sarah out of the final ditch, I lose my footing and go under the water. I come up immediately, ineffectively wiping my face, and reach up to grab Sarah's hand.

But it doesn't feel like Sarah's hand.

"You got this," a deep voice says, and I forget all about the mud covering my face, whipping my head up to see my starting line hunk holding my hand. His half smile returns as we lock eyes, and my breath shakes from my mouth, mud sputtering off my lips. "And I got you." He yanks me out of the ditch as if I weigh nothing.

Once I'm on solid ground again, hunky guy lets go of my hand, winks at me, and takes off running with his buddy.

I'm left speechless, staring after him. I don't even know what to think. He's still just as hot as he was on the starting line, even now, covered in mud.

I startle when Lisa calls my name, pulling me back to the real world. I jog to catch up with my friends. Luckily, the next couple of obstacles are easier ones, because with the way my knees are wobbling, I wouldn't be able to scale anything without falling off.

As we reach one of my favorite obstacles, the vertical wall, I've regained my stability. At the wall, I put my back to it and drop into a squat. I act like a step stool for my friends.

Lisa is the last and she sits atop the wall with her hand extended down. When I shake my head, she huffs a breath. "I should've known you'd want to to do this one yourself. Okay, we'll be waiting for you," she says before climbing down the other side.

With a huge grin on my face, I back up. I need room to get a running start so I can jump and shimmy my way up the eight foot vertical climb. Of course, when I get back far enough, a few other racers are now working their way over the wall, so I have to wait.

"You got this?"

I glance over to find my muddy hunk standing next to me, his mud-covered eyebrows arched in the most adorable way. A wry smirk crosses my lips, and I nod. "Oh, yeah. I got this."

I dash toward the wall, my adrenaline pumping furiously. I scale it no problem, but instead of jumping over, I straddle the top and wave formy gorgeous race partner to follow. I watch him lick his mud-covered lips, spitting almost immediately before he takes off. He, of course,makes it up without issue, but he's also got at least six inches on me, making his climb shorter.

When he gets to the top, he copies my straddle of the wall, facing me. "I'm Sam," he says and offers me his hand.

I shake it firmly. "Brynn."

He stares at me, that half smile melting my insides, and I can't do anything but stare back. Everything stops. I can't feel the sun baking my mud mask. I can't see the other races topping the wall around me. I can't hear anything except the beating of my heart.

"Brynn! Come on!" Lisa's sharp shout severs the moment.

I clear my throat, giving Sam a quick grin. "Gotta go!" I leap off the wall, jogging to my friends without looking back.

"Who was that?" Lisa asks, jutting chin over her shoulder.

I shrug. "Some guy complimenting my climb. Guess I impressed him."

She gives me a knowing look and starts jogging.

The rest of the race goes as expected. We do the ice bath, the ladder climb, and the warped wall, but skip the electroshock jaunt. I skip it because I still have metal pins in my wrist from when I broke it at age seventeen. My friends skip it because I suspect they're wusses.

When we cross the finish line, volunteers hand each of us a gray t-shirt with the word "Finisher" across the back, and a can of beer. As my muddy fingers leave their mark on the sleek fabric, my sense of accomplishment materializes before my eyes. My chest fills with pride of yet another Mud Down completion.

The four of us happily cheers our drinks before heading to the food truck area. While I'm standing in line with Lisa, I look over to find Sam sitting at a picnic table, a beer in his hand. When our eyes meet, he smirks and lifts his beer like he's cheersing me from afar. I nod, lifting my can as well.

"Is that the same guy from earlier?" Lisa nudges me with her elbow.

"Yeah." I can't even stop the smile from conquering my face.

She shoves me away. "Go talk to him."

"What? No." My adrenaline spikes at the thought.

"Just go." Lisa pushes me hard enough that I stagger forward, and Sam notices. Now I have no choice but to talk to him. Even if reluctantly.

I walk toward his table, the butterflies in my stomach fluttering a mile a minute. He watches me the entire time. His smile grows bigger with each step I take. When I reach the table, I say a quiet, "Hey."

"Hey," he replies without taking his eyes off me. "Nice job finishing."

"You too."

A throat clears next to him, and Sam does a double take at his friend. "Oh, sorry. This is Paul." He motions between me and Paul. "This is Brynn."

My name sounds so natural on his tongue, so fluid. I wonder what else he could do with his tongue?

"Sup?" Paul says with a jut of his chin. "Saw you on the course today. You're fucking tough."

Sam elbows Paul, scoffing at his swearing.

I chuckle. "Thanks."

A silence settles between us, so Paul stands up. "I, uh, need another beer. I'll be right back." And with that, he's gone, leaving me with Sam.

He motions for me to sit, so I do. "Sorry about Paul. No manners, that one."

"It's okay." I shrug. "He's right, I am fucking tough."

Sam laughs, hanging his head for a moment before meeting my gaze again. "I like that."

Thank God I'm still covered in mud, because his flattery surely has my cheeks as red as a candied apple. "So, is this your first Mud Down?" I take a sip of my beer.

He nods. "You?"

My can still at my lips, I hold up five fingers.

He gapes. "Wow. So, you're like, an expert at the course then?"

I swallow my drink. "Something like that."

"You'll have to share all your secrets with me."

I shake my head. "No time. My friends and I are going into town directly after this to get ice cream."

"Ice cream? No shower first?"

I laugh. "The interesting looks we get are always great."

"I'll bet." Sam's gaze scans my face as if tracing the muddy outline. "I hope the ice cream is worth the attention."

"Oh, it is. There's an old-timey soda shop that has the best butter pecan." My mouth waters just thinking about it.

"I'm more of a mint chocolate chip guy, myself."

The idea of tasting Sam's mintiness makes my mouth run dry.

"Brynn." Lisa taps my shoulder. "We got our bags and we're gonna take a picture under the finisher sign before we go. Here's your phone." She hands me my phone, winking at me before glancing at Sam. "Hey, man."

"Hey."

She turns back to me. "Hurry up, okay?"

I look at Sam with apologetic eyes as I stand up. "Sorry. Gotta go."

"Shit." Sheer panic seems to overtake Sam's face as he pats all his pockets. "I'd ask for your number, but I don't have my phone yet."

My heart skips a beat. He wants my number? "Well, here," I say, handing him my phone. "Put yours in mine."

A delighted smile crawls over his face as he types and hands it back to me. I chuckle, reading what he input. "Sam Mudboy? Is that your real last name?"

He shakes his head. "It's Eastman."

"Well, nice to meet you Sam Eastman," I say as I tap my screen. "See you around."

"Wait," he calls after me. "Do you have a last name?"

I turn my chin over my shoulder. "Guess you'll find out when you check your texts."

Also By Christine Layne

Because of Blake – Available on Amazon

Mud, Love, and Chemistry – Available on Amazon

Acknowledgements

This is my second novel which I have self-published, and although the process became more streamlined, it was still quite the endeavor. I want to thank each and every one of you who helped me on this journey! It's not over, but hopefully will get easier over time.

To my loving, supportive husband:

Thank you for believing in me, and supporting the idea that writing isn't just a hobby. It's my passion and I thank you for recognizing that.

To my children:

Thank you for keeping each other occupied in order to give mommy the time and space to work.

To my awesome critique partners, Shayna Astor and Tara Brodbeck:

Saying "thanks" to two of the most awesome critique partners doesn't seem like enough. You have both been invaluable in the process of everything I've ever written, and I couldn't do any of this without you. Your advice, criticism, and general sounding board abilities never cease to amaze me, and I cannot thank you enough for everything you've done.

To my wonderful writing group:

Thank you for keeping me sane and reminding me that everything is a work in progress.

To my fantastic editors, Mackenzie and D.P.:

Thank you for making my book and my writing better. Your hard work does not go unnoticed!

Thank you **Coffin Print Designs** for my gorgeous cover!

To my ARC team:

Thank you, as always, for taking the time to read my book before it was available to the public, and for leaving your fantastic reviews. You gave me my start and I greatly appreciate it!

And, most importantly, to my readers:

If this is your second time reading my work, thank you so much for the compliment! It means the world to me that someone not only liked my first novel, but liked it enough to read my second! I hope I can continue to produce stories and characters you love!

If this is your first go reading one of my novels, I thank you for taking a chance on an aspiring author. I hope you loved my book as much as I did, and I hope to see you in the future.

Readers are what make the author world go around. Without you, we wouldn't be here, so from the bottom of my heart, thank you so very much!

About the Author

Christine Layne is a romance author who loves to tell stories about people falling in love against the odds. Though writing is her passion, Christine also enjoys painting, spending time with her children, or watching movies with her husband, as long as she has a cup of tea in her hand.
Follow me for the latest updates, teasers for upcoming novels, giveaways, and more!

Instagram @christinelayneauthor
X (Twitter) @ChrisLayneLove
TikTok @Christine.layne40
Facebook Group: Christine Layne's Creations